"WARNING:

DON'T PICK UP *THE POPE OF GREENWICH VILLAGE* UNLESS YOU'VE GOT THE NEXT FEW HOURS AVAILABLE, BECAUSE IT'S NOT EASY TO PUT DOWN. . . . VINCENT PATRICK REALLY KNOWS HOW TO TELL A GOOD STORY."

—*Playboy*

"GO OUT OF YOUR WAY TO READ IT. . . . fine writing from a considerable talent. . . . Life in Little Italy has never been better depicted. . . . A slick, polished, gifted novel"

—*Chicago Sun-Times*

"EARTHY AND OUTRAGEOUS . . . IRRESISTIBLE READING!"

—*Cosmopolitan*

"QUITE EXTRAORDINARY. . . . Besides an alert ear and a sharp eye the author has the priceless gift of unpredictability. . . . Vital storytelling"

—*Newsweek*

more . . .

"SIZZLING . . . ENGROSSING. . . . Patrick writes with gusto and humor about the denizens of New York's Little Italy and of the Irish cops who find it politic and profitable to cooperate with the Mafioso."

—*West Coast Review of Books*

"Tough, violent, throbbing with grim vitality. . . . The dialogue alone makes *The Pope of Greenwich Village* worth the price of admission. . . . A GREAT FIRST NOVEL"

—*Minneapolis Tribune*

"A SOCKO NOVEL! . . . One of those heart-warmingly deadly wonders we haven't seen for far too long"

—*The New York Post*

"VINCENT PATRICK, LIKE GEORGE V. HIGGINS, MARY GORDON AND JOHN GREGORY DUNNE, MINES TERRITORY RARELY ENCOUNTERED IN MODERN FICTION."

—*The New York Times Book Review*

THE
POPE OF
GREENWICH
VILLAGE

VINCENT PATRICK

PUBLISHED BY POCKET BOOKS NEW YORK

FOR TESS FORREST

 **POCKET BOOKS, a Simon & Schuster division of
GULF & WESTERN CORPORATION
1230 Avenue of the Americas, New York, N.Y. 10020**

chapter

1

Charlie looked toward the door, thinking he could slam it closed behind him just hard enough to tilt the little print hanging beside it, then call her from work later and apologize. She would stay angry for an extra few hours, but it would cut short the headache that was just starting and was going to dog him through his whole shift. He decided against it, and walked to the window instead, to watch the line of cars below feel their way past the yellow barricades of a Con Ed excavation. They crawled through single file, bumper-to-bumper, with several drivers pressing down on their horns as cars in front hesitated. The horn blowing had been constant all afternoon—maybe that was causing his headache.

"You don't even bother to lie to me carefully, Charlie," she said. "It's insulting to be lied to so obviously."

He answered without turning. "I'll lie better, Diane. I promise. A new leaf gets turned over tomorrow. All my lies will be first-rate. You'll feel a lot better."

She turned on the faucet in the small bathroom sink

1

and splashed water on her face. That was to let him know that she was crying, or about to, Charlie thought.

"Why don't we fight over at your place, Diane? We can walk it in a few minutes and it won't be so goddamned depressing. Four hours awake in this room is like doing time."

"Where does this leave us, Charlie? I don't want to sit like a fool worrying that you might be dead somewhere, while you're having a good time in some after-hours bar and don't have the decency to call."

He turned from the window. "That's the beginning of the cassette again. You have an automatic rewind on it, Diane?" He took his coat from the closet. "It's half past five. I don't want to be late for work, Ronnie can't leave until I get there."

Pulling the hanger off the rod reminded him—the hat chick from the Honey Bee had promised to stop by for a drink if she got off before midnight. If she did, Charlie would want to stay out late. He should go out the door and slam it, he thought. Make the picture move. Stay angry. It would give him an easy way to come home late after work.

He decided not to, and called back that he would talk to her later. If he was going to have to fake being angry to get out for a few hours, he might as well be married.

Halfway across the lobby he paused, and called, "Any mail?"

The desk clerk shook his head without taking his eyes off the tiny Sony screen. Charlie looked past him and saw that the cubbyhole was empty, then continued through the overheated vestibule onto the street. He turned toward Third Avenue and adjusted his scarf higher on his neck. It wasn't too cold to walk if the air remained still. He would make his stop at

Twenty-fifth, try to squeeze two hundred out of Edelweiss on the ring, and have twenty minutes for a scotch at the Forge before starting work. It would be a bad night—he could sense it. For half a block he thought about calling in sick, then forced himself to keep going. The shylocks would think he was avoiding them, and he would only wind up bouncing all over the Upper East Side, then going after hours, dropping their payments over the bar and hung over in the morning. Even with the scarf, he felt his shoulders hunch up against the cold. He walked quickly, relieved that there had been no mail.

The old man was behind the window. Charlie cursed to himself—the son always looked more generous. He waited while a skinny Puerto Rican kid ahead of him held up a camera case.

"What do you have there?" the old man asked.

"Camera."

It wouldn't fit through the narrow opening under the glass. The old man motioned toward the doors on his left, then pressed a buzzer that allowed the kid to open the outer door. The kid placed the camera on the floor and came back out, closing the door behind him. After the door latched shut, the old man opened the inner door and carried the camera to the window. He examined it distastefully through a pair of bifocals for half a minute, then shook his head slowly.

"There's a company business card pasted in the case. I'm going to pass on this one."

He placed it between the double doors and buzzed. The kid shrugged and picked up the case. "Cheap Jew bastard." He said it loudly, but with no malice.

The old man ignored him. "What have you got?" he asked.

Charlie slid the ring off his pinkie and pushed it

through the opening. The old man slipped a jeweler's loupe into his eye socket and rotated the ring beneath it.

"What do you want on it?"

"Two hundred."

"A hundred fifty."

"The ring's worth a thousand. Better than a thousand. There's over a carat of perfect diamond in there."

Edelweiss shrugged. "What it's worth or not worth I'm not saying. What I'll give on it is one fifty."

Charlie started to protest, then looked into the old man's face. He slipped his watch off and slid it under the glass. "Give me fifty on the watch."

The old man glanced at it and nodded. "Some identification," he said, and stamped two tickets. He copied off the driver's license, then slipped four fifties under the glass with the tickets.

Charlie added them to the two fives folded in his money clip. Suddenly annoyed at being without the watch, he said, "Fuck you, Edelweiss," as he left the store. Behind him, the old man stared through the glass.

He walked south a block, letting his anger dissipate in the cold air, then saw an empty cab. He hailed it and rode the six blocks to the Forge.

Billy Dolan was setting up the bar for the dinner shot. Two scotches and half an hour with Dolan gave Charlie the lift he needed. They had tended bar together four years ago at Major's in the garment center. Billy Dolan would steal a hot stove—he was known as Billy the Kid among bartenders who worked as his partner. As a team, he and Charlie had done very well for themselves, finally being fired from Major's together. When they had gone to an after-hours joint to commiserate, Billy had pulled from his coat the framed twenty-dollar bill with GOOD LUCK and a signature that had hung on the backbar at Major's.

They had left the framed, glass-covered twenty on the bar to pay for their drinks and a tip.

Dolan was squeaking through at the Forge; there wasn't enough bar action for legitimate tips and barely enough for stealing. Tonight he had eight customers at the bar and was working contracts with six of them—only one couple was paying for every drink. He joined Charlie for a drink while they checked up on mutual acquaintances on the bar circuit. Charlie enjoyed the warm, empty bar enough to decide at six o'clock that Ronnie, the day man he was due to relieve, could screw himself—he would have a third scotch and be ten minutes late. At a quarter past six he swallowed the last of it, slipped his remaining five under the empty glass, and left. Billy was due to go off at midnight. Charlie invited him to drop by the Good Times for a nightcap.

Ronnie was cranky.

"You think I like this place, Charlie? That I don't want to leave?"

The bar was crowded and the reservation book full for a Wednesday.

"It was Diane, Ronnie. She's running a hundred and four and we ran out of aspirin. I had to get to the druggist."

Ronnie shrugged. "Paulie came in half an hour late, so I been working short a waiter. Nothing new there. He's your cousin, Charlie, but the kid pushes it to the hilt. And I been on the phone with reservations half the day. Christ, don't they know how bad the food is here? A toilet in the men's room overflowed during lunch, and at one-thirty with the floor jammed and a strong second lunch shot coming through, two immigration guys come in and pinch Mucho the bus-boy for not having a green card. You can't even bribe the bastards to wait an hour these days—you don't know who's wired. I spent half an hour bussing tables. It's been another great day at the Good Times. To top it off, my night manager comes in to relieve me twenty minutes late."

"Have a drink, you'll feel better."

"I will."

"Has Nicky been in yet, Ronnie?"

"No. Tell him the machine's been out of Marlboro for almost a week, for Christ's sake. And J-three on the jukebox sticks. Twice a day the bartender has to run out from the service end to reject it. I taped a note to the side of the box."

He put his topcoat on and walked toward the front door. Halfway down the bar he held up his hand and spread his thumb and index finger an inch apart. The bartender filled a rock glass with vodka and ice cubes. Charlie watched Ronnie down it in one long gulp, then leave without a backward look. He would likely stop somewhere for half an hour to calm down before going home. Charlie hoped he wouldn't pick the Forge. Billy Dolan was sure to mention his being there and tomorrow he would have to swallow the embarrassment of being caught in a small lie.

Nicky showed up at 8:30. He replenished the cigarette machine first, then emptied the jukebox. The whole place was moving smoothly, and Charlie took a few minutes to sit at the corner table and watch Nicky stack quarters. Charlie slipped two of the crisp fifties from his money clip and handed them to him.

"Good, Charlie. What's that leave?"

"Six more weeks."

Nicky nodded. He would adjust whatever hieroglyphic records he kept after he left.

"I'm thinking about my own place, Nicky. Would you be able to put a box in?"

"That's nice, Charlie. From a night manager to an owner. Very nice. You got a place in mind? Something definite?"

"No. I'm maybe six months away from making a move. I'm not sure what I'm doing. I been thinking about leaving the city altogether. Maybe go to New England and get a nice restaurant. Something out in the country. Or maybe stay in the city and open something in Manhattan."

Nicky continued to stack quarters. "What are you going to do in New England?"

"Who knows, Nicky. It would be a fresh start."

"In Boston or Providence I could put you onto good people. Where you could borrow if you had to. If you stay in New York, anyplace in Manhattan or Brooklyn, I could put machines in. The territory don't matter—just so we been doing business before. I'd make you a nice deal, too, Charlie."

"What?"

"Standard split. Seven cents a pack on cigarettes. Fifty-fifty on the box. And it would be worth a five-hundred-dollar loan with no juice."

"None at all, Nicky?"

"Zero. I give you five hundred, you pay me fifty a week for ten weeks, then I renew for five hundred. I'll run like that for the first year with you. You'll need money, too, the first year or so. Every time you renew, Charlie, it's a hundred in juice you're saving. Six hundred I'm supposed to get back each time."

He pushed a stack of quarters marked with red ink across to Charlie. "Even these, Charlie. Most guys now, you ask for red ones, they tell you red quarters went out with high-button shoes. I still give out red quarters." He paused and counted the stacks. "You got a nice week here. A hundred twenty-eight. You want something for yourself, Charlie? It's up to you."

"I'll grab fourteen bucks. Cover my day's carfare."

He pocketed fourteen dollars. Nicky put fourteen into his bag.

"That's a hundred left. My piece is fifty. Leaves fifty even for the house. I'll throw some change in so it looks right."

He scribbled out a receipt and handed it to Charlie, along with a cigarette report slip and fifty dollars. Charlie put it all into a money bag, closed the zipper, and stored it in the strongbox under the register. Nicky stretched a rubber band around his stack of knocked-down cigarette cartons and moved to the end of the bar for his J & B rocks.

Charlie turned to Paulie, who was standing with his tray, waiting for a drink order to be filled.

"You were late again."

Paulie didn't look up from his book of checks. "Ronnie's been making his daily rat report?"

"He's the general manager, Paulie. Anyplace else, they would have thrown you out four times already."

Paulie motioned with his head toward Nicky. "They stick with J and B, the old-time wise guys."

Charlie smiled.

"What do you guess he ends up with in his pocket at the end of the year?" Paulie said.

"Nicky Dum Dum?"

"How many locations he got?"

"Say eight. Ten at the outside. He can't have more than ten."

"And what kind of money you figure he has out on the street?"

"Eight, nine thousand. Call it ten," Charlie said. "Christ, just between me and Eddie the bartender, we're into him for two grand."

Paulie shrugged again. "He's got to wind up with fifty large, no? Even after expenses on the machines and kicking money back to his crew boss, he's got to wind up with a thousand a week. Half the cigarettes go into his machines are swag, too. He trades a Caddie in every two years, don't he?"

Charlie laughed. "He does. You ever been in it? He gave me a lift once. There's a movie, *The Grapes of Wrath.* The inside of Nicky's car belongs in the movie. The whole back seat is loaded with spare parts for his machines. Loose, in a big pile. All the upholstery is torn and greasy. He puts cigarette butts out on the floor. Then every two years he trades it in."

Frankie Shy showed up at ten. He ordered an amaretto on the rocks and grunted what seemed to be a thank you when Charlie motioned to the bartender that the drink was on him.

"What number came in today, Frankie?"

"The Brooklyn number? Four seventeen. What did you have?"

"Five seventy-two. Combination. I been playing it steady for a year now and it never hit."

That would cover their conversation for the night, Charlie decided. He took a twenty and a five from his pocket and put them on the bar in front of Frankie. "Keeps us up-to-date."

Frankie nodded. He pulled a folded wad of bills from his pocket, leafed through the outside hundreds and fifties until he reached the twenties, then added Charlie's bill to the pile. He let the five sit on the bar.

"My book says nine more weeks, Charlie."

Charlie nodded, and motioned to the bartender to refill the amaretto, then pretended to see something in the rear dining room that needed his attention. He stretched up on his toes, excused himself to Frankie, and walked quickly to the dining room, his eyes straight ahead, knowing that to pay any attention to the customers would be to invite a complaint. He made it to the kitchen and stood for a few moments just out of reach of the swinging doors, until the dishwasher, a young Argentinian, slid open the door of the machine and released a cloud of steam that Charlie felt on the back of his neck. He moved further into the kitchen.

Walter was already well on his way, which meant that one of the waiters was bringing him vodka from the bar. At this rate he would never make it to closing; and without a second cook, Charlie would wind up peeling off his jacket at eleven o'clock and coming into the kitchen to expedite. He thought for a minute, watching Walter work the range, sweating into a pan of veal marsala he was sautéing, and decided that it must be Paulie bringing in the vodka. The party of twelve on the north station had asked for him as their waiter. He must be working a contract with them and the vodka was the price Walter got to let half the food go out of the kitchen without a dupe. It was Paulie's style—if you didn't watch him every minute he would put the place on wheels—and the fact that Walter would soon fall facedown into a frying pan full of veal scallopine wouldn't worry him. Paulie looked out for number one.

Paulie came through the swinging doors just as the dishwasher was squeezing past Charlie in the narrow aisle between the salad bar and a worktable, holding above his head a handful of frying pans from the pot sink.

Paulie shouted, "Cut that out, you Argentine degenerate! Leave our manager alone. That's my cousin's ass you're rubbing there." He reached across the table and shook his forefinger at the dishwasher's face. "That shit might go over in some filthy little jail in Caracas, but this is the U.S.A."

The Argentinian leaned back against the salad bar, his eyes wide. He spoke no English. Paulie continued past the steam table to the waiters' ordering station, strutting loudly on the tile floor, five-foot-three, even with the slight high heels that caused his arches to ache after every shift. He held up a dupe and shouted at Walter as he reached the station, "Ordering, you Albanese dummy! One broccoli da rob and a hot antipast. Then hold a veal parmigiana with, and a linguine marinara."

He slapped the dupe onto the shelf above the steam table, put two orders of spaghetti on his arm, then paused as he passed the dishwasher. "No humping the manager, Julio. It's family."

Charlie followed him through the doors, and slowed up as he passed the party of twelve. Con Ed office workers in from Queens, he decided, in Manhattan with their wives to celebrate someone's promotion or birthday. They were on their main course. He asked if everything was all right, and took a fast inventory of the table. He could have predicted it by the oversize bellies each of them carried. There were eighteen entrees on the table, being shared family-style. These were fifteen-thousand-a-year guys—not paying with plastic, either: hard-earned green. Half those dishes were being left off the check or they wouldn't have ordered them. And none of them was from the pasta side of the menu.

He caught up to Paulie at the end of the bar, returning a martini that wasn't dry enough.

"Am I crazy, Paulie, or is Walter half-whacked?"

Paulie looked wide-eyed. "Walter the cook? The Albanese?"

"You know another Walter in the place, Paulie?" He shook his head.

"Somebody's been feeding him vodka. One of the waiters."

Paulie frowned and took on a doubtful expression. "Nobody would do that, Charlie. Who would do that? Nobody here would give that space case a drink. The waiters know better." He paused for a few moments, then added, "I can't vouch for the busboys."

Charlie remained silent while the bartender added gin to Paulie's drink. Just as Paulie turned to go, Charlie said, "The big party on N six, Paulie. How are they?"

He could sense Paulie stiffen.

"They're all right, Charlie. Some of the guys come in for lunch sometimes. Working guys. Nice people."

"What's the check like?"

"Nice check, Charlie. They'll run eight, nine a head by the time they're done."

Charlie motioned toward Paulie's checkbook. "Let me look at the check, Paulie."

Paulie looked at him quietly for a moment, then asked, "What for, Charlie?"

" 'Cause half the items aren't on it, that's why." Paulie began to protest, but Charlie cut him short. "We'll both walk up the end of the bar, borrow two hundred apiece from Frankie Shy, and bet it on the check. If you have more than twelve entrees listed, you win. And I count eighteen on their table. *Three* of which are steaks, you little pimp. I'll go double or nothing just on whether you've got a single steak on your check."

Paulie fidgeted in the affected, little-boy style he used when caught in a lie among friends. He waved his finger back and forth slowly in front of Charlie's nose. "Careful of that double or nothing. You'll lose your ass on that bet."

"The check, Paulie."

He pulled it from under the thick rubber band on the cover of his book, then held it back. "You were in, Charlie. Serious now. You were in for a sawbuck."

There were nine entrees listed. No steaks.

"But, Jesus *Christ,* you're greedy. At least list twelve. One for each person, just to show some respect for the management."

"You're in for a sawbuck, Charlie."

He handed back the check. "You bring another drop of vodka into that kitchen and I'll bounce you out of here. Throw Walter a pound for forgetting the dupes. But no more booze."

He watched Paulie walk away and thought for a moment about pouring a scotch, then decided to wait another half an hour. Drinking on the job before midnight was a symptom he wanted to avoid. A minute later he decided to hell with it. He wasn't about to lead his life by a list of little rules that might not be right anyway. He caught the bartender's attention, pointed at the Teacher's, and felt his throat loosen up as he swallowed the first sip.

He had to think back five years to remember a time when things were as grim. Right now he was six weeks behind in payments to his wife, he still owed money to two shylocks, he was way overdue for five hundred's worth of new clothes just to work in, and he was six months into the worst streak of losing horses he had ever gone through. He looked at his wrist to check the time and felt a surge of anger when he remembered that his watch was gone. The brass pendulum clock at the end of the bar said 11:30. It might be accurate or it could be twenty minutes fast if Paulie had got to it. The little maniac sometimes set it ahead when no one was watching so he could get out of work early. The kid was a cross he had to carry. Diane would call soon in any event. Just what he needed to round out his troubles—a twenty-one-year-old who should have been a fast piece of ass and had developed instead into a long-term affair. She looked to him for advice and stability. Advice and stability—it struck him as incredible. And now she was starting to bitch if he came home late without calling. He pointed for another scotch.

If he had gone to Nevada in '65 he wouldn't be jammed up now. Nevada had been the one real shot in his life, and that was ten years gone now. Jimmy Roselli had held open a dealer's slot on the strip for six months, until Charlie said "maybe" for the third time and the offer died. By now he would have been a pit boss, with a closet full of suits and a year-round suntan, stopping after work each day for a rubdown in the hotel steam room.

There was nothing in sight, either. Seven months away from being thirty-five and nothing on the horizon. He would have to make a move. It had been in the back of his mind for a while now. Something heavy, which would mean sticking his neck out but which would net him maybe fifteen thousand if it worked. He could settle up debts and still have ten big ones to use toward his own place.

He sipped the scotch and considered it. The last time he had made a serious move was five years ago, when he was still with Cookie. They had found a lump on her breast and he had needed money fast to get her out of Bellevue and into Mount Sinai. He had waited for a rainy evening, then gone uptown to the Chez d'Or on East Fifty-fifth, dressed in black waiter's pants, a double-breasted black jacket, and carrying a peaked chauffeur's cap and a huge umbrella. He

had several numbered tickets printed with the Chez
d'Or name and, above it, in large letters, Free Valet
Parking. He tucked himself into a doorway next to
the restaurant, just out of sight in case the maître d'
looked out, and passed up half a dozen possibilities
until a deep green Mercedes sedan that would bring
fifteen thousand on a lot pulled up. As the woman
opened the door, Charlie met her with the umbrella,
bridged the gap to the sidewalk awning, then leaned
into the car and offered the fifty-year-old business-
man behind the wheel a ticket.

"We have valet parking service now, sir. Shall I
take it?"

He had bagged the Mercedes and a dollar tip to
boot, then stretched his luck by parking it only two
blocks away and hurrying back for a second shot. He
grabbed off a Continental and drove it straight to Joey
Hubcap's garage in Red Hook. He took a cab back,
picked up the Mercedes, and drove back to Joey's,
then came home with forty hundreds folded in his
money clip for three hours' work.

Now a four-thousand-dollar scam wouldn't do it.
He needed fifteen to get it together, and that meant
something heavier than swiping a couple of cars. It
meant something that might rate a five-to-ten sentence
if it went sour.

He finished his scotch and wondered when the
phone would ring with Diane's call. The bartender
filled his glass. Charlie sipped it, and decided that he
had better come up with something fast. If the table
stakes were five-to-ten, then those were the stakes.
He was still too young to start playing it safe.

chapter

▌▌

He mulled it over for a week. Nothing presented itself. Walking to work each day to exercise off what was becoming a continuous hangover, he considered several minor scams. None of them would net more than a few thousand. The big-money schemes that occurred to him were all too heavy—snatching some corporate president's kid, or going after the armored truck that delivered each Friday to First National City on Fifteenth Street. The risks were more than he was willing to gamble with. He didn't need that kind of money. Ten or fifteen thousand would do it, which meant a twenty-five-thousand-dollar score split two ways, or call it forty thou if it needed a three-man team.

On Thursday he caught the fifth race Exacta at Aqueduct. The OTB price was just over three hundred, and he had it twice. It was his first break in months. The six hundred took a few weeks' pressure off with the shylocks. Friday night he paid the day manager to cover his shift and went bouncing on the

East Side to celebrate, then ended up going after hours with Paulie. He woke up Saturday afternoon in a studio apartment on York Avenue. The hat chick from the Honey Bee was next to him. With no makeup in the daylight, she looked to be pushing fifty. In the shower he found crabs crawling on him and he had to call a drugstore for a bottle of A-200 before finishing the shower. By the time he shaved and found a cab, he was nearly an hour late for work. He worked through the busy Saturday shift depressed from the alcohol, the crabs that he could feel needed another treatment, and the thought that the money was gone. He hadn't gotten around to redeeming the ring and watch from Edelweiss. It came back to him that he would have to make a move.

His thinking slowly homed in on grabbing off a tractor trailer. It would keep him out of the big leagues of armored trucks or kidnapping. That was fine; judges didn't hand out suspended sentences for hijacking, but they didn't whack you with fifteen to thirty either. It would need only two people, which was also fine. That would mean a load worth twenty-five thousand, which ruled out cigarettes but didn't push him into the fur class either. Pharmaceuticals would do it. Carefully selected pharmaceuticals. A load of the right pills driven into a Manhattan warehouse could mean splitting twenty-five, with half a break, thirty-five, thousand—just three or four hours after nailing the truck. And it didn't need six months of planning. It could be done in three or four weeks.

He thought about a partner. Billy Dolan crossed his mind, but he would prefer to stick with an Italian. Someone from the East Side or the Village, with a stake in not being marked a rat if things went sour. Someone who dated back to being kids together and still carried that kind of loyalty. He developed a men-

tal list of ten people who qualified, and slowly elim-
inated the couple of serious psychos, anyone hooked
up tight with neighborhood wise guys, and the con-
sistent losers. He zeroed in slowly on Paulie. The kid
was a screwball to take on as a partner, but there was
a blood tie there. If things went bad, Paulie would
stand up.

On Monday he asked Paulie to hang around for
a drink after work. They walked to the Dublin Pub,
which stayed open until four and where they wouldn't
bump into anyone who would interrupt their conversation. The bartender clocked them for people in the
business and smelled a pound for himself. He free-
poured full rock glasses of scotch, then saw that they
wanted to talk and moved away to the end of the bar,
beneath a fake sod ceiling and a framed sign saying
that "God Invented Alcohol to Keep the Irish from
Ruling the World."

"How old are you now, Paulie?"

Paulie frowned. "Twenty-eight, Charlie. You know
that. Twenty-eight in February."

"Twenty-eight. And where are you going, Paulie?"

He shrugged. "Home, Charlie. I'm going home. I
got nowhere else to go."

"I don't mean tonight. Where are you going in life,
Paulie? What do you see ahead of yourself?"

Paulie interrupted. "Stop, Charlie. I don't need this
shit after working all night. I thought we were having
a drink. Two minutes you'll be asking me why I
live next door to my mother and my aunt and telling
me how soon I'll be thirty. I don't need it, Charlie.
Please don't join my uncle Angie and the rest of them
trying to make a man out of me."

"I meant with money. Where are you going finan-
cially? Taking home two-ten, two-twenty a week in
tips and pay and you're robbing what—another hun-

dred? Where is three and a quarter a week going to take you? You take a girl out and drop eighty bucks."

Paulie took it as a compliment. He nodded modestly. "More than eighty, Charlie. I like to live good. Lobsters, some wine, a couple of sambucas after dinner. I know how to spend. When I drop eighty bucks on my night off, I figure I got away cheap. Like I robbed twenty."

"So where is it all leading you? What if the job at the Good Times folds? Suppose the old man flies in tomorrow from Acapulco or Jamaica or wherever the hell he is this month and fires half the crew? It could happen, Paulie. I saw him do it a year ago. Got a bug up his ass that everyone was stealing too much and he fired half the crew. What do you do then?"

Paulie waved to the bartender for another round. He was quiet while the Irishman pumped the bottle over their glasses to emphasize that he was pouring with a heavy hand. Paulie sipped his drink slowly, his pinkie extended almost straight. Charlie sensed that he was about to drop a bombshell, his idea of an ace in the hole to answer Charlie's question.

"Soon I won't have to depend on waiting tables. I'll hold on to the job for a while, but I got something *big* going for me."

"What?"

"You got to keep it quiet, Charlie. I don't want no one to know for another week or two. Till it's final."

"I won't say a thing. What's the big thing going for you?"

Paulie sipped his drink again, raising his chin slightly in an aristocratic way. "I own a third of a tur-row bed."

He waited for a reaction.

"A what?"

"A *turrow* bed. A fucking *race*horse. Since last Thursday, I own one-third. Now I'm just waiting for the state racing commission to okay the license. My character record isn't perfect, and I been told they run a double check on Italians."

"A thoroughbred! Are you crazy, Paulie? What the hell are *you* doing with a racehorse? Who's in with you, two busboys?"

"Jimmy the cheese man and Tommy Botondo from Bleecker Street. We each got a third. We kicked in four thou apiece and bought a beautiful filly from a farm upstate. They delivered her last week to Aqueduct. We already lined up a trainer."

"Where did the money come from? Where did you get four thousand?"

He acted embarrassed. "I had to go on the street for it."

"Are you nuts? Taking home three and a quarter a week and the way you live, you'll never meet shylock payments. And the feed bills haven't started coming in yet, and vet fees, and vitamins, and extra rubdowns. You're crazy, Paulie."

"She's beautiful, Charlie. Big. A big filly. She's gonna win a lot of money. I feel it."

"You're a fucking *waiter,* Paulie."

"Starry Skies, her name is."

"What do you know about horses, Paulie? What does Jimmy the cheese man know? Either one of you ever *rode* a fucking horse? A real horse?"

Paulie smiled and shook his head slowly from side to side. "I don't have to know nothing in this deal. We got in on a swindle with this horse—it'll make you drool, Charlie. This beats printing twenties in your basement."

Charlie waited.

"This horse's father won the Belmont Stakes."

"Paulie, any horse wins the Belmont, its yearlings get sold at auctions for maybe two hundred big ones."

"That's exactly it, Charlie. We got her for twelve grand. We robbed her. It was like shoplifting, buying that horse. You know how racehorses have babies, Charlie?"

"Of course I know."

"They don't fuck, Charlie. You own a couple of horses worth maybe a million apiece, you don't set them loose in some field to fuck. It's too easy to get hurt, you know, Charlie? How many times yourself, you pull a muscle or something screwing? And that's in a nice soft bed. These great big stallions get horny they can easily kick the girl horse in the head or something. These champion stallions, they never even get laid, the poor fucks. They take their sperm and inject it into the other horse with some kind of tube."

"They call it artificial insemination, Paulie."

"That's it. Well, Jimmy the cheese man got in with the groom for this champion horse." He lowered his voice. "Just between us, Charlie. It don't go no further—on your father's grave."

He waited for Charlie to nod.

"We got this champion's sperm. The groom jerked this horse off. Beat his fucking meat right in the stable. He sold the tube to a horse farm upstate. My horse's mother got some of that tube. You know what that means, Charlie? You bet the horses. It means the first couple of races my horse goes off at big, big odds. Her papers say her father was some piece of garbage. But she's got the champion gene, Charlie. Horses ain't like people—they can't make themselves better than they're born. With a horse, it's all in the gene, Charlie. It's the fucking gene does the running, not the horse.

The horse got nothing to do with it. They either got the gene or they don't."

"How are you going to keep up shylock payments, Paulie? What did they nail you for?"

"A yard a week. It's with Nappy—he gave me a break." He took a long swallow of his drink. "I'm worried, though, Charlie. It don't leave me enough every week. It's going to be tight for a while."

They sat quietly for a few minutes. The bartender was in a conversation with a customer who had to be a cop, off duty or on. Charlie broke the silence.

"I'm jammed up for money, too, Paulie. I've got to make a move. Something that'll net me maybe fifteen large. It needs two people. You want to jump in?"

"What is it?"

"Pharmaceuticals. A tractor-trailerful. We grab a Jersey load at one of the turnpike stops. One of us holds the driver in a little van until the whole rig has been dropped off in New York, unloaded, and left somewhere on the docks. All clean. Whoever does the driving comes back, we leave the driver tied up in the van and go home. Figure five hours. Six tops. Thirty big ones, nice and easy. You can be a playboy with your turrow bed and I climb out of a deep hole and have a little something to put me into action."

Paulie became serious. "Too heavy for me, Charlie." He ticked his points off on his fingers. "It means a gun. Armed robbery. It means holding the driver. That's kidnapping. It means crossing the river. That's federal. Forget it, Charlie."

"They're technicalities, Paulie. If it did go sour, they'd use those to negotiate with. They'd press it for hijacking."

Paulie lifted his drink and extended his pinkie out

straight again. He was about to drop another bombshell, something comparable to his announcement of being a horseman.

"I got something better in mind. We're about ready to go and we need a third man. You want in?"

It took Charlie completely by surprise.

chapter

Paulie arranged for the three of them to meet on the following Thursday. They would have dinner at Caballini's on Prince Street. Charlie knew it as an overpriced family-owned place that might seat forty people when it was jammed. He was the first one there.

"I'm early, I'll have a drink," he told the owner, and took one of the three stools at the tiny service bar. He sat with a scotch and thought over again what Paulie had told him about Barney, the third man on the team. Charlie had insisted on being told nothing about the job until all three of them decided they were happy with one another. He only knew that there was a safe to be cracked and that Barney was along to crack it. A solid, married guy who had done some time a while back. Now he was past fifty. He lived in the Bronx and worked as a clock repairman. It had likely been five years since he had been on any kind of score. Paulie had met him a few years ago through a friend who had once handled some swag TV sets for him. He had looked him up two weeks ago and found that he wanted in.

Paulie arrived before Charlie finished his scotch. He paused just inside the doorway and smoothed down his overcoat collar, waiting to be recognized. The owner greeted him loudly by name and asked after his mother and aunts while they shook hands. The attention pleased Paulie. He introduced Charlie to the owner, Gino, who made a show of lifting a reserved card from a cramped three in the center and leading them instead to a roomy corner table. He scolded Paulie as he seated them.

"But you should tell them who you are when you make a reservation. You don't want a table in the aisle."

Paulie shrugged and gave him his modesty smile.

"You must go for a bundle in here," Charlie said, after Gino had left.

"I go for a few. Two people drop forty here for dinner nice and easy, Charlie. You want to make a little noise, you go for sixty or seventy. This asshole Gino used to go out with my aunt Josie a hundred years ago. She dumped him for some guy turned out to be a bum. He still wants to rub it in by playing big shot."

"They do well here?"

Paulie nodded. "Very. But meanwhile, his wife is in the kitchen breaking her hump, and the two of them live here six nights a week. Another successful family restaurant."

He tore a slice of bread in half and stuffed it into his mouth. "You open your restaurant, Charlie. I'll take the horse."

Charlie was about to bug him about the horse when Barney came in. He could easily be a cabdriver on his night off, Charlie decided. Five-nine or -ten, with the beginnings of a belly that showed after he hung his coat. He wore a dark suit that had never been in style and a tie pulled as tight as possible into an old-time knot. He looked as though his socks might not match.

Gino led him to their table. He had a nice handshake, Charlie thought, but the glasses bothered him. They were just thick enough to give him a dopey look. His fingernails were clean and trimmed though, and he asked for Punt e Mes on the rocks, which helped offset the glasses.

They concentrated on ordering appetizers, Paulie calling their attention to the stuffed artichoke and the broccoli salad, then adding on an order for "a couple of dozen small clams, tiny and cold. We'll split them around. And bury two bottles of Orvieto in the ice for later."

After each of them had taken the edge off his appetite with a few slices of bread, Charlie turned to Barney. "Paulie tells me you can crack safes."

Barney nodded. "Some. The kind we'll run into on this job I can get into."

"What kind can't you get into?"

He thought for a minute. "Banks. The big jewelry houses. Pretty much anything wired up to Holmes. I'm no big-time safe man, I'm a hotshot locksmith. People got a half a million or so to protect, they buy the kind of box that I don't know how to open."

"You're sure about opening this one, though?"

"If it's not wired, I'll get into it. I might need four, five hours, but I'll get in. He says it's not wired."

They both looked at Paulie.

"Guaranteed. I've seen it."

"You done any time, Barney?"

He buttered a fresh slice of bread carefully, then nodded. "Goes back to forty-seven. I did a pound at Coxsackie."

Charlie raised his eyebrows.

"Breaking and entering. Big furniture company in Yonkers. They had a bug on one of the inside doors. The guy next to me, kid named Rudy Miller, they shot him right between his shoulders. Didn't even bother with an ambulance. The guy doing lookout got away clean."

"They never caught him?"

Barney smiled. "That's why I did the pound. That, plus the kid getting killed. You know what it is—once there's shooting, the judges get heavy. Even if it's some asshole cop does the shooting. We had no guns."

The waiter brought the appetizers and the wine. Paulie ordered three pieces of manicotti as a next course, then they passed the dishes around the table and ate quietly for a few minutes.

"What do you do now?" Charlie asked.

"I fix clocks, mostly. I got a little shop in the Bronx that a couple of rich collectors send stuff up to. Then there's half a dozen antique dealers in Manhattan keep me busy a few days a week overhauling and repairing. Ninety percent of the work with them is chimes. You could almost make a living in this city doing nothing but chimes."

He filled his mouth with several stalks of the cold broccoli, swirling them first in the film of olive oil on the plate. He nodded approvingly, and waited to swallow his food before talking again.

"I grab another fifty here and there from a couple of people on the Bowery sell used cash registers and adding machines. Their mechanics get stumped, they call me in."

He reached across the table, placed a clam on Paulie's plate, and took the remaining one for himself. He chewed it thoughtfully, for longer than was necessary.

"Look, Charlie, I'll lay it on the table. I'm not a full-

time professional thief, not since I came out of Coxsackie. I was thirty. Since then, I been on half a dozen
scores—three, four thousand a clip—when I'm pressed
to the wall. In between I hustle. For a while I had a
scam going with the phone company was out of this
world. It died a sudden death three years ago. Now I
got a hook into one of the airlines so I get swag tickets to move a couple of times a year. Mostly I do
legitimate work. Clocks. I used to do watches and some
camera repairs, but I can't work that fine anymore."

"So why take this shot?" Charlie asked. "It sounds
like you're comfortable."

Barney removed his glasses and held them out to
Charlie. "Four years ago I didn't need glasses. Look at
these. Four more years they'll fit me with the bottoms
from Coke bottles and tell me to buy a shepherd. I'm
fifty-eight, with a twenty-year-old retarded kid my wife
won't let go of. I got a two-family house that's got a
little left on the mortgage, then I may even see a few
every month if the neighborhood don't go colored. I
need a score right now. A single shot for ten, fifteen
large to give me some kind of cushion. I can set up a
real shop for that. Sell clocks, besides just repair them.
Something small and quiet, on a side street in Manhattan, with a kid to handle the close work. I need one
nice score to stock the place, and that means I got to
stick my neck out. This is the best thing I've run across
in a year."

"You looked it over?" Charlie asked.

Barney nodded. "Except the safe. What I've seen
looks fine. Going in ought to be a joke."

"Three people can handle it?"

"If my eyes were what they ought to be, two of us
could do it."

"And what do we net?"

Barney pointed at Paulie.

"There's got to be thirty grand in there. Not a nickel less. There could be fifty."

"You're sure of that, Paulie?" Charlie asked. He turned toward Barney. "You can't believe *anything* he says."

Barney raised his eyebrows.

"I mean it. I've seen a party come in at midnight and sit on his station—because they look like stiffs, he tells them the chef had a heart attack twenty minutes ago and the kitchen is closed. And he looks like a little funeral director while he escorts them to the door, asking didn't they hear the ambulance. Lies aren't even lies with this guy."

He turned back to Paulie and spoke deliberately. "Tell me if you're not sure, Paulie. Tell me now. If we open that safe and find peanuts in there, I'm going to want your throat. Right on the spot."

Paulie shook his head slowly in disbelief, then poured more wine into their glasses. "This is guaranteed. That's all I'm going to say. It's A-one guaranteed." He lifted his glass. "You want in, Charlie?"

Charlie shrugged, then raised his glass. "I got to be crazy, but it beats hijacking a trailer. When do we set it for?"

"You got any questions, Barney?" Paulie asked.

Barney sipped his wine and looked at Charlie. "This is nice." He leaned forward and spoke while he read the label on the bottle. "Yeah, I've got a couple of questions. You don't mind?"

"Ask."

"Paulie tells me you're cousins."

"Fifth. Maybe sixth—I can never figure it out. His father's great-aunt back in Naples was a cousin of someone on my mother's side."

Barney nodded. "With Italians, that makes you about as close as twin brothers in an Irish family. Either of you owe any time? You got anything hanging over your head?"

They both said no.

"What's pushing you? Neither of you are pros. Why take the shot?"

Charlie answered. "I'm in hock for a little and I need another ten to get started in my own place."

"You ever been on a burglary?"

"Not since I was a kid. It's the one fall I took, in fifty-seven. A warehouse on Washington Street."

"You did time?"

"They suspended it. I copped a plea."

Barney raised his eyebrows. "You were lucky."

"I was seventeen."

Barney inclined his head toward Paulie. "How about him?"

"This maniac wants to own a horse. He never in his life owned a dog, but he just bought a horse."

Barney looked interested. "I thought you lived on Carmine Street. Where are you going to keep this horse?"

Paulie became exasperated. "Where am I going to keep it? At the track, for Christ's sake! It's not a fucking pet, it's a racehorse."

"The horse will make him a big shot," Charlie said. "One of his friends must have got a bigger pinkie ring. The horse will pick up his standing two or three notches."

"You ever do any time, Paulie?" Barney asked.

Paulie broke off a fresh piece of bread and pushed it into his mouth without buttering it. He spoke with his mouth full. "What's the matter with you, are you crazy? Do I look like I could afford to do time? I'm not a tough guy, I'm five-foot-three. They send me upstate, some big militant nigger is going to grab me in the shower and ram it up my ass. I know guys bigger than me who went away straight as arrows, came back two years later screaming fags."

Barney nodded. "It's not a joke. Twenty-five years ago, when I was away, you could do your time nice if you wanted. Now the niggers run it, unless you fall into one of the cushy places. Wallkill. Allentown if it's federal. Those places got quality prisoners. Judges who were on the take. Crooked government guys. But you land somewhere tough, Auburn or Attica, the niggers run it."

Paulie pushed another piece of bread into his mouth. "I don't intend to do no time. All this talk about doing time makes me nervous. You guys in or not?"

Barney nodded, Charlie shrugged, and they clinked their three wineglasses.

chapter

IV

Bunky Ritter entered the Fishouse through the Mott Street doors. He checked out the room as he crossed the few yards to the front of the bar, instinctively, rather than from any real expectation that someone would be there who didn't belong. It was one more of his nineteen-year-cop habits, he thought. It would stay with him the rest of his life, like reaching to unstrap his revolver as soon as he got home.

The Fishouse had a fair-size crowd for midnight, mostly overweight, middle-aged Italians and Jews from uptown, night people who were able to sit down at 1:00 A.M. and put away a bowl of calamari in extra-hot sauce. The women had napkins tucked into their collars and leaned well over their plates to protect hundred-dollar pantsuits from tomato sauce.

The small bar was nearly full. There was a six-for-five guy from Spring Street with a hooker who stood a full head over him; two couples waiting for tables; and a pair of well-dressed Chinese, speaking English softly. Bunky decided they were local wise guys.

He took the first stool and waited for the bartender to finish pouring for the Chinese.

"Coffee, Bunky?"

He nodded.

"You do the four-to-midnight?"

"Yeah. I just came off." He spilled three heaping spoons of sugar into the coffee and motioned with his head toward the end of the bar. "Who are they?"

"The chinks? They're good people." He dropped his voice even lower. "Neighborhood guys. They're with Eddie Grant."

"I'm surprised. Everybody says the Chinese are moving out on their own. The word is they don't need the wops anymore, they run their own action."

"It don't happen overnight, though, Bunky."

He sat quietly and watched the two Chinese in the backbar mirror. There was no animation to them. They never interrupted one another the way Chinese do. Bunky decided they had learned their behavior from watching the Italian wise guys, it hadn't come from Hong Kong. It might be worth mentioning them to Flynn. Carlucci had sent him word just a month ago that all his people were out of Chinatown and payments had dropped because of it. And Bedbug Eddie Grant was one of Carlucci's people. It could also be that Eddie had some action going without the old man knowing it. That would be worthwhile information— that Carlucci was slipping that fast with his underbosses. He had smelled something like it for a while now. Nothing specific, just a faint whiff of disrespect now and then that would never have been there a year ago. It should be explored. The stakes were too high for him to be playing in the dark.

Eddie Grant came through the door and interrupted his thoughts. They shook hands easily, and Eddie moved onto the stool next to Bunky's. The bartender wiped the bar thoroughly and cleaned the ashtray, a small ritual performed as a sign of deference but also done to relieve his nervousness at having an East Side boss at his bar.

"Have something," Bunky said.

Eddie's face went sour and he patted his stomach. "What can I have?" He glanced at the back bar. "Amaretto. A little amaretto. And a cup of coffee."

The bartender was still wiping with quick, short strokes. "Brown coffee, Eddie, or black?"

"Black coffee."

He filled a short glass with espresso and a pony glass with amaretto, set the bottle on the bar, and made a show of moving out of earshot.

"You want to take a table, Bunky?"

"No, let's stay here. It's noisier." He pointed toward the jukebox and smiled. When he spoke again, he moved his lips carefully but allowed only a whisper to come out. "Just in case you're wired."

Eddie smiled. "*I'm* the wise guy. *You're* the cop. You're the one who's supposed to be wired."

"No more, Eddie. Read the papers. Only cops get pinched now. The wise guys are all too busy testifying."

Eddie nodded. "You ain't far wrong, Bunky. It's all fucking upside down. The whole world is upside down."

They sipped their coffee.

"When you walked in, Eddie, did you clock the two chinks?"

He nodded. "Why?"

"I just don't like them. The Internal Affairs people are so goddamn devious now they use anyone. I'm sure they got a line into the Chinese."

"These two are okay. They run some light action over on Division Street."

"They run it themselves, Eddie? Or maybe you got a piece of it?"

It caught Eddie off-guard. His face hardened. "What are you saying, Bunky?"

"Just that the two chinks are with you. No big thing."

Eddie finished his espresso. "So this little weasel bartender has a fucking big mouth."

Bunky looked noncommittal. "Does Carlucci know you still got people in Chinatown?"

Eddie looked into Bunky's eyes for a few moments, then shifted his gaze toward the window on Mott Street. His voice dropped even lower. "Carlucci don't know it, Bunky. Carlucci hardly knows what time it is anymore. Don't ask too much more. I'll only lie."

"It sounds like he's on his way out, Eddie."

He shrugged. "You said it, not me."

"Where is that going to leave me, Eddie?"

"Right where you are now. If anything, you'll come out ahead a few. Carlucci's got the first quarter he ever hustled. The new guy will throw in another few yards a week for the bagman. You'll do fine, Bunky."

"It's someone who's moving up?"

"What's the sense? I told you, I'll only lie. Just don't say nothing to your people about me being in Chinatown. With those greedy bastards we'll have a whole *mishkadenze* on our hands."

Bunky wagged his finger. "Please, Eddie—greedy bastards is no way to describe the highest-ranking officers of New York's finest. And what's a *mishkadenze*, anyway?"

Eddie was surprised. "I always took you for half a wop, Bunky."

"Irish and German. I just have dark hair."

"That's a laugh. I told you everything was fucking upside down. The biggest bagman ever in New York and he don't know what a *mishkadenze* is. A mess. Like a mishmash with a dozen people in it that gets worse and worse and takes a long time to straighten out." He rubbed his stomach with both hands. "I got an appetite sitting here. Let's order some mussels and talk business."

Eddie went through two bowls of mussels in medium-hot sauce.

"Carlucci got a gripe, Bunky. He says your people ain't earning their money. The after-hours joint on Seventy-fifth Street got busted Sunday night. That all comes out of the Village, Bunky. Your people know that."

Bunky shook his head slowly. "Let me explain something. Didn't the old man ever hear about Knapp, Eddie? Things are different. You guys don't even realize how different. It used to be a captain was on the pad, he let word filter down through the whole precinct that such and such a location was protected. Every lieutenant, every sergeant, every cop in the precinct knew to leave it alone—even the honest cops couldn't touch it. Knapp changed it, Eddie. Those days are gone. Tell Carlucci to look around him—cops pay for their dinners now. You run a bar now without making regular payoffs and the cop on the beat says thanks if he gets a bottle of Cutty at Christmas."

He reached across and took a mussel from Eddie's bowl. "Carlucci thinks too small, Eddie. Like some old-time speakeasy owner. The stakes are bigger here. The brass have more autonomy since Knapp. They get to make their own decisions more. They set more policy. Carlucci and the others aren't buying protection for every after-hours gambling location in the city, they're paying so all the effort goes into things that don't affect them too much. You're paying so a dozen inspectors and captains decide that massage parlors don't have priority. So that the guys they push for the organized-crime unit aren't the really sharpest kids on the block—and those are the guys get assigned, believe me. That hasn't changed. Cops still move into slots according to who their rabbis are, and you guys are paying off the rabbis.

"You know who's assigned to after-hours enforcement, Eddie? For the whole midtown command? A big four cops—and two of them moonlight days driving cabs, so they spend half their shift cooping. You know who worked them into that slot? The guys I bring the bag to every month. So the other two guys finally came down on a location Sunday. You got to take a pinch once in a while. Tell Carlucci to relax, he's getting plenty for his money."

Eddie chewed the last mussel.

"Makes sense?" Bunky asked.

Eddie nodded. "Makes sense. But mention it to them anyway. That was *my* action up there, Bunky."

Bunky left the Fishouse an hour later. He walked slowly across Bayard to the Bowery and mulled over what Eddie Grant had said. There was no question that Carlucci would be out within the month. And Bunky sensed that it was Eddie Grant moving up—he smelled it between the lines in everything that had been said. He wondered what it would mean. Eddie Grant had always come through as calm and sensible, but people didn't call him Bedbug Eddie for no reason. He had a wild reputation. It would likely be a nice, corporate-style turnover of power, but there were never guarantees. Bunky was to tell this to his people. If there was a *mishkadenze,* they shouldn't panic; the same arrangements would continue when the dust settled. There would be a big sweetening-up on this payment to calm everyone's nerves—a package of a hundred and fifty thousand. It would be waiting for Bunky in the safe on Saturday.

He crossed the Bowery to catch a cab heading up-town and turned his back to the cold wind coming down through the bridge approach. In the distance, at the end of Bayard Street, the wall of the Tombs cut off the view west. It made him uncomfortable. He let two cabs pass, waiting for the roominess of a Checker in which to stretch his legs, then hesitated before giving a destination. He thought of going uptown to Ann's, fin-ally gave his own address instead, then sat back and propped his feet up on the jump seat. By the time they were halfway across the bridge, his muscles began to relax. He turned and looked south for a minute, past the double string of lights on the Brooklyn Bridge to the Statue of Liberty, then reached under his shirt and peeled off the lower strip of tape that held the bug against his abdomen. He scratched softly with his thumbnail. It had begun to itch two minutes after he walked into the Fishouse.

The tape would be dated and the circumstances identified, then it would go with the other half-dozen in his dresser. That was more than enough of Eddie Grant. Now he needed the golden voice of Inspector Ed Flynn to round out his collection. Saturday, when he delivered the money to Flynn, he would get one more recording. Both ends would be covered then. With luck he would never need any of them, but— God forbid—if things ever did go sour, he planned to be sitting on a hell of a stack of chips to bargain with.

chapter

V

Charlie woke up slowly. He pulled the covers up under his chin and lay still in his own warmth, waiting the few seconds it would take to discover how hung over he was. There was only a light pressure behind his eyes, but his mouth was completely dehydrated. It would be bad. He could either get through the day on aspirin or put a little alcohol into his system fast. Maybe Diane had a cold can of beer in the refrigerator.

He found a Heineken and emptied the bottle in two long draughts. If the kitchen clock was right, it was 11:30—Diane would be back from the dentist any minute. He couldn't find another beer and decided to shower and shave before putting anything else into his stomach. When he came out of the bathroom, she was in the kitchen, pouring two cups of coffee.

"How did you do with the dentist?"

"Fine. It was just a filling."

She opened the venetian blinds and cleared a space on the coffee table for their cups, then carried in a pot of water from the kitchen and poured some into each of the plants that lined the windowsill. Each time she poured, water trickled down the side of the pot and dripped onto the sill.

"That pot's no good for that. You ought to get one from the florist, with a long spout."

She answered without looking up. "This one works fine."

He was tempted to ask about the row of tiny puddles, but decided against it. His body hurt too much for an argument he would lose anyway. Maybe it was her teeth bothering her.

"Are you working tonight?" she asked.

"Why not? I always work Wednesdays."

She continued to water the plants, dribbling a fresh little puddle beside each one.

"What makes you ask?"

"Nothing important, Charlie. It's just my birthday. Remember? You promised we would go out to dinner."

"Jesus, I never got anyone to work my shift. Ronnie's on today—maybe he'll do a double if I work for him tomorrow. I'll call him now."

"Don't bother, Charlie. It isn't that important."

He sat quietly on the couch, watching her delay at the window. She was waiting for him to get up and make the call. He would do it if he weren't so hung over, he thought. His head was just too heavy. He decided to slip out of it.

"You're sure, Diane? If it's important, it's no big deal for me to call Ronnie. He won't be happy, but he'll do it."

"I said it wasn't important." She watered the last plant and sat down with her coffee. "I brought in a quart of beer if you want it. It's in the kitchen."

He went in and filled a glass. From the way it poured, he knew it wasn't cold enough.

"And I stopped by the Brentwood," she called. "The desk clerk gave me your mail. It's next to the beer."

There was a bill from Wallach's for two hundred dollars about to be turned over to a collection agency, and a letter from a city marshal informing him that parking violations on his car over the past eleven months amounted to nineteen hundred and fifty dollars without interest. If the money wasn't received within ten days or suitable arrangements made to pay it, his salary would be garnisheed and the car impounded. He leaned against the stove and shook his head slowly, then drank down the warm beer and read the letter again.

"What's the matter, Charlie?"

He refilled his glass and walked back to the living room, still shaking his head. He spoke softly. "I don't *believe* this. I don't fucking *believe* this." He held up the marshal's letter. "It's Cookie. She must be collecting three tickets a week on the Buick, and it's still in my name. I'm responsible for them."

"Let her pay. That's only fair."

He waved the letter. "What the hell good is it for her to pay? Every cent she gets comes from me." He looked at the letter again. "Nineteen hundred and fifty bucks. She must be parking on the fucking sidewalk!"

He drained the glass of beer and felt the pressure in his head ease off some more. Diane took the glass from his hand and returned it filled.

"I can't take a garnishee. The old man will let me go as soon as he hears about it. He hates them."

"I don't think he's allowed to, Charlie. I'm almost sure it's illegal."

"Illegal? What the hell does that mean? I don't work for General Motors, Diane, I work for the Good Times Bar. What am I going to do, sue Frawley to get my job back?"

"Yes, if you have to. That's your right, Charlie."

He felt his anger begin to focus on her, then remembered it was her birthday. "Maybe you got a few years of college, Diane, but you don't understand what happens on the street. I don't care what the law says I can do, I can't sue Jack Frawley for my job. It's not *practical*."

"What will you do, Charlie?"

"I've got ten days. I'll have to make some kind of score in the next ten days. Meanwhile, I ought to do something about that car—get it away from her, or get it out of my name."

"Can't you just demand it back? It's your car, Charlie."

"You ever know any girls with the name of Cookie?" She shook her head.

"If you ever run into one, watch out. Any girl ends up with the nickname Cookie is someone you don't fuck with. The first one I ever knew was a pretty little girl who kicked my ass from one end of a schoolyard to the other, with the whole third grade watching. Cookie Penna. All the Cookies I met since are the same way—you aggravate them, they take a swing at you."

"Your wife would fight you? Physically?"

He rubbed the back of his head. "I got eight stitches in my skull from her. And not all at once—five and three. Both times she waited till I turned around. She whacked me once with a ceramic lamp, and the second time with an iron that thank God wasn't plugged in. There's an awful lot of guys I would sooner tangle with than her."

He walked to the window and looked out over the low roofs and water tanks of the West Side. If this were Cookie's birthday, she would be dragging him out to dinner by his hair, hangover or not. Diane would let him off the hook. He should remember to stick with WASPS from here on in, he thought.

"What *can* you do, Charlie?"

"Nothing. The only thing is to go down to Mulberry Street one night and just drive the car off. It's not worth it. It would start a war."

"With whom?"

"Her whole crazy family. These are really whack-adoo Sicilians. They're maybe a hundred years behind in the way they think. She's got two older brothers, pick-and-shovel guys who sit down to dinner and drink their wine out of the bottle, like Coca-Cola. She's the baby. Anybody makes baby Cookie cry, these animals go to work on him. There are six uncles who are worse."

"Couldn't you go to a lawyer?"

He frowned in disbelief. "A *lawyer?* Diane, when Cookie and I finally split up, I got my separation from the Mafia. The uncles wouldn't let me leave her and somebody was going to wind up getting shot. When push comes to shove on the East Side, it's a tiny Sicilian village—you don't go to a lawyer to settle a beef, you go to a local boss. I had to see Carlucci. It was a mess."

"You're kidding me, Charlie."

"I'm not. Carlucci called a round table in the back of a social club on Mulberry Street. One hundred percent greaseball-style—glasses of espresso for everybody and the anisette bottle in the center of the table. Her oldest uncle presented their case, all in Italian. He wore a suit he must have bought in Palermo and a tie that made his face all red. Carlucci just sipped his espresso and let his eyes close half the time. Then he handed down a decision. First to the uncle in Italian, then to me in English. There was to be no more arguing, no more threats of violence. I was allowed to leave Cookie, but I had to do the right thing with money—a lump sum of two thousand, and a hundred a week forever. And she got the car."

"Was it a fair settlement, Charlie?"

"Fair, my ass. I had to go on the street for the two thousand, to one of Carlucci's people. I wound up paying eight hundred in juice. I'm sure the son of a bitch figured on it, too. How would he give me a fair shake? My father wasn't Italian. My mother's family raised me in the neighborhood, but it's not the same as being a hundred percent Italian. On top of that my mother's people are Neapolitan. For an old-time Sicilian like Carlucci, Naples is northern Italy. He had it in for me anyway, the old man. He'd never admit it—would have made him look petty, but when I was nine years old I used to beat up Carlucci's fat little nephew. Guido, the kid's name was. Him and an Irish kid from Hudson Street. Lester McQuigan. I had the two of them terrorized. In the fifth grade I got some whacky kid's idea and started my own religion. I made the two of them join—the only members. We used to run fake little Masses after school. McQuigan ran home and told his mother, after I made the two of them crown me pope. He thought he would go to hell. We had a regular little coronation in a basement on Carmine Street, the two of them kneeling on the cement floor until their knees hurt, then they put a little crown on my head. We cut it up out of Guido's father's fedora. A beautiful soft gray felt, with little points cut all around it. They were so scared of God blinding them or something, they refused to make me pope of the whole world—they tried to say I was only the pope of Carmine Street. I finally compromised on Greenwich Village. They both held the cut-up little fedora—all four hands on it—and set it on my head, while Guido said, 'We crown thee, Charles Moran, the Pope of Greenwich Village.'

I blessed them both with some ratty water from a puddle under a steam pipe.

"It was the high point of my life, for about two days. Until Lester McQuigan ratted to his mother. First the nuns whacked me silly, then Guido's father found out about the fedora and that I made Guido kneel down for half an hour. He caught me in the playground, in the middle of a punchball game. I got the worst kick in the ass of my whole childhood. Like a football. I swear he lifted me two feet off the ground.

"'*Il Papa de villaga,*' he hollered. '*Disgraziad! Meta Scapa Ungoula.*'

"Three weeks, I limped. And the name stuck for a long time. Paulie still calls me the pope sometimes."

"And you think Carlucci would remember that for twenty years?"

"Il Papa, he mumbled to me, when he set the two-thousand fine. He smiled at me."

"And what about your kids? You never see them?"

He shrugged. "You know what happens, Diane? The first couple of months I broke my ass to see them every Sunday. The zoo. The ferry. Cinerama. I left money at every Carvel stand in the city. Half the time Cathy is crying over something or other and Vinny gives me nothing but tight lips and a frown all day. He's eleven. He's already beginning to grunt like the uncles. I can *see* this Sicilian blood running through him. And I'm sure Cookie and the animals spend all week running me down to them. Then one Sunday I've got to work, and a few weeks later I'm so hung over I just can't get out of bed. And both times at the end of the day I was happier. And my guess was that the kids were, too. I just kind of let it drift. It's been almost a year. I wouldn't know what to say to them if I saw them tomorrow."

He walked to the kitchen and poured the last half-glass of beer from the bottle. It would be enough to finish off his headache. The marshal's letter wasn't so grim either, when he considered it. Once he left the state, all they could grab was the car. Which was fine. And the hundred a week to Cookie could stop. Carlucci owed nothing special to the Sicilians—he would shrug his shoulders and get rid of them with some crap in Italian about how the girl was better off with Charlie gone. Carlucci couldn't make a dime out of family fights. The first time neighborhood people came to him, it built up his stature. The second time was a pain in the ass.

In the living room Diane began to loosen up with arm-swinging exercises. That meant she had a one o'clock class at the mime theater and from there would go directly to work. Each time she reached toward the ceiling, the cashmere sweater she wore stretched across her breasts and slid up enough to expose a strip of white skin with her navel like a depressed bull's-eye in the center. Just below it a narrow band of black nylon showed—the elastic strip of bikini panties she wore under the dungarees. He watched her rise up, then ease down on her toes in a slow rhythm. She didn't have to leave for another half-hour, time enough for some fast action. It would put the finishing touch on his hangover, but when it was over she would definitely ask him not to work so they could celebrate her birthday.

She may have sensed what was on his mind; her pelvis seemed to thrust forward a little bit more than the exercise demanded. It wasn't worth it, he decided. If he came directly back after work, he could still get laid, without the dinner and three hours of TV later.

He took two eggs from the refrigerator and scrambled them while she settled into a yoga shoulder stand. She pushed up onto her shoulders, her back and legs perfectly vertical up to her toes. Her hair fell into a circle on the rug. From the kitchen it created the illusion that her body was a piece of sculpture cemented to the floor. He knew that she would hold the pose, absolutely still, for three or four minutes, breathing deeply.

He slid the eggs onto a plate and ate standing up, chewing slowly and concentrating on Diane to detect any tremor of her muscles. It reminded him of the poor shape his own body must be in after years of abuse. When he got settled in New England he would enroll in a gym—skip some rope each day and bang away at the light bag for half an hour. Maybe learn to ski. In two or three months his body would be like a rock.

He thought for a moment that he might tell her about New England, ask her to come along, then decided that it would be simpleminded. She was beautiful, but Boston must be loaded with beautiful women. He had made that mistake once with Cookie. Six years ago, after a four-thousand-dollar day at Belmont, he had gone on a weekend junket to the Dunes and had taken Cookie along. The bartender he worked with then couldn't believe he was taking his wife to Vegas. "Charlie," he had said, "when you're going out to eat in a fine steak house, you don't take along a McDonald's hamburger."

He had turned out to be right. Cookie had stood behind him counting every chip he lost and tugging at his sleeve to quit if he ran ahead two hundred. She had dogged him through the casinos, jinxing every table she came near, until he had dropped the entire four thousand from Belmont. By the time they reached the airport, he had left behind another twenty-five hundred in markers that would have to be made good in a week. On the airplane his body finally rebelled at the three days of constant pounding it had taken. He had kneeled in the cramped bathroom and vomited into the chemical pool until his insides ached, then gone back to his seat and crouched into it, suddenly so depressed that for a few minutes he thought he was going to cry. There was no fresh start in sight. For the first time in years, Cookie became tender.

A week later, during a screaming fight after he had spent the night with a stewardess in Flushing, he had justified it by telling Cookie that the bartender had called her a McDonald's hamburger. "You're twenty-five pounds overweight!" he had shouted. "You're a big fat Mac, and I spent the night with a trim little stewardess." She had picked up a vase; then, instead of throwing it, had sat on the edge of their bed and cried, holding the vase with both hands. He hadn't realized how much it had got to her until years later, during the round table with Carlucci. Halfway through the old uncle's plea in rapid Sicilian dialect, Charlie distinctly heard him cry, "Bigga Mac!" He had often thought that the two thousand had been the price Carlucci had put on that insult.

Diane lowered herself out of the shoulder stand into a sitting position, crossed her ankles, then stood without using her arms. She kept her back to him when she spoke.

"My mind became very clear during that shoulder stand, Charlie. It always does—I think the extra blood flow to the brain feeds it a lot more oxygen. I haven't come out and spoken my mind. And I have to."

She turned toward him. "I didn't go to the dentist this morning. I was at a clinic. I'm pregnant, Charlie."

He felt the hangover return. His eyes ached again. He leaned against the kitchen doorjamb and rubbed his palm across his forehead.

"Tell me one thing, Diane—"

She interrupted him. "Don't, Charlie. Please don't

ask me if I'm sure it's yours. I know it's what you're going to do."

"Jesus *Christ,* Diane! How could you think I would ask you that? I know better than that."

She saw right through him, he thought. The way Cookie did. What the hell was the matter with him that every last broad he hooked up with could read him like a book? The chubby Sicilians and naïve blond WASPS from Maine.

"I'm going to have the baby, Charlie. I'm not going to pressure you to stay, but I want the baby. You do whatever you think is right."

chapter

VI

Barney twisted the gooseneck stand to bring the magnifier into his line of vision. He focused on the escapement wheel and decided there was no way to salvage it; the teeth were worn down to slivers. The clock itself was a seven-foot-tall grandfather built in 1872, not a production model. That would mean milling and case-hardening a new wheel. Barney decided to go to lunch first. He switched off the bench lamp and pulled on his overcoat. The material felt thin between his fingers. He looked down and realized that the coat was badly worn, already frayed at the cuffs. At best he might get the winter out of it. He double-locked the shop door and rattled it several times, then walked quickly toward Westchester Avenue.

Hanratty's had the noontime regulars spotted along the bar; retirees' row, Barney called it, a dozen pensioned-off subway conductors, telephone installers, or Con Ed clerks, patiently working through their daily shot and a beer ration. They gazed up at the silent cable-TV news written across the tube. The usual crew of local shopkeepers was clustered down at the service end, chewing on club sandwiches or hamburgers. Barney shifted a stool closer to them and responded to the greetings with a nod. Tim Riley was tending bar, the Thursday relief man. That meant a heaping plate of corned beef and cabbage as the special. It also meant several good bar stories out of Riley.

He was already leaning forward in storytelling position, his right foot lifted up onto the edge of the sink, protruding from under the apron. He was speaking in a near whisper—his County Kerry conspiratorial voice. The subject of the story must be someone further down the bar. Barney realized that Riley was talking about Francis Cullen, an old-timer sitting under the TV who had years ago been a cop.

"He was on the mounted force, in the late thirties, when there were a lot more horses being used in midtown. Four different times the horse come marching into the station house alone, at the end of an eight-to-four tour, looking for his bag of oats—Cullen meanwhile in one of the West Forty-sixth Street gin mills gulping Seagram's Seven out of a coffee mug. Purposely wouldn't go to the stable, Francis claimed, where someone might just quietly feed him and forget about Francis. No, the horse would go right up the few steps of the station house and clomp across the floor with his noisy shoes, then stand in front of the desk sergeant and look him in the eye, waiting to be fed.

"Come four o'clock, every day, the horse would quit work like a union man hearing the whistle. Head west on Forty-sixth, he would, stopping at each saloon along the block and poking his head into the front door. Every bartender in the neighborhood knew the horse. If Francis didn't turn up, it was back to the precinct alone for the horse.

"Francis detested the beast—Kevin was its name. It's never been easy, you know, the mounted force. All that crap people believe about a policeman and his horse loving one another—nothing of the kind. Every shift is spent with the animal. A man can never duck into a movie house, or into a friendly girl's apartment for a few hours on a bitter night—the damned horse is always along. A big, stupid animal that can't be hidden in a doorway. It's only a matter of time till the man and the beast come to despise one another. Francis often said that he had spent whole tours in the rain cursing at the animal, who would do nothing but stare straight ahead with his big, watery eyes. 'He plays dumb, but the bastard knows how to torture me,' Francis would say.

"Then Francis fell head over heels for a red-haired bimbo living in Hell's Kitchen, just off Tenth Avenue. He had himself a snootful along Forty-sixth one night, and at ten o'clock went up to her apartment, pulling the horse behind. The big lunk of a Polish super goes charging off to the station house to complain. Francis never could explain to the sergeant what the horse was doing on the third-floor landing of this tenement building, hitched as secure as you like to the banister. And Kevin must have taken a liking to the warm hallway—it took the sergeant and three husky patrolmen to push and pull the animal down the three flights of steps. On the way up, the horse had left a steaming pile of horseshit in the middle of the second-floor landing—it's why the super went to the sergeant in the first place. Francis always claimed the horse had done it spitefully. 'Kevin never in his life shit at ten P.M.,' he told me. 'He was always so regular he could have been using Carter's Little Liver Pills.' "

Gerald Boyle, who had the TV shop next to Barney's, interrupted. "I always wondered how he got on the cops at all, with the speech impediment he's got. The man damn near needs a pad and pencil to hold a conversation. And when he's nervous, getting a clear sentence out of him is hopeless."

"It wasn't always so," Riley said. "Francis had a bit of a stroke just a few years ago. It affected his speech something awful."

"So that's how Cullen was bounced off the force," Boyle said. "It's no wonder the old sot is bitter. Imagine being fucked out of a pension by some Polish super!"

Riley used the break to fill their glasses. Barney decided on a light scotch and soda.

"That wasn't it at all," Riley said. "Back in the thirties, they wouldn't fire a cop over a minor thing like that. Francis was transferred—to the four-two in the south Bronx, which covered the Mott Haven railroad yards. A stinking beat for a mounted cop. And didn't they transfer the horse with him! Francis claimed it was the one bit of perverse satisfaction he got— that the horse was sent off to the boondocks, too.

"Francis stayed off the sauce completely for two weeks, but in winter the wind is something fierce across those open tracks. He took to tucking a flask under his greatcoat and cooping for a few hours inside an empty boxcar. He would set a couple of planks up to the car door and lead the horse right in with him. Claimed it gave him a feeling of security he never felt in Manhattan, having Kevin under his thumb that way. 'The animal won't be causing mischief, as he did whenever he cared to go traipsing along the sidewalk of Forty-sixth Street poking his long nose through every set of saloon doors he saw, like some cranky wife.'

"It was the freezing January of nineteen thirty-eight that done poor Cullen in. It dropped to near zero for a week running and forced him to buy himself a bigger flask. Sure enough, he overdid it—the flask held just a bit more than he could handle in his cozy boxcar coop. The very first night he had it he fell asleep—and woke up rattling along at a steady pace across the Jersey meadows, with the New York skyline fading away behind and the horse standing beside him just as calm as you please. 'Staring off into space, he was. Waiting for four o'clock, no doubt,' Francis said. 'The only thing the narrow-minded beast ever thought about was the bag full of oats would get hung on his head at the end of his shift.'

"Francis could have hopped off the train every time it slowed for a curve, but he couldn't persuade the horse to jump. Francis said, 'He stood quivering like an old biddy caught halfway across Fordham Road when the traffic light changed. As we approached the Delaware border, I went so far as to threaten him with me service revolver—pressed the barrel right up against his nose. The creature may as well have had his hooves set into concrete. He wouldn't budge.'

"When the train finally stopped, the jig was up for poor Francis Cullen. Near midnight it was, and him already eight hours overdue, in full uniform and leading a horse across the freight yards in Baltimore, Maryland. 'The beast was so hungry he was nibbling me collar,' Francis said. 'Even in that predicament he could think of nothing but his stomach!'

"They had to send a van down from New York to bring the two of them back. It was all over for Francis. The horse was never even disciplined."

Riley made a tour of the bar, refilling glasses and emptying ashtrays. Cullen, too, had a retarded kid, Barney knew. In her thirties and still at home. He had taken an early retirement from a brewery job just a few years ago. Barney guessed that contacts in the department had arranged for him to get into the union right after he was bounced off the force. From a good pension job to a fair one, but both pension jobs, while Barney had spent his life looking to pull a fast one. Now the old son of a bitch had something to fall back on while Barney was pushing sixty and still scrambling. And Cullen had a little extra pension going for him that only Barney knew about—a ring of fourteen keys that had once belonged to Barney and now netted Cullen a comfortable hundred a week, tax-free.

Barney had shared a cell in Coxsackie for six months with a soft-spoken Puerto Rican kid called Joe Loco, a wiry ex-gang fighter from St. Ann's Avenue in the Bronx. The kid was quick-witted and curious and looked to Barney for advice. Six years later, Loco had walked into Barney's shop and presented an idea. Outside, in the trunk of his car, were fifteen pay phones, pried off walls with a crowbar during fifteen separate burglaries in different parts of the city. Loco was sure that Barney could disassemble them and figure out the key system used by the telephone company for collectors to remove the full coin boxes and replace them with empties. "If the fifteen phones ain't enough, Barney, say so," Loco had said. "I get you however many more you need to figure out the system."

Barney had deciphered it all after sawing through the tenth box: A set of fourteen keys would allow any coin box in New York City to be removed. He worked day and night cutting the keys. Before the week was out, he and Loco were in action.

It had been a beautiful scam while it lasted. Over a frantic Labor Day weekend they had hit Kennedy, La Guardia, and Newark airports for hundreds of boxes and split nine thousand dollars in quarters, dimes, and nickels. They eased up then, whacking out a dozen restaurants along Queens Boulevard on a Tuesday afternoon and maybe doing a line of cigar stores on Flatbush Avenue that Friday, grabbing themselves an easy deuce apiece each week.

Then Joe Loco disappeared. A year later Barney heard that he had been stabbed during a game of eight ball in a poolroom on Southern Boulevard; he had bled to death on the sidewalk a block away, heading in the direction of Lincoln Hospital. Barney had continued at an easy pace for another two years, knocking down a quiet few hundred a week.

Until Francis Cullen had spotted him going into a drugstore booth on upper Broadway one afternoon, and studied him closely enough to sense that something was wrong. His old cop instincts went to work and he followed Barney through six more stops, then shook him down for the ring of keys. For three years now Cullen each week had emptied a hundred dollars' worth of coin boxes. "Maybe a bit heavier toward Christmas," he had told Barney over a drink, "what with all the holiday expenses. I'm not about to become greedy at the start of me golden years. I see it as an extra pension coming in, from the telephone company instead of the police department."

He had lifted his shot glass and tapped it softly against Barney's, then drained it and nodded appreciatively. "It's a first-rate set of keys you cut there, Barney. I'd recommend your work to anyone. Have another," he had said, and patted Barney's shoulder. "It's a pleasure to be able to buy a drink for a craftsman of your caliber."

Barney was afraid to cut a new set of keys. He was convinced that Cullen would eventually be pinched, and ten minutes later would have cops tearing the shop apart. Barney had written it off as finished, deciding it was great while it lasted but that every scam had a natural life-span. When they died, it was best to walk away ahead of the game, with no hard feelings. Cullen had no such idea. He had confided to Barney that before his liver gave out he intended to pass the keys on to his son, who was five years short of retiring from the police department. "Michael will know just what to do with the little key ring—he hasn't been fifteen years on the job for nothing. This will be worth more than a beat in Harlem. It's a regular little annuity I'll be leaving him."

Now Barney sipped the scotch and soda. It would have to be his last if he was to have a few beers with the corned beef and still hope to machine a new escapement wheel this afternoon. He looked down toward where Cullen was, then removed his glasses and scrubbed them with a cocktail napkin, knowing as he did it that it wouldn't help. It didn't. The end of the bar was still a haze—a blur of color on the television screen; the oval neon Rheingold sign suspended inside the front window; what Barney knew were potato chips clipped onto a vertical rack at the front of the bar; and a figure hunched forward that would be Cullen, with his beak full of busted blood vessels and the magic key ring safe in his pants pocket.

Barney's stomach tightened up with a surge of anger. This fat and happy old barfly who was still pissed off at some long-dead horse was sitting on the keys, while Barney was about to go on a score that could easily put him away for five if it went sour. And it would be tough time to do, looking forward to coming out of the gates nearly blind at sixty-three, rehabilitated and ready for a fresh start, two years shy of what for most people would be a social security pension but for him would mean zero; he had never in his life owned a social security card. How the hell would Nora get along for five years? Welfare, he supposed.

And Roger? Would welfare cover him, or would they stick the poor soul into Willowbrook?

He couldn't blame his life on Cullen; he had planned ahead while Barney had been busy chasing next week's pot of gold. The shot he had missed was right after the war, when his record was still light enough for him to have fought his way into a locksmith's license. By now he would have been knocking down a comfortable twenty-five a year and looking forward to a small condominium in Florida.

The bartender set down a corned-beef plate and a beer. His body didn't need the calories, but he was sure that his eyes would go long before his heart anyway. What he needed now was a solid little business that would get him through the next ten years and maybe let him accumulate enough to keep Roger out of the public institutions after Barney's eyes or heart finally did go. He stuffed his mouth with corned beef and took a long swallow of the cold beer. If the score didn't go sour, it might work out yet. At age fifty-eight, another big if. If Nora hadn't wanted a baby too late in life, Roger wouldn't be a problem now. If Cullen hadn't seen him that day on Broadway, if the nasty old bastard had been hit with his stroke two years earlier, if Barney had gone into locksmithing . . . *if*. Now, if these two kids knew what they were talking about with this trucking-company safe, there might be a little pot of gold at the end of this week's rainbow.

chapter

VII

Paulie's brother was waiting for him in the hospital lobby. Up close there was the fish smell on him, which meant that he had come directly from work.

"I think we need passes to go up, Paulie."

Paulie headed for the bank of elevators. "Come on! These yo-yos try to throw you out, they're going to smell from fish for three days."

They were alone in the elevator.

"I didn't have time to run home and shower." He sniffed loudly. "I got no sense of smell. Is it that bad, Paulie?"

"Don't worry about it, Vito. I've smelled it a lot worse. The chloroform helps kill it."

They found the old man sitting up in bed. Each of them kissed him.

"How do you feel, pop?"

"I feel lousy."

"So what do they say?"

He drew his forefinger across his stomach. "They want to cut me."

59

"For what, pop?"

"For what! For fifteen hundred bucks they get for an hour's work. These people beat the Mafia when it comes to shaking someone down. Carlucci don't make fifteen hundred an hour."

"They say what it is, pop?"

"The ulcer's bleeding again. Karlinsky says they got to open me up."

"Karlinsky's gonna do it, pa?" Vito asked.

"Karlinsky don't operate. He's got another Jew does the cutting. They spread the money around, these people. A third guy feeds you the gas, he whacks you for three hundred. I can go on Mott Street tomorrow and get someone killed for the same money this guy gets for giving gas. The Italians always worked too cheap."

Paulie brought his palms together in a position of prayer. "But, Jesus *Christ,* pop. Six months ago Karlinsky warned you—watch your diet!"

"I did."

"My ass you did. When I saw you two weeks ago at the Primavera, you had your face in a bowl of scungilli—shoveling them in like somebody heading for the electric chair in the morning."

"I had a yen for it, Paulie." He reached to the end table and lit a cigarette.

"Karlinsky lets you smoke, pa?"

He inhaled deeply. "Who is he, Vito, the pope? This guy knows *everything?*"

He puffed at the cigarette quietly.

"This whole thing ain't fair, Paulie. I'm fucking cursed. My father—he should rest—he drank a bottle of wine with every meal and he used to grind red pepper on his marinara sauce. Eighty-three when he died. The last meal he ate was a couple of bracioles you could have busted a plate-glass window with.

They never even repeated on him. I ate bland every Tuesday of my life since I was twenty to keep my system clear. When I was living with your mother, she never had a drop of olive oil in the house wasn't Bertolli, no matter how tough things were. It's all I keep in my apartment now, and it's up to thirteen fifty a gallon."

He ground out the cigarette and coughed. "I'm cursed."

"You'll be fine, pa."

"You had to mention that bowl of scungilli, Paulie —I suddenly got a yen for them you wouldn't believe. Meanwhile I'm sitting here bleeding inside. How's your mother?"

"She's fine, pop."

"She won't be up to visit?"

They looked toward Vito.

"I don't think so, pa. She says you brought it on yourself."

"She gave me plenty of help. For twenty-five years the juices were boiling inside me. She knew just how to stir them up."

He lit another cigarette.

"My aunt Maria—she should rest—told me before I got married, 'Vincie, this girl will give you nothing but *agina*.' Christ, was she right. In nineteen thirty-nine she blew a *three-thousand-dollar* score for me. You know what three thousand was in nineteen thirty-nine? That's where this ulcer got started. I was running numbers on Pleasant Avenue and she was supposed to—"

"We heard it, pop. A hundred times. You're getting all red in the face for nothing."

"I want to be sure it's on the record with you kids. In case this operation goes sour. What's the use of talking? How's the job, Vito?"

"It's good, pa."

The old man sniffed loudly. "What do you do, Vito, you waltz around the market all day with a striped bass? Why don't you look for work in a meat market?"

"I didn't get home to shower."

Paulie heard someone enter the room behind him. An enormously fat man in a white nurse's uniform glided through the door, holding a pleated paper cup in each hand. He looked Vito over carefully as he crossed the room. "Pill time, Mr. Lastrangillo." He turned toward Paulie and Vito. "You'll have to leave for a few minutes. There's a little sitting area halfway down the hall."

"He can't swallow pills with us here?"

He held up a thermometer. "Tempy time, too."

They walked toward the door as the old man took the paper cups. He called to them, "If I scream, you come in and drop this fat fag out the window!"

The nurse laughed. "Enough fooling, Mr. Lastrangillo. Let's roll over now."

Paulie and Vito walked slowly through the corridor.

"I think pop's right, Paulie. That guy looks queer. I don't like the way he looked me over."

"No kidding. I happen to *know* him, except he don't recognize me. That's Fat Waldo the Waiter. While he was going to nursing school, he worked nights on the floor at Cody's. It's a steak house up the street from the Good Times. The bartenders and waiters there couldn't believe this guy. He ain't just gay, this is a total degenerate. Anything that's warm and that moves, he tries to get his dick into it. Guys, broads, animals—it don't matter. He gets horny at the end of a night shift, he nails one of those Fourteenth Street junkies nodding on the sidewalk near Luchow's and throws them a sawbuck. If there's nothing else doing, he'll cruise the subway looking for action in the men's rooms. I know half a dozen people watched him bang a goat at a New Year's party on the West Side."

"He ain't Italian, is he, Paulie?"

"Polack. From Rumania, or someplace. His parents still live on a farm upstate. Five years ago they went over to Europe and brought him back a wife. A tiny little eighteen-year-old that can't weigh more than ninety pounds. Fat Waldo's got to run two ninety, three hundred. This little broad was so innocent it took her a year to wise up to him. By now she must be as degenerate as him. He used to bring guys home at three in the morning, lead them into the bathroom, and tell her he was showing them his new electric razor. He used to run the razor so she would hear it buzz while he was doing his number. You know Jimmy Dee, the bartender?"

Vito nodded.

"They worked together at Cody's. Jimmy was behind the bar cutting fruit when a brand-new chef, a Chinaman who had only been there four hours prepping vegetables for dinner, comes running out of the kitchen screaming in Chinese. Fat Waldo had been shucking clams next to the Chinaman and got so carried away he lost control. He grabs the chink, pins him up against the reach-in box, and puts a fucking hickey the size of a saucer on this guy's neck. Jimmy said it was so purple the poor guy must have been pinned against the box for a full three minutes. They heard him screaming in the kitchen but figured he was on the phone with another Chinaman."

"The chink didn't go after him?"

"He wanted *out*. He never even came back for his four hours' pay. This guy is powerful, Vito. You get three hundred pounds hugging you tight and sucking the side of your neck for three or four minutes, you just want out."

"How did he get away?"

"One of the colored cooks walked in the kitchen while it was going on and whacked Fat Waldo on the back of the head with a cast-iron stock pot. He said it took three solid shots before the fag loosened up on the Chinaman. Fat Waldo claimed the Chinaman was just starting to like it. He swore that the last thirty seconds he felt the chink's tongue trying for his ear, but the cook claimed no, he never would have broke them up if that was so."

"They didn't fire him, Paulie?"

"Fags are great waiters. The Chinaman didn't even have a green card. A Chinese kid named Po Ching who was bussing tables at Cody's when it happened told me the poor bastard had only been in the country six days. He nearly suffocated coming across the Canadian border jammed in with thirty-five other chinks inside an empty gasoline tank truck. They climbed out of the hatches on the American side into two feet of snow, sucking for air like a bunch of mosquitoes just been hit with spray. Five hundred apiece the driver whacked them for. For a guy got nothing going for him but a teamsters card, that ain't a bad score, Vito—eighteen large for a half-hour run."

"This fat fag really figured he could score with the Chinaman?"

"No. According to the people who worked with him, the fag gets so passionate he loses control. He can't help himself. And you *can't* turn the son of a bitch off. No matter what you do, he's going to use you. Jimmy Dee and him were putting away stock in the liquor room and Fat Waldo must have watched Jimmy keep on bending over and reaching up. After twenty minutes he lost control. He suddenly grabs him around the waist from behind and starts dry-humping him. He's panting like a polar bear and telling Jimmy that he loves him. Jimmy finally squirms around, hits him a shot in the nose makes him bleed, then belts him two or three more times around the eyes. All the while Fat Waldo is pumping away, face-to-face now. He's finally hurt enough so he lets loose, Jimmy hits him a shot on the forehead nearly busts a knuckle and Fat Waldo's knees buckle on him and he's on the floor in a heap."

"Jimmy Dee went to work on him, Paulie?"

"He was about to when the degenerate gets hold of his ankle, begins slobbering on his shoes hollering, 'More! More! Beat me, I deserve it.' Jimmy said if he had started kicking him, the son of a bitch would have come."

Vito shivered a little. "This queer makes a move for me, Paulie, I break his legs."

"You better do it quick, Vito. Jimmy Dee told me over a brandy that the scary part is if the fag had hung on two more minutes Jimmy would have been in real trouble—he thinks he was starting to like it."

Waldo came out of the room and walked down the corridor toward them. He stopped and said, "Your dad said for just Paulie to go in, the other one should wait." He winked at Vito and wrinkled his nose as he started to walk again. "You're a cute little thing, but change your perfume, honey."

Paulie left Vito and went into the room. "What's wrong, pop?"

"Nothing. I want to talk for a few minutes without Vito. We got a problem, Paulie."

"What's the problem?"

"This operation. What if I don't make it, Paulie?"

"Don't be crazy, pop. It's an ulcer operation. People don't die from ulcer operations."

The old man pointed furiously toward the ceiling. "My sweet ass they don't! People croak in that operating room every day from tonsils, appendix, from fucking cataracts! Don't you see the papers, Paulie? These Jews sew you up, sometimes they leave half the hospital inside you. Rubber gloves, sponges, scissors, the fucking surgeon's wristwatch. Forget about the chances you'll drop dead because they feed you too much gas or they let some kid do the cutting, or some fucking supergerm they don't know how to fight gets in there. Don't kid yourself, Paulie, they wheel me into that room they might as well be wheeling me into the casino at Caesar's Palace—I'm in a real crap game."

Paulie squeezed the old man's hand. "Don't be crazy, pop. It's only a lousy ulcer. Maybe you should get out of here and go into Columbus. It's all Italians there. Half the nurses are nuns, from the other side. And you get an Italian doctor you might not be so worried he'll leave something inside you."

The old man shook his head. "Paulie, let me tell you something you shouldn't forget. You want to eat good, hang out with Italians. For doctors, go to Jews. For surgeons especially. They don't really believe in God. Not the same way we do. Somebody's going to stretch you out on a table and slice you like a leg of veal, you don't want some old-time greaseball believes it's really in God's hands. You die, they'll say it was God's will. The nuns are worse. They'll say a rosary over you instead of running for a tank of oxygen. The Jews keep working."

"So then relax, pop."

"What are you going to do, Paulie? Suppose I did go. What's going to happen to you? And your kid brother? You're in hock to your ears all the time, and he clears a yard a week chopping the heads off fish —every Puerto Rican kid pushes a rack through the garment center makes that. And neither one of you

can read. This day and age, Paulie, you don't know
how to read, you might as well be born with a club-
foot."

Paulie punched the railing of the bed lightly. "What
do you mean I can't read? You never seen me read
the *News,* pop? I read the *News* every morning."

"You look at the funnies, Paulie. And the pictures.
Tell the truth."

"I read! I read what it says under the pictures. The
titles. I read it slow, but I read it, pop."

The old man lit a cigarette. "Nicky tells me you
bought a horse."

"Nicky who?"

"The nose. He says you bought a racehorse."

Paulie looked down modestly. "Not a whole horse,
pop. A third. There's three of us."

The old man closed his eyes for a few moments,
then opened them and seemed surprised that Paulie
was still beside the bed. "You're twenty-eight, Paulie.
You got to stop behaving like you're fifteen. Your
mother's not doing you no favor bringing manicotti
over twice a week and washing your laundry. The
Rockefellers own racehorses. Big-shot Mafiosos own
racehorses. Waiters don't own racehorses, Paulie."

He closed his eyes for a few moments.

"You went on the street for the money?"

"Most of it."

"To who?"

"To Nappy."

"For how much?"

"Twenty-eight hundred."

"What's he banging you for?"

"A hundred a week juice for as long as the loan is
out. He went light on the interest, but I can't pay no
principal in pieces. I got to get back the whole twenty-
eight hundred in one piece."

"You got no gripe there, Paulie. But how the hell are you going to make the payments?"

"I'll make them, pop. The horse has got to run in the money a couple of times, too, no?"

"Where did the rest of the money come from?"

"Another twelve hundred. From the loan company. Value Finance, on Canal Street."

"They gave you money? What's wrong with them? Paulie, you can't get fifteen cents' credit at a department store, you're working on a phony social security number—how the hell did these people hand you twelve hundred?"

He adjusted his cuff links. "It's nothing, pop. You throw a hundred to the guy who makes the loan. You deal with the assistant manager. He writes the loan for thirteen hundred, you take twelve, and a yard goes south to him. There's no problem."

"What if you can't meet all these payments, Paulie?"

"Pop, you got to *see* this horse. As soon as you're out of here, we'll ride out to Belmont. It's like the country there, nice wood barns and grass all around. Starry Skies, her name is. A big brown filly with a white patch between her eyes. This horse is going to make money, pop. I feel it in my bones."

"Paulie, I don't wish you any hard luck. I hope this horse makes a million. But mark my words—if I don't come out of that operating room you remember this, and maybe then you'll listen to some of the other advice I gave you—this horse is going to cost you money. You'll never see even a little piece of baccalà out of this deal."

He reached for another cigarette, discovered that the pack was empty, and crumpled it.

"It's better you don't smoke, pop."

"Jesus *Christ*. I'm surrounded. Everybody tells me

I can't eat and I can't smoke." He dropped the crumpled pack onto the night table. "I should have been tougher with you, Paulie. With Vito, too. My brother whacked his kids a lot more, and they're better off for it. Look at Nicky. He's only three, four years older than you, he's got two kids, a little house on Staten Island, he trades in an Olds Ninety-Eight every two years, and he's sitting in a soft job with the butcher's union."

"Pop, I don't have nothing against the nose—he's my first cousin—but he ain't my idea of a big success. Soft union job or not."

The old man's face got red. "How can you say that, Paulie? Don't you *see* the difference? Nicky knocks down twenty large a year just in salary, for Christ's sake! He's got a half a dozen trees he can go out and shake for fifty whenever he needs it, and at Christmas he shakes maybe two thousand down—no taxes. How can you say he's not a success, Paulie? You're in hock for thousands and all you got going for you is a million-to-one shot on a fucking horse."

Paulie stabbed the air with his forefinger to make his point. "Nicky the nose ain't even *Napolidon,* for Christ's sake! He takes after his mother all the way, pop. With money especially. He's fucking Genoese through and through. He don't go for spit. You stand at a bar with him, pop, you got to embarrass him into reaching for a tab. His Ninety-Eight is double-parked outside, all Simonized, but meanwhile he tips bartenders with *change,* pop. The nose shines his own fucking *shoes!*"

"So what do you call a success, Paulie?"

"Knowing how to *spend* it. I take a broad out, I drop sixty on dinner. I never ordered a brandy in my life wasn't Cordon Bleu. Last year I took five hundred from *shylocks* for two tickets to Sinatra at the Garden.

Two-fifty a ticket! I sat·three seats away from Tony Bennett. I took a girl whose name I don't even remember now. And, pop, I enjoyed every minute of it. I'd do it again tomorrow if he was in town. That's success! Twenty-five years from now I'll still remember Sinatra with his tie loose, singing 'My Way,' while the nose sits on Staten Island counting his nickels like some old greaseball and covering up his fig trees every winter with tin cans and tar paper."

"The old greaseballs don't have such a bad life either, Paulie. Wrapping up fig trees and squeezing a big vat of grapes in the cellar every year ain't exactly a sentence."

"It's dull, pop."

"So is owning six lousy jukebox locations spread all over the Bronx. That's what Philly Mack ended up with. Your uncle. Six jukeboxes and a tired little saloon in Astoria that grinds out a yard and a half a week for him. With the Con Ed meter jumped. He's sixty-three and spent his whole life the way you're starting out—a half a thief. So what's he got now?"

"What about Uncle Pete, pop? Pete Grillo's your closest friend. You think he's got such a tough life?"

"Pete Grillo is a fully made wise guy. Pete Grillo got a button, Paulie. Use your fucking head—Pete's a Mafioso, you're a waiter. How the hell can you think of ever being Pete Grillo?"

He closed his eyes for a minute, then opened them. "I ain't so sure Pete's got such a great life either, Paulie. He don't look so happy to me, even with a new Caddie every year. I'll take the fig trees on Staten Island."

They looked at one another quietly. Paulie moved closer to the bed and touched the old man's hand. "What are you trying to say, pop?"

"Just you should think ahead, Paulie. I worry that

you'll get your back to the wall if you're not careful with the shylocks and take a shot at something might put you away if you get caught. You're a waiter. Don't think so big."

Paulie squeezed his hand. "If I don't see a way out of waiting tables all my life, I'd pack it in now, pop. I don't care if I read slow, I ain't going to be a waiter all my life."

He winked at the old man. "But I'm not going to do time, either, pop. I'm only five-foot-three."

chapter

VIII

The place was on Greenwich Street—a narrow, five-story loft building with a grimy brick front and a vertical line of boarded-up windows where the freight elevator ran. A large sign on each window and a dull red bulb warned firemen that it opened into a shaft. The street-level store had been converted into a tire-repair shop for trailer trucks. A loading dock and freight elevator beside it seemed to be used only by a doll manufacturer who occupied the second and third floors. The trucking company office they would hit was on the fourth. The top floor belonged to Local 1 of the Amalgamated Leather Belt Cutters Union.

Barney had decided they would go onto the loft building off the roof of an adjacent tenement. Only a narrow alley separated the two buildings, with the tenement parapet a few feet higher than the loft. A ten-foot ladder would span it comfortably. Paulie's eyes had grown wide when he heard it, and he had said, "I don't work above the first floor without a net, Barney. What is this—Topkapi we're busting into? I'm no cat burglar. I'm a waiter and a small-time thief." He had later asked Charlie privately, "You think this guy knows what he's talking about, Charlie?"

"He better, or we're all in trouble. I got my fingers crossed."

"I wish he would get himself some contact lenses, Charlie. Even when he's talking sense, I take one look at those magnifiers he wears and he looks like a yo-yo. They're just so fucking *thick*."

The next afternoon Barney ran a hundred feet of movie film for them that showed every detail of the building roof clearly. "No big deal," he had said. "I took one of those fifteen-dollar helicopter flights around lower Manhattan and slipped the pilot a double sawbuck to hover for a few minutes. Told him I was shooting footage for a low-budget film."

The film showed a small skylight in the center of the roof. Barney said that the ladder used to bridge the roofs would get them down nicely from the skylight.

"The skylight won't be bugged, Barney?" Paulie asked.

"It's ten to one against it. People usually let those alarm systems go stale, unless they really got something to protect. Who's going to bust into the belt cutters union?"

Charlie glanced up from his *Daily Telegraph*. "The FBI. Who the hell else goes into union offices?"

Barney nodded.

"What if it is bugged?" Charlie asked.

"If it is bugged—*if*—then it's definitely just hooked up to a bell. That place *couldn't* be wired into Holmes. Whatever Mickey Mouse setup might be on that skylight has got to be a joke to disarm."

"So when do we go in?" Paulie asked.

"Saturday night. Nine-thirty or ten. Just in case we do run into a hard time, it gives me thirty hours or so."

"What about a car?"

"We rent one. A small van. A truck attracts a lot less attention on that street." He looked toward Charlie. "You drive a shift?"

He nodded.

"You better give me your license—I'll need it for your description. I can have a phony made up by Saturday morning. You can use it to rent the truck. Cost us a yard."

They agreed.

Charlie drove the truck slowly through the surrounding streets, watching mainly for parked police cars.

"Especially along the docks," Barney said. "If they're going to coop anyplace, it's there. And from the docks we'll be silhouetted against the sky—we'll be like ducks in a shooting gallery crawling across that ladder."

"You'd think the cops would be scared to go near those docks, guns or no guns," Paulie said. "You ever see some of the SM fags walk into those old terminals at night? Big motherfuckers. Everything they're wearing made out of raunchy black leather. Some of them got fucking *chains* slung over their shoulder. I drive through West Street some nights, it looks like the Hell's Angels are holding a meeting. Big, mean bastards, and every one of them queer as a three-dollar bill. It's enough to scare the shit out of you." He shuddered a little. "I heard some mornings the cops find *cocks* in those buildings. Laying on the floor. These fags get so carried away beating up on people they chop a guy's *cock* off. You think that's true, Charlie?

You think they really find cocks laying around in there, or it's bullshit?" He shuddered again.

"Who told you that?"

"Tommy the cop. He works the Sixth Precinct. He claims plenty of mornings they find cocks laying around, but they just keep it quiet so people don't have something else to get up in arms about."

"You mean they sweep them under the rug, Paulie?" Charlie asked.

"I don't know what the hell they do with them. They probably just kick them into the river."

They rode silently for a block, then Paulie shook his head from side to side. "What do you think happens to the poor bastards who *lose* their cocks? Can you——"

"Jesus Christ, kid, change the subject," Barney said.

Paulie shuddered slightly, but kept quiet for a few minutes. He whistled between his teeth until Charlie asked him to stop.

"What's in the suitcases, Barney?" Paulie asked.

"The two small ones are tools. The one you're sitting on is oxyacetylene tanks and a torch. There's some food in there, too."

Paulie was surprised. "What kind of food?"

"A nice imported salami and Swiss cheese. Italian bread. Mustard. Plastic cups. Some concentrated apple juice and two big thermoses of coffee."

"You got an *appetite,* Barney? I couldn't eat a thing all day."

"That's what the food's for. Three or four hours in there, you'll be starving."

Charlie stopped for a light, then turned onto Greenwich Street. "You had to wrap the ladder up like that, Barney?" he asked.

"It looks a lot better carrying a long, skinny box than dragging a ladder across the sidewalk at ten o'clock."

"Where do we park it?"

"Right in front of the apartment house, where any solid citizen would park."

Charlie pulled up beside the empty curb and cut the lights and the engine.

"Wipe off everything might have fingerprints on it," Barney said. "The wheel, the knobs, door handles, the rearview mirror. Sounds like bullshit, but you never know. Paulie, you carry the case you're sitting on. Charlie, the two small ones. Try to make them look light. I got the ladder. Don't look up and down the block. Get it in your heads that we're one hundred percent legitimate. We *own* the fucking place. We *belong* here."

They moved easily across the sidewalk and into the vestibule, hesitating for only a few seconds while Barney reached forward and opened the inner door with a plastic strip. They walked up the five flights without seeing anyone, hearing the same television programs at each landing. The strong odor of cooked cabbage permeated the third and fourth floors.

"People are going to *eat* that stuff?" Paulie whispered, and pinched his nose. "They'll die. For sure, they'll die."

Barney negotiated the stairs carefully, steering the leading edge of the boxed ladder up into the stairwell each time he turned. When they reached the roof door, he motioned for them to stay put while he caught his breath. After a few minutes he told them, "I go first. Then you, Paulie, then Charlie. Close the door behind you soft and easy, and *tiptoe* across this roof. There's people right under us and they'll be able to hear a dime drop. When we reach the edge, just crouch down while I set up the ladder." He zipped his jacket closed. "Nice and easy now. We head to our left. Short, light steps, and there's no rush."

He pushed the door open slowly. The cold, steady wind blowing off the Hudson hit their faces. The sky was clear. They made their way to the edge of the roof silently. Barney set the ladder down, slit open the corrugated wrapper with a penknife, and jammed the flat carton between two vent pipes. He swung the ladder into position with Charlie's help. It sloped down at an angle.

"I go first. Charlie, you hang on to this end of the ladder. It won't lay still by itself. Hold on like a vise —you let it slip six inches and I go down."

Charlie braced his knees against the parapet and clenched a rung with both hands. He leaned forward slightly and peered over the edge. Below the third floor the brick walls disappeared into the darkness; he could barely make out a row of garbage cans on the ground. Barney backed onto the ladder, pressing his body against it and feeling with his feet for the rungs. When he was stretched out fully, he told Paulie to set the suitcase on the ladder in front of him. He backed across to the loft roof, sliding the suitcase along the ladder rails, then made the trip twice more with the tools.

"Paulie, you come next. Come across backward, like I did."

Paulie sat on the parapet and swung his legs onto the ladder, then inched himself over until he was on it fully, lying on his back.

"On your stomach, Paulie!" Barney whispered.

"Fuck that," Paulie whispered. "I look down and I'll freeze here for a week."

He grasped the sides of the ladder and pulled himself across in short jerks. Charlie came across easily, while Barney steadied his end of the ladder. They pulled it across and laid it on the roof.

The skylight wasn't wired. Barney opened one of

the tool cases and took out work gloves. He dropped two pairs near them, pulled on his own, then dug back in the case and located a roll of wide gaffer's tape. There was enough light for him to work by. He criss-crossed the skylight with strips of tape, then folded a bath towel over one pane of glass and rapped it with the side of a hammer, a short, hard blow. A few pieces fell to the floor below and tinkled in the silence. Most of the glass clung in small pieces to the strips of tape. He removed the pieces carefully until the entire pane was gone, then took a small, folding umbrella from the case. He reached down into the skylight and opened the umbrella, upside down, then set the towel and broke out three more panes. They cleared the slivers of glass from the frame in a few minutes. The empty grid of metal reminded Charlie of a huge black chessboard.

Barney took a long pair of cutters from the case.

"They'll cut it, Barney?" Paulie whispered.

"They'll cut case-hardened steel. This stuff's just galvanized. You could go through this with nail clippers."

Charlie and Paulie held the frame while Barney snipped it around the edges, then they lifted it out and set it on the roof. They packed the tool case and lowered the ladder carefully through the opening. Barney went first, then stood with his arms stretched wide above his head, squinting up toward the skylight while Charlie lowered the cases on a rope.

They left the ladder in place and used flashlights to get their bearings. They were in an office of the belt cutters union, a room with a bare wood floor, several desks, and a full wall of filing cabinets. One of the doors opened onto the corridor. Barney went out first and pushed the elevator button. Nothing happened.

"It's off for the night. They turn it off about seven-thirty."

Charlie nodded approvingly. "You've been doing your homework, Barney."

Barney pointed toward the front of the building. "The freight elevator is over there. We'll check it when we're downstairs. It's nice to know where everything is."

The stairwell was lit with red bulbs. They carried the cases down the flight of steps quickly, then stood in the hallway to get their bearings. There were three doors.

"Cheap operation," Barney said. "This kind of door, they usually have gold-leaf lettering on the glass. Like upstairs. This outfit just leaves them blank." He turned toward Paulie. "Which one?"

"The middle or the front. It don't matter, the offices are connected."

Barney examined each lock. "They're both a joke. Let's do the middle."

He opened it with a pick in a few minutes. They stood inside the doorway and moved the flashlight beams over the entire room. It was poorly furnished, with waist-high mahogany partitions separating old wood desks. The linoleum floor tiles were worn through to wood in spots.

The safe stood against the wall, a four-foot-high gray block with double doors. All three flashlight beams stopped on it. Barney walked to it and squatted on his haunches, Indian-style, while Charlie and Paulie stood well behind him, holding their lights steady. Barney first examined it from top to bottom, then moved around to each side. He shone his light into the small space between the back of the safe and the wall, then rapped the safe all over with his knuckles. After a few minutes he returned to his squatting position in front of it. He wiped his glasses clean with his handkerchief, then moved his face very close to the dial and examined it for several minutes without moving his head.

Paulie whispered to Charlie, "I think he's *sniffing* the fucking thing."

Charlie motioned for him to be quiet.

Barney stood up and stretched his legs.

"How does it look?" Charlie asked.

"It's a dressed-up tin can. Good for fires. A couple of hours, I'll be in it. Let's get set up."

They laid out the cases on the floor. Barney took out a small floodlight mounted on a photographer's tripod. He adjusted it to shine away from the front windows onto the safe door, then had Paulie plug it into an outlet. He first turned the dimmer switch until the brightness was just enough to work with, then rotated an iris lens on the lamp can and concentrated the light beam into a small circle that centered the safe dial perfectly. The large case held a small folding stool with three telescoping legs. Barney adjusted each leg height and tightened the locking nuts. He set it in front of the safe and placed a circular plaid cushion on it.

Paulie nodded approvingly. "Maybe you got a couple of broads tucked away in the case, too, Barney?"

Barney lifted a large electric drill from the case and tightened a fine, diamond-tipped bit into the chuck. "It pays to work like a gentleman, Paulie. Clocks or safes, it don't matter, you're better off working comfortable and neat. The job comes out better, too."

He pulled a small bundle of aluminum tubes from the case and screwed them together to form a stand for the drill. He adjusted the leg heights until the tool contacted the safe door just to the right of the dial, then tightened a wing nut that locked the drill to a slide on top of the stand. Charlie plugged it into an outlet.

"Paulie, you keep an eye on the street. Just don't park yourself right in the window. Watch the elevator shaft—it's pitch-black in that corner and they only got a little gate across it, comes up to your knees. Charlie, maybe you could pour some coffee?"

He removed his jacket and laid it across the safe, then unbuttoned the top of his shirt and planted himself on the stool. The drill turned slowly, with little noise. He pressed against it firmly and began humming a tune that Charlie couldn't make out.

Bunky Ritter finished shaving. He patted on witch hazel and called out, "Ma, do I have a clean T-shirt?"

"It's out here. On the chair."

The television was tuned to one of the quiz shows, with the voice off completely. She was at the kitchen table, underlining and circling entries on the *Racing Form,* her head pulled back to read the fine print clearly. She lit a cigarette and pulled the ashtray closer.

"You know anything about Trusty Dream? A four-year-old filly."

"No. Do you want the set off, ma?"

"She's in the third at Aqueduct. Six furlongs. One-thirteen her last time out and they've dropped her a class. That could be a nice place bet."

"Should I turn the sound up, ma?"

"Just leave it alone. I can't think straight if I have to listen to them screaming and jumping. It's nice to just watch them sometimes." She tapped the paper with her pencil. "They've got Imarazzo on her. He gets the five-pound bug and she's running against stiffs, except for Green Grip." She tapped the paper harder. "I like this horse."

He buttoned his shirt and pulled open the closet door to look in the full-length mirror. "Do I have a clean handkerchief?"

"In your drawer. You could use a haircut soon. The back is starting to go over your collar."

He felt the back of his neck. "I'll drive out Monday before work. Pete's never busy on Monday."

"Why do you go back to Myrtle Avenue for a haircut? There must be someplace closer. He's not even a good barber."

"The barbershops are all beauty parlors now. They don't cut your hair anymore, they style it. And blow hot air on it. You walk out looking like you're wearing a wig. Pete cuts hair so you look like a normal human being."

"His boy, Frank, was the dumbest thing ever went through Saint Joseph's. Sister Theresa told me that. In confidence."

She sucked in a long puff of the cigarette.

"That's terrible for your heart, ma. They tell you that every checkup. At least go to filters. And the highball isn't helping you, either."

"A little whiskey is good for the system. And the cigarettes aren't what gave me a heart attack, thirty-seven years of living with your father and scrubbing hallways for the Jews did it. While he played chess! The only superintendent in Brooklyn who spent four evenings a week at the Times Square Chess Club. Meanwhile, yours truly crawled up and down the stairways all day like an aging Cinderella. I knew every tenant in every building we ever had by their shoes. It's the first part of them you see, kneeling in a hallway with a bucket."

She ground out the cigarette. "You remember what it was to call garbage after dinner every day of your life. Look at this." She pulled up the right sleeve of her blouse.

"I know, ma. Your right arm's bigger."

"Twice the size of the left one. That's from pulling dumbwaiters up and down five-story buildings."

He reached across the table and squeezed her bicep lightly. "Anyway, the muggers won't get you while I'm gone. Calling garbage had its good points."

She sipped her highball and looked down at the racing charts. "It could have been worse, Walter. Crazy kraut that your father was, he was decent. And didn't drink. I could have easily married some donkey who would have been in a gin mill every night instead of the chess club. I still remember how he cried when they poisoned Lady. Twenty-three sixty Kylee Avenue we had. The coal bin was too small and the boiler went on the bum once a month all winter. It was nineteen forty-two. They poisoned Lady because she was a dachshund. Imagine. I still see your father carrying her in from the yard. Like a long, stuffed doll in his arms. She was actually all wet where his tears were falling on her."

Bunky pulled on his overcoat. "The end of next year and I'll have my twenty in. Then we head for Phoenix, ma. Sunshine and clean streets. I'll teach you to play golf. With that dumbwaiter arm, you'll drive the ball a mile."

"And what exactly will *you* do, Walter?"

"Maybe open a liquor store. Something nice, with a good stock of wines. Put a couple of bonded clerks in and I'll have plenty of time for myself."

"On a second-class-detective's pension?"

He winked. "I've got a little saved."

She drew a little circle next to an entry in the sixth. "Is that why you need the little recording box and adhesive tape that you've got in your pocket now? To keep track of your savings?"

He was surprised. "Just forget all about that, ma. There is no little box."

She shrugged. As he opened the door he called, "Chain it behind me."

"I will. Tell me, do you want twenty to place on this Trusty Dream in the third? They've got her way under-priced, just on performance."

"Yeah, ma. Put down twenty for me," he said, and locked the door behind him.

He drove in along Bay Shore, visualizing the liquor store in Phoenix. Roomy, with wide aisles, and well lit, near a supermarket in one of the shopping centers, with an entire wall of California wines. For the first year he would go in every day; after that, maybe three times a week to check the receipts. Bonded clerks, a good inventory system. There would be plenty of time for golf. And all of it with enough money stashed away for a sprawling, one-level house, something southwestern. Maybe even Mexican-style, built around an inner courtyard. A little separate wing for his mother. He would have to remember to suggest installing a tiny dumbwaiter in her wing. So she could keep her arm in trim.

He would be going out at forty-one. And he had paid his fucking dues for every one of the twenty years. When all the dust settled, it had been a mistake to ever take the exam—he could have done more with those years. It was a shit way to spend your youth. You could make your bundle once you decided to, but there was no way to buy back twenty years' worth and ever again see the world exactly like other people did. But forty-one was young enough to have a couple of kids if he did it fast. Ann was anxious as hell—she wasn't even interested in marriage unless he wanted a few kids. The more he had thought about it, the more he had gotten to like it. He still hadn't mentioned marriage and kids to his mother. When he did, she would hardly look up from the *Racing Form,* but after he left the house she would pour a double highball for herself and be tickled pink.

He turned onto the expressway at Fort Hamilton and looked at his watch. Eleven-fifteen. Another five minutes to the tunnel, then up West Street. He would be out of Greenwich Street by midnight and have the satchel in Flynn's hands before 1:00—less fifteen thousand in crisp fifties for his own tin box. He turned up the heater and thought some more about the racks of wine in the liquor store.

Paulie saw the car make a full stop at the corner, then take the turn onto Greenwich. It was the second car to come through the street in the past half-hour. He stretched forward a bit as it slowed and pulled alongside the opposite curb. After the headlights went off, he watched for the door to open. A minute passed. Nothing. He glanced back toward the safe. Barney was leaning patiently against the drill, working on his fifth bit. Charlie was behind him, sipping coffee. Paulie decided to say nothing unless someone got out of the car. It was probably some kid getting a fast hand job. No point disturbing the master mechanic for nothing.

Bunky sat for a minute and watched in the side mirror for headlights. He decided to tape the bug to his stomach now; when he had the money with him wasn't the time to sit and begin tearing off lengths of adhesive tape. He reached in and pulled his shirt up out of his belt. This would be the first time he'd bugged Flynn. He was less nervous recording the Mafiosos—they couldn't smell a bug the way a New York City police inspector could. The Mafiosos were probably taped a lot less frequently than the inspectors, he thought. He would have to be very careful about leading the conversation, just get what he could naturally. Maybe drop John Hanrahan's name in—the more inspectors, the merrier—but no one else's. Don't get greedy. To get nailed by Flynn would be no better than being nailed by Eddie Grant. Flynn and the brass in with him would put a contract on Bunky as fast as the wise guys would. With even less chance of being caught.

He pressed the last strip of tape across his stomach and tucked in his shirt. As he opened the door he glanced up at the fourth floor and stopped short. Had something in the window moved? It seemed crazy, but he could swear that something at the side of the window had moved. He slammed the door gently behind him and crossed the street. It was probably some kind of reflection, but he intended to go up the steps holding onto his .32.

Paulie jerked his head away from the window and felt his heart speed up. Whoever it was had looked up at the building. He edged back slowly and watched the figure cross the street. Paulie realized suddenly that he wasn't heading for the apartment house, but for the loft. His throat constricted and he croaked his words. "Someone's coming!"

Barney turned off the drill. "Where?"

Paulie pointed his finger at the floor and pumped his arm up and down. "Into the building."

"Grab the cases, Charlie," Barney said quietly. He yanked the electrical cord loose, then hugged the drill and tripod to his chest and lugged them behind a desk. "How many?" he called.

"One guy."

"Cop?"

"He's wearing street clothes, Barney. Some kind of lumber jacket."

"Come back here and grab the light. Get everything out of sight. Nice and easy."

They cleared the room and crouched behind a desk in the rear corner.

"What do you think?" Charlie asked.

Barney shrugged. "One guy. As long as he's alone, he's not a cop. Probably a boss from one of the companies in the building. Forgot to take something home for the weekend or something. Who the hell knows."

"What if he's from here?"

"From here ain't too bad. Chances are he won't even look at the safe close enough to see the holes. If he does, we bluff him. Pretend we got guns and tie him up. It's if he's going upstairs that we're in trouble. He sees the ladder and the skylight and it's all over."

"So what do we *do,* Barney?" Paulie's voice became insistent. "We're like three fucking rabbits sitting here!"

"We sit. Nice and quiet. And we keep our fingers crossed. Nothing else makes any sense."

Paulie clenched his hands together and whispered, "I'm cursed. I'm fucking cursed."

Bunky came up the four flights of stairs on the balls of his feet, close to the wall with his neck stretched forward and his head lowered to see up into the stairwell. He kept the .32 pointed ahead. At the fourth-floor landing he stopped and listened, then pulled open the stairwell door slowly. He stepped into the hallway, stood still in a partial crouch for half a minute, then moved down the corridor slowly, lightly trying the knobs on each of the three doors. All of them were locked. He walked softly to the door nearest the front of the building and used his left hand to insert his key, then pushed the door open gently with his foot, most of his body pressed against the wall. After a few moments, he went into the room in a half-crouch, looked around, then straightened slowly and walked toward the front window. It could easily have been his imagination.

Paulie stiffened when he heard the key go into the lock. Barney squeezed his arm hard and put his fingers to his lips. "Let me handle it," he whispered. He shifted his head a bit to the right as the door pushed open. It gave him a fair view of the room.

Bunky relaxed as he walked across the front of the room. It had been his imagination, or a reflection. He reached the window and looked down at his car, then noticed the half-filled Styrofoam cup on the windowsill. He dipped his left forefinger into it, felt that it was lukewarm, and realized at the same time that he was outlined in the window, as Barney half-stood and called, "Freeze! Freeze, you son of a bitch, or I'll blow your fucking head off!"

Bunky plunged toward his right, into the darkness, his arms extended down to break his fall. His hands never found the floor. As his body kept going, it flashed across his mind that he was going into the freight-elevator shaft—his knees hit the top of the low steel gate. He let go of his pistol and felt the cold set of cables hit his face, heard his own scream reverberate in the shaft as his body picked up speed.

chapter

IX

Charlie leaned forward and peered down into the elevator shaft. The flashlight beam showed a figure sprawled on its back on the plank floor of the car, forty feet below. One leg was bent back at the knee, tucked under the body. Charlie stepped back.

"Nothing moving down there."

"What did he hit?" Barney asked.

"The floor of the car—it's got no roof on it. It looks to me like it's parked on the first floor."

Paulie moved further away from the elevator. "What are we standing here for? Let's get the fuck *out* of here."

Charlie looked at Barney and nodded. "Makes sense."

"It doesn't make sense. We don't know whether this guy's dead or alive. If he's still breathing, our best bet is to get out of here and call an ambulance fast. If we're lucky, we get ourselves out from under a murder rap."

Paulie's eyes widened. "Murder rap! What the hell

are you talking about? Nobody got murdered here. Nobody came within twenty feet of that yo-yo. He dived into that hole like a fucking gopher."

"Let me break the sad news, kid. You commit a crime, someone dies during it, it's murder one. End of story."

Charlie nodded. "He's right."

"But, Jesus *Christ,* why can't I get a break?"

"You got a break, Paulie. The state ain't burning people now for murder one. That's your break. It's only twenty-five to life. You could be out in fourteen." He turned to Charlie. "You want to run down and take a look?"

Charlie shrugged. "He may be right, Barney. Our best bet might be to beat it. Right now."

Barney shook his head furiously. "Listen to me. First order of business is to find out whether he's alive down there. If he's not, then we don't call anyone. The more time passes before they find him, the better." He took off his glasses and wiped them with the front of his shirt. "Another thing. I don't want to sound like a bleeding heart, but keep in mind, that poor fuck down there might be dying right now."

They stood quietly for a few moments. Charlie looked at Paulie.

"You want to run down there, Charlie, it's fine with me," Paulie said.

Charlie walked down the stairs softly. Twice he started to hurry, then held back, anxious to be done with it but afraid of what he would find. He heard Barney call down for him to cover his face with something, just in case.

The door into the first-floor shop was locked. He started to call Barney, then decided that his nerve was going and kicked out quickly with his heel just below the handle. The door swung open. He hesitated in the doorway and breathed in the sweet rubber aroma of the shop, then moved quickly past a small hill of scrap truck tires to the freight elevator. As he swung his leg over the steel half-door, he shifted the light beam onto the sprawled figure. The head was centered in a small puddle of blood. Charlie stepped across the wood floor on the balls of his feet. He took a deep breath, removed his work glove, and reached in under Bunky's shirt to feel for a heartbeat. Nothing. His hand touched the recorder taped to the abdomen, then he saw the empty shoulder holster. The badge was in a trouser pocket, its outline pressed into the leather flap that covered it. Charlie wondered for a few moments about the recorder, then instinctively pulled it loose and dropped it into his jacket pocket. He went up the stairs two at a time.

Barney and Paulie were waiting in the hallway. They looked at him expectantly. He held out his hand in a thumbs-down position.

"Morto."

"You looked close, Charlie?"

"As close as I wanted to. The back of his head looks like there might not be much left. I didn't roll him over to see."

"You guys were serious about a murder rap?" Paulie asked.

"I got some even worse news. That's a dead cop down there."

Barney spent several minutes convincing them to open the safe before leaving. "We're talking about ten more minutes. Fifteen, tops. It won't change the rap one way or the other, and I'd like to walk out of here with something in my kick for all the work."

They stood to the side while Barney resumed drilling. Charlie decided to say nothing about the recorder; he could always mention it later if he chose to. He watched Paulie, who shifted his weight from foot to foot.

"You're *sure,* Charlie?" he whispered. "Maybe you're wrong. My kid brother, Vito, got knocked cold once on the steps to Saint Anthony's. You would have sworn he was dead, Charlie. Maybe this guy is just out cold."

"Stop dreaming, Paulie. He's dead. And he's a cop. That makes it worse than murder one. They can burn you for killing a cop."

"Maybe he ain't a real cop. Maybe he's a fucking phony. An impostor. There's hundreds of guys walking around making believe they're cops. Shaking people down and what not." He looked up and crossed his hands in prayer. "I swear on my mother I'll make novenas the rest of my life if this guy's not a real cop."

Charlie felt a headache coming on. "Barney, for Christ's sake. You're not fixing a clock. Can't you hurry?"

Barney ignored him. A minute later he pulled the safe door open. The only contents were on the top shelf, a vinyl attaché case and three rolls of stamps. Charlie felt the pain in his head intensify. He turned to Paulie. "There better be money inside that case, Paulie. I mean that. If you gave us a bum steer on this, you're in some fucking trouble."

Barney laid the case on the floor and opened it. It was packed full with neat stacks of fifties and hundreds, bound with rubber bands.

"Jesus Christ! How much is there, Barney?" Paulie asked.

He closed the case. "This ain't the place to count it. It's a whole lot more than twenty-five or thirty grand, though."

They would drive the van to West Forty-eighth

Street, transfer the tools to Barney's car, and lock the attaché case in the trunk. Charlie could hold the trunk key while he returned the van to the Hertz office.

"Leave it parked outside," Barney said. "With the keys on the sun visor. I don't see why the cops should trace it, but, if they do, nobody's going to remember you."

"Where do we meet?"

"You know the all-night diner at Forty-third and Tenth? You can walk it in ten minutes. The way the place is set up, we can put the car in the parking lot and keep an eye on it from the booths."

Driving uptown, Barney gave the money a quick count.

"Jesus! There's something like a hundred and fifty thousand here."

Charlie whistled. "What do you think?" he asked.

"To tell you the truth, it scares the shit out of me."

After they switched the tools, Charlie pocketed the key and stood beside the car as Paulie slid into the passenger seat next to Barney. Charlie leaned forward so his shoulders came between the car body and the open door, just as Paulie began to pull it closed. Paulie looked up over his shoulder. Charlie leaned further into the car, his face close enough to Paulie's ear so Barney wouldn't quite be able to hear him.

"You got some explaining to do, Paulie. I want to hear more about this trucking company when I get back to the diner. A hundred and fifty large is sitting in a cheesy safe and a plainclothes cop is wandering around the joint on a Saturday night—it smells more and more like one great big fucking jackpot you waltzed us into."

Paulie started to protest. Charlie slammed the door shut before the sentence was finished. He stepped into the van and ground the gears absently, then drove at a moderate speed down Tenth Avenue. There wasn't a sign of life on the street. A large square of corrugated sheet broken loose from a bale cartwheeled across an intersection in the wind. He slowed for a light and became aware of the weight in his jacket pocket—the slim, custom-made tape recorder that had been taped to the cop's belly. The damned thing was one more joker in the deck, he thought.

Paulie poured three packets of sugar into his coffee, then crumpled the empty wrappers and dropped them on the floor. He bit deeply into a jelly doughnut and spoke with his mouth full.

"What the hell do we do now, Barney? You ever been in this kind of a jam before?"

Barney stared out the window at Tenth Avenue. He shook his head no, slowly.

"You think that guy was really a cop, Barney?"

"Of course he was a cop. What the hell brought him in there is what I'd like to know."

"You don't think somebody saw us and called it in?"

"Yeah. And the local precinct sent out a plain-clothes man. By himself. With keys to all the doors." He pointed with his thumb toward the car in the lot. "That case full of money is all wrong, too. Who leaves a hundred and fifty thousand cash sitting in that tin can over a weekend? In a cheap attaché case. The whole thing smells, kid."

He stared at Paulie and waited for a reply. Paulie stuffed the remaining half of the jelly doughnut into his mouth and shrugged. "Where the hell is the waitress? Three parties in the whole place and she can't handle her fucking station." He caught the counterman's attention and called for more coffee and another doughnut. "You want one, Barney? They're delicious."

"There's nothing we should know about this trucking company, is there, Paulie? Nothing you're holding back?"

"I wouldn't do that, Barney. You got the whole story on it."

"Well, I'll tell you what I think, Paulie. I think you're full of shit."

Paulie waited until the waitress set down the coffee and doughnut and was out of earshot. He pulled a napkin from the dispenser and wiped the sugar from his mouth.

"Just where the fuck do *you* get off to tell me I'm full of shit? Charlie hollers at me sometimes like I was a kid, Barney, that's a different story. Me and Charlie are related. Me and Charlie are both from the neighborhood. We go back twenty years together. With all his joking, he respects me. I like to clown around a little, but don't let it fool you, old man. You start talking to me like some schoolteacher, I'll tell you to hold on to your goggles and go take a flying fuck for yourself."

Barney stared at him for a few moments, then wiped his glasses clean. Paulie cut his fresh doughnut in half. He selected the piece with the least jelly, bit into it, and pushed the plate with the remaining half across the table to Barney.

Charlie came into the diner and slid into the booth beside Barney.

"You figure out anything?" he asked.

"Paulie says there's nothing he didn't tell us. We know everything he knows."

"On my mother, Charlie."

"You're not lying, Paulie? Even a little bit?"

"Charlie! On my *mother*. What am I, crazy? I'm going to hold back on you now? We're in this thing together, Charlie."

Charlie looked at Barney.

"I think he's full of shit," Barney said softly. "I told him that five minutes ago. I still think so."

Paulie pointed his finger at Barney's face. "And I'll tell you once more, I don't give a good fuck what you think." He turned toward Charlie. "I don't have to listen to that kind of crap from him."

"You gave us the whole story?"

"Absolutely."

Charlie turned toward Barney. "End of story. We drop it."

Barney said nothing.

"Let's get the money split up," Paulie said.

"This money can't be spent for months, now. Am I right, Barney?"

Barney nodded.

"But we're going to whack it up now—no, Charlie?" Paulie said. "We don't spend it. Fine. But I want to hold my own money."

"We'll split it up. Just no spending."

"I'll dump the tools," Barney said. "They're as bad as fingerprints. The crime lab people can tie them right to the scene in ten minutes."

"There's not much else to do," Charlie said. "We make novenas now."

"What kind of badge did that cop have?" Barney asked.

"Ordinary badge. A little small, maybe. Not as big as the kind a uniformed cop wears."

"That's nothing. That was a three-quarters—all the cops use them. A cop loses his shield he's docked a month's pay. Automatic. So they buy a three-quarter size—it's legal for stores to make them up—and carry that instead. Was it gold or silver, Charlie?"

"Gold."

"That means he wasn't just plainclothes. He was a detective, or a sergeant, at least."

"It's going to get hot, Barney?" Paulie asked.

"With a dead detective? You bet your ass it is. Just don't flash any money around. The three of us stick together and do the right thing, we can come up on our feet on this."

Paulie signaled for the waitress and grabbed the check. While they waited for change at the register, Charlie took a toothpick and chewed on it lightly. He decided to hear what was on the tape recorder before saying anything to them. Barney was absolutely right that they had to stick together, but Charlie's experience told him that if things got tight and they were pushed into a corner, each of them would start looking out for number one.

chapter

X

Barney offered to drop them at Charlie's hotel. They sat quietly during the ride down Broadway, Paulie squeezed between them in the front seat. When they pulled up at the hotel entrance, Charlie waited at the car until Paulie was halfway across the sidewalk, then he leaned into the open door.

"You understand what happened back at the diner, right, Barney?"

"With Paulie? I understand, Charlie."

"I had to back him, Barney. It's like you said—fifth cousins on my mother's side of the family are like twin brothers on my father's side. That's where my allegiance had to be."

"Forget it, Charlie. You were on a spot. Thanks for explaining it." He put the car in gear. "Between you and me, though, the kid knows more than he's letting on. We're in a fucking swindle here, Charlie—we're in way over our heads. Be nice to know what the hell it's all about."

Charlie nodded, and stood for a few moments at the curb as the car pulled away.

He said nothing while they walked up the two flights of steps to his room. He chained the door behind him and broke open a tray of ice cubes from the tiny refrigerator while Paulie smoothed the blanket on the bed and laid out his share of the money. Charlie filled two rock glasses with ice and scotch. He set one beside the neat stacks of bills on the blanket, then sprawled into the torn easy chair and swallowed half of his scotch.

Paulie counted out his money, removing the rubber band from a stack and slipping it onto his wrist, then counting aloud and forming little stacks of ten bills each, finally recombining them into a single large stack, aligning the sides with his fingers as he would a deck of cards, then slipping on the rubber band. He placed each counted stack to his right, building them into an interlocking pattern like a neat pile of bricks.

Charlie sipped at the scotch and watched him for a few minutes, then asked, "What do you think, Paulie?"

Paulie finished counting a stack, then answered without looking up. "This is really a score, Charlie. I counted on fifteen apiece, twenty if we stepped in horseshit. I never even dreamed of fifty." He cocked his head and riffled a stack of hundreds near his ear. "This is like hitting the lottery, Charlie."

"Are you *crazy,* Paulie? Are you fucking *nuts?* What kind of score? There's a dead cop back there!"

Paulie slapped the pile of bills in his hand down on the blanket. "Jesus Christ, is that all you and Barney can talk about? It's the only thing I've been hearing for two hours now. It's not our fault some hard-on cop decides to hop into an elevator shaft. I'm sorry for the guy, Charlie, I really am. But it's got nothing to do with us."

"It's got everything to do with us. Listen to me, dummy. We're going to be wanted for *murder.*"

Paulie shook his head vigorously. "No! It was *not* murder. I don't want to hear the word. That was a suicide, Charlie. That asshole committed suicide." He put his hands over his ears and continued to shake his head. "Don't talk to me about murder!"

Charlie swallowed the last of his scotch, then stretched forward to the night table for the bottle and refilled his glass. Paulie returned to counting and stacking. Charlie watched him, and after a minute realized that Paulie was whistling very softly between his teeth. He listened closely. He was sure Paulie was whistling "My Way." His stomach tightened in spite of the liquor.

"What possessed me?" he said softly. "What could have possessed me to tie up with this retard?"

Paulie continued to whistle. Charlie reached across and tumbled over the neat stack of bills.

Paulie looked up, surprised. "What's a matter, Charlie?"

"I'll buy you a set of fucking blocks for your birthday. Right now, listen close, Paulie. I mean it. You tell me exactly how you got on to this trucking company. Exactly."

Paulie frowned. "There's nothing—"

"You're lying. When you frown like that, you're lying, you little pimp."

Paulie widened his eyes into his hurt-little-boy look. "Charlie! I'm surprised at you, Charlie."

"The truth. Something ain't right here, Paulie. You're not leaving this room until I know what you're holding back."

"Nothing, Charlie. I swear I'm not holding nothing back."

"You swear?"

"I swear."

"On your kid brother Vito. Swear on Vito. He should get cancer if you're lying, Paulie. You just say out loud that you want Vito to get stomach cancer if you're lying. Then I'll shut up."

Paulie picked up his glass of scotch and sipped it before answering.

"That ain't fair, Charlie. Vito got nothing to do with this."

"If you're telling the truth, Vito can't get hurt, Paulie. You're telling the truth, right?"

"You got any more scotch, Charlie?" He held out the empty glass.

"Say it, Paulie—I swear on my kid brother Vito that I'm not holding back anything from Charlie. Vito should get slow stomach cancer if I'm lying."

"But Jesus *Christ!* You don't leave a guy no room."

"Room for what?"

He looked away from Charlie's eyes. "Maybe I didn't tell you every last detail, Charlie. I figured you didn't have to listen to hours of details. It didn't seem that important."

Charlie held his breath. "What wasn't that important?"

"About Eddie."

"Eddie who?"

"Eddie Grant. You know—Bedbug Eddie. From Mulberry Street."

"What about him, Paulie?"

"I think it's his trucking company, Charlie."

"You think?"

"I'm pretty sure."

"How sure?"

"What's the use of kidding ourselves, Charlie? He owns it."

Charlie covered his face with both hands and shook

his head from side to side. "Unbelievable! Paulie, you wanted to commit suicide, okay, but why drag me into it? What's *wrong* with you?"

"What do you mean what's wrong? We're sitting on fifty big ones apiece, Charlie. There's nothing wrong with that."

"Bedbug Eddie's money! That's the fucking Mafia's money. Paulie, that's a worse jam than the dead cop. We get nailed for the cop, we get a trial. We get some kind of a shot. Eddie Grant will parcel-post pieces of us to our relatives. He's been known to do it, Paulie."

"Eddie Grant ain't going to know a thing. You sound like some scared old fag, for Christ's sake."

Charlie reached for the scotch bottle and filled their glasses. He forced himself to relax. They sat quietly for a few minutes and sipped their drinks.

"Who tipped you, Paulie?"

"A kid—Frankie Wheels from Bleecker Street. He drove a truck for them for seven, eight months."

"They going to be able to trace it to him, Paulie?"

He became serious. "No. Two, three times over a drink he talked about how the company did a lot of business off the books. That a lot of cash went through the place. It was strictly bar talk. He never even knew I was interested."

"Were you ever up there?"

"Just once. A couple of months ago. For two minutes. I walked in and asked for a job. I looked around. I walked out. There was just a lady behind a desk."

"This kid from Bleecker Street—you see him much?"

"Maybe twice a month. He hangs out in the Gallery. If I stop there for a drink on my way to work, I see him there."

"But you never let on you were interested?"

"Please, Charlie! I'm not fucking *stupid*."

Charlie laughed.

"If things really go bad, Charlie, I could reach out."

"To who?"

"Pete Grillo. Worse comes to worse, Pete Grillo could bail us out maybe."

"What the hell is Pete Grillo going to do for us?"

"He's my *goombah,* Charlie. I still call him uncle. And he's on Eddie Grant's crew."

"All the more reason he'll want your eyes. They find out it was you who ripped off Eddie's money, it'll mark Pete lousy for the next ten years. You live in some fucking dreamworld, Paulie."

"If I ask him, Charlie, he'll go to Eddie for me. Pete treats me like his son. He spanked me in the middle of Carmine Street when I was nine because he caught me robbing from Lambaise's."

Paulie began to stack his money neatly again.

"You figure he'll spank you again for robbing a hundred and fifty grand from his crew boss?"

"Worse comes to worst, he'll go to Eddie for me. I'll make retribution. If Eddie gets his money back, he ain't going to kill me."

Charlie finished his drink. "Look, Paulie, we got only one chance going for us here. Listen close. We can't spend a nickel. Not five cents, Paulie. We've got to make believe we don't have a cent for the next six months. We sit tight and say rosaries, and if we don't show people a penny we stand a chance. You understand?"

Paulie nodded.

"Say you understand, Paulie."

"I understand. We can't flash any big money around. It makes sense."

"Not big money—*any* money. Not a penny."

"Charlie, we don't have to be crazy either. We should be careful, but we don't have to go crazy. Nobody's going to notice a hundred bucks here and there."

"No! Not a penny."

"Okay, Charlie. Not a penny. I didn't mean the kind of money people would notice. I meant like an extra hundred on a weekend. In a restaurant uptown. Maybe two nice custom shirts from Bauman. That's all I meant, Charlie. Nickel-and-dime stuff."

Charlie picked up a stack of hundreds from the bed and held it close to Paulie's face. "Just sit on every cent of this, Paulie. You don't even take off one of the rubber bands. *Cabeesh?*"

He nodded.

"We're going to have the cops looking to destroy us, Paulie. And we got the biggest psycho in the Mafia looking for us. You make one of your dumb moves that gets me nailed, Paulie, you'll wish Bedbug Eddie got hold of you instead."

Paulie stood up and started to pack his money into his pockets. He took the bills from Charlie's hand.

"What do we do about Barney?" Charlie asked.

"What about him?"

"We ought to let him know about Eddie Grant."

"For what?"

"So the guy knows what he's up against, Paulie."

Paulie shrugged. "Barney got his fifty large. We got to look out for him, too? What are we, family?"

Charlie tugged at Paulie's sleeve. "This is serious, Paulie. You're a little bit pissed off at him, but the poor fuck is sitting up in the Bronx, he can't see six feet ahead. You saying we don't owe him that much of a break, Paulie?"

They stood beside the bed, Paulie ready to leave. Charlie held his sleeve lightly. After a minute Paulie nodded. "Go ahead and tell the old man." He walked to the door and unchained it.

Charlie called to him as he stepped into the hallway. "Why, Paulie? It wasn't right not to tell me."

"You would never have taken the shot, Charlie."

"You're right. Not with the Bedbug's money. You should have found someone else."

"There was no one else. And I needed the fifteen I figured I'd get. I don't have time, Charlie. I'm pushing thirty. This horse is my shot. If I don't make my move now, I'll never get the chance."

chapter

XI

Big Ed Flynn paused before descending the steps of Saint Patty's and fished a roll of Tums from his great-coat pocket. He chewed three tablets quickly, then sucked on another one. The heartburn had started when Ritter failed to show with the money late Saturday night. He had gone through six packs of Tums on Sunday, swallowing a dozen whole tablets just before midnight to hold him until Communion this morning. When he got out of bed three hours ago, his stomach was still producing acid. It had gotten worse when the call came that Ritter was dead. Several times during Mass he had been tempted to leave; and as he received the host, he had been unable to resist the wish that it was an antacid tablet. He would have to pick up a Mass card to send to whatever family Ritter had left behind. God willing, the son of a bitch hadn't left a big fat trail from the dagos straight to Flynn's office; the Internal Affairs people wouldn't go for an outright cover-up, but they wouldn't dig one inch deeper than they had to, either, when it involved deputy chiefs. He started down the steps slowly, wondering how the hell Ritter had let himself get creamed.

Behind him, people from the Mass began coming out. Two fire chiefs he had known over the years from different K of C affairs fell into step with him. They walked the three blocks to the Waldorf beside him, complaining in turn about the effects of the latest budget cuts. When Flynn asked what was new in the south Bronx, the younger one groaned.

"I was in Cornyn's last night with a battalion chief just coming off a shift at the Bathgate Avenue house. The poor bastard looked ready to fall off his stool. His company had made forty-seven runs, five of them fires. Can you imagine? Forty-seven runs! He told me if this shit keeps up, the city will be down to four boroughs soon. To top it off, the department has gotten so tight the firemen up there have to buy their own yellow paint, for Christ sake."

"For what?" Flynn asked.

"For the outside of buildings. Half the tenements in the Bronx have burned five or six times."

"Who the hell is burning them?"

"The landlord, the first time out. For the insurance. A month later, some tenant gets tired of being cold and figures Welfare ought to put him up in a hotel for a while, so he buys five gallons of kerosene and touches it off again. After that, the junkies burn it to get at the brass pipes, and the kids do it for whatever reason kids burn things. Roasting mickeys or something. Frying bananas more likely with that crew."

"And what about the paint?"

"The firemen don't want to put their asses on the line for an abandoned building. They paint a big yellow square on the outside wall. If there's any kind of hazard—if a floor is out or the stairwells are gone—

they paint diagonal slashes into the square. It tells the company who responds to the next fire not to go in. And the fucking department won't pay for the paint. The men in each firehouse chip in for it."

"It's no better with us," Flynn said. "I've never seen morale lower."

He chewed another Tums, wanting a cigar but forcing himself to wait until after breakfast. He left the firemen at the entrance to the ballroom and looked toward the dais for the police table. Tom Sheridan, who would be retiring as chief of detectives in another year, was already seated. Flynn braced himself for the conversation.

"Hello, Ed. Did they get to you yet?"

"About Ritter? I got a call at home halfway out the door. What the hell happened?"

"They found him at the bottom of an elevator shaft. A loft building down on Greenwich Street. A maintenance man in a toy factory gets in every day at four A.M. found the body."

"Pushed?"

Sheridan shrugged. "It looks like it from the little I got on the telephone. A radio car responded and they called Homicide. Two detectives from Manhattan South went in. When they saw the badge, they got to me just before I was leaving for the Mass."

"Will you be staying for the breakfast?"

Sheridan smiled. "Only. It's a perfect excuse for me to duck out before Cooke gives us the hungry-Catholic-children routine."

"There's no hint of what the hell went on, Tom?"

"It makes no sense yet. There's a safe was broken into in the building. Some trucking company." He put several sections of grapefruit into his mouth and chewed on them for a few moments. "You knew him a bit, Ed. Could Ritter have been part of a safecrack-ing?"

Flynn shook his head. "I knew him very little—he kept to himself pretty much. But I never had reason to think him a thief. I'm sure he grabbed his few hundred at Christmas, but nothing more."

And that's little enough of a lie about not knowing him, too, Flynn thought. He himself had been on one end of things, Carlucci on the other. Ritter had been right in the middle, and Flynn never comfortable with him socially—he seemed more like a hoodlum who had got himself into the department than a cop who had decided to look out for himself.

People from the Mass began coming through the doors in a steady stream and moving in clusters to the numbered tables.

"The Internal Affairs people will be snooping all over," Flynn said.

"They're already at the scene. John Kessler is run-ning it himself."

Flynn moved his hand through a tiny sign of the cross. "For the department's sake, let's hope Ritter was clean, Tom."

Gene Boyle and John Hanrahan slid onto the chairs next to Flynn.

"Had you heard from old John Lawlor, Ed?" Boyle asked. "I spoke with Helen over the weekend. He's in poor shape."

"Kidneys again?"

Boyle nodded. "And the liver. The doctors say it's a race as to which goes first. He's in Montefiore."

"Had he gone back on the sauce, Gene?"

"Six weeks ago. They told him bluntly, the next drink will kill you. They refused to serve him in Man-nion's— Pat Crowley turned him down cold. They had one hell of an argument. And Mannion's was the only gin mill in the neighborhood he would drink at any-more. He's been saying for years that the rest of them had surrendered to the niggers."

"How is Helen handling it?"

"Like a saint. She's a strong woman, Ed."

Tom Sheridan leaned into their conversation. "Is that John Lawlor you're talking about?"

"Did you know him, Tom?"

"Barely. We shook hands once at an Emerald Society dinner. I knew that he was well liked."

Flynn nodded. "He was good, John Lawlor. The two of us were sworn in together."

"And he went out a patrolman?"

"After thirty-four years. He would have stayed longer but for the way the job changed. They had his retirement dinner at old Alex and Henrey's when they were still on a Hundred Thirty-eighth and Cortlandt. Half the people at this table went, the man was that well liked. He never gave anyone up. Joe Connors, who was deputy commissioner then, showed up."

"And tied on a hell of a load, too," Hanrahan said.

"He did. And this was for a patrolman."

"Doesn't he have a son on the force?" Sheridan asked.

"Had. Terry, a fucking maniac if there ever was one. He's with Fire now. During the preliminary investigations for the Knapp hearings, his name popped up so often that Connors had him resign. He set him up nicely over at Fire, too, which the crazy son of a bitch didn't deserve."

"Was the boy that greedy, Ed?"

"He wasn't greedy at all. He was putting next to nothing into his pocket. It was all bar bills and seven-course dinners on the arm. That kid came out of the academy and got sent straight to the one-seven. There's no one in the department can remember a rookie ever being assigned to the one-seven. It's what came of having Connors for a rabbi. When the maniac finally had to be transferred, they put him into the one-nine! Kept him up on the gold coast!"

"There's no one eating hamburgers in those two houses," Hanrahan said. "That whole Upper East Side is steaks and shrimp cocktails on every tour—plus the fanciest whores in the country to lean on for a bit of free trade."

"And, sweet Jesus, but Terry Lawlor could do it, too. The boy didn't know what it was to order off the middle of a menu. One of the investigators told me that Lawlor's name was mentioned by so many restaurant managers, he was convinced the man had to weigh three hundred pounds."

"Why was he transferred, Ed?"

"The lunatic went from bad to worse. He was so hard to work with, what with the constant drinking and screwing on duty, that he couldn't keep a partner. They put him in a one-man car! It had to be the only one in the city. Anyone else would have lost his seat, but Lawlor's rabbi said no, no foot patrol for Terence, let the boy ride alone. It was a license to suck on a bottle of scotch each tour. Finally the fool clocked a sergeant in the locker room at the end of a shift. Knocked him cold. And not a regular guy, who would settle it himself. He punches some Hebe—Murray something or other. The biggest bagel face in the precinct, and Lawlor belts him. That's when they moved him over to the one-nine."

"What kind of cop was he?"

"Good. A good cop—drunk or sober. You'd be happy to have him beside you going up a dark fire escape."

The waiters arrived and began thumping down plates of eggs along the table.

"I remember him a bit when he was a kid," Hanrahan said. "He was an altar boy at Tolentine for five or six years. And look how he turned out."

Flynn laughed. "A hell of a lot being an altar boy means. Half the perverts loitering in subway toilets can recite the offertory for you in perfect Latin."

When Cooke started to arrange his index cards, Tom Sheridan quickly wiped up the egg yolk from his plate with a piece of toast and stood up. He winked at Flynn and said he would see him downtown, then walked quickly across the room, still chewing. Hanrahan came down the table and sat in the empty chair. His eyes were wide—he had heard about Ritter during breakfast. He whispered close to Flynn's cheek even before he was seated.

"Jesus, Ed, Ritter is dead. That's why he never showed up Saturday night."

Flynn felt himself flush. He smiled a bit for the benefit of the people at the table and tilted his head toward Hanrahan's ear. "John, half the inspectors in the department are watching us this instant and you're turning pale in front of them. It isn't clever, John."

Hanrahan nodded, and turned in his chair as Cooke started to drone a long thank you to the Catholic Charities workers at the front tables. There were enough blacks among them for Gene Boyle to comment softly that the Waldorf would soon be serving grits at these affairs. As Cooke implored the rest of the room to dig deeper into their hearts and their pockets than ever, Flynn lit a fat Don Diego and pretended to concentrate on the cardinal's speech. He sipped his coffee and puffed slowly, and considered what might be done about Ritter.

The key to it would be the Internal Affairs shooflies. He needn't worry about Tom Sheridan—he wasn't one to give a man up. If his people came across something, he would likely tip off Flynn and then look the other way. It was the shooflies who would rush right in to their boss with anything they found. And where it went from there would depend upon how definite it all was. John Kessler was honest as a bishop, but he wasn't happy running Internal Affairs and he understood the politics of the job. He had to pay as much attention to public relations for the department as he did to keeping the house clean. Opening up this can of worms, with four deputy chief and assistant chief inspectors inside, along with a dozen chiefs, would not endear him to the commissioner. He would also be marked lousy by everyone in the department. Still, if something showed up that was too blatant to ignore, Kessler would go ahead and do it. The man had come up as a loner, and had always been just a bit of a prick, too.

Of the people who were taking, it was his own sister's husband—quart-a-day John Hanrahan—that he had to worry about. Flynn glanced beside him at Hanrahan, who was listening intently to whatever Cooke was saying. The capillaries in his nose were broken beyond repair and his eyes were nearly pink this morning. What with worrying about Ritter all weekend, he had likely poured an extra quart of high test into his belly. He would be a weak link for sure under any kind of pressure. The last time they had eaten lunch together, Hanrahan's meal had consisted of three straight-up martinis and a large, raw Bermuda onion that he had chewed up and swallowed like an apple before going back to the office. Flynn remembered him when he had been a chief, running a precinct in Queens. Hanrahan would send a patrolman out to a nearby bar for what he called a "flute"—a Coke bottle filled with gin. "A flute for the captain," the cop would say. And sometimes make three trips during a tour. The man had become a regular sponge.

People began to applaud, and Cooke sat down.

"He's okay," Gene Boyle said. "He's not another Spellman, though."

Flynn laughed. "Indeed he's not. Harry Kaufman—God rest him—before he retired always said that Spellman could have worked for the UJA, he was that good at emptying a roomful of wallets."

The crowd started to break. People from different tables came together in small groups to talk while others edged around them and made their way to the door. Half of them lingered at their tables over a final cup of coffee. A waiter found Flynn and said there was a phone call at the desk from the chief of detectives' office. Tom Sheridan was on the line.

"Something peculiar has popped up, Ed. It mustn't go any further."

"What's that?"

"The safe that was cracked belonged to the oil-and-vinegar crowd. I've got a young guy from the organized-crime unit looking at it. And brace yourself for this one, Ed." He paused, then said slowly, "Ritter was wired."

Flynn's throat tightened. "What!"

"Ritter was wired. There are marks on his belly where adhesive tape was peeled off and the little mike is still taped on his chest. There's no question he was wearing a recorder."

"Jesus Christ."

"It's not to go further, Ed."

He hung up. Flynn placed the phone down and crossed the lobby slowly. He searched his pockets for a roll of Tums—the heartburn would return in the next few minutes. At the ballroom door he caught

Hanrahan's attention and motioned for him to come out.

"Let's get out in the fresh air for a few blocks. We can talk."

They walked down Park Avenue toward the mouth of the General Building.

"Tom Sheridan just called me. Ritter was wired. The little cocksucker had a recorder taped to his belly."

Hanrahan stopped short on the sidewalk. "Jesus, Mary, and Joseph! What's on it?"

"God only knows. Whoever killed the son of a bitch has it. Sheridan's people found the mike still taped to him."

"Who the hell done it, Ed?"

"From the time I left the house right through Mass I would have sworn the guineas did it. Now I don't think so. Sheridan says they owned the safe that was opened. That must be how Ritter made his pickups. They're not about to kill a cop and leave him to be found in their office. They would have shipped him across to a private little plot in Jersey and been done with it."

"So who was it, Ed?"

"The maggots who cracked the safe is who it was. Ritter must have barged in on it like some kid out of the academy and they killed him. These thieving bastards killed a cop, John, and took our money, too."

A radio car slowed as it turned into Forty-fifth Street. A woman cop was driving, looking straight ahead into traffic, but the recorder saw them and straightened up in his seat quickly. He cupped his cigarette and touched his eyebrow in a salute.

"Jesus, will you look at the hair on him," Flynn said. "And did you ever dream you'd see a female behind the wheel of a radio car, John? Look at her, too, chewing on a wad of gum the size of your fist."

Hanrahan shook his head. "It's hopeless, Ed. I was up in the Twenty-fifth last week and I could have sworn I was in with a pack of fucking hippies someone had put uniforms on. Hair and mustaches like some tribe of apes, and a nigger sergeant at the desk with an Afro on him would scare the living shit out of me in some hallway. It was like a visit to the Bronx Zoo. There were four prisoners in the holding pens were better groomed than the policemen. There's no sense kidding ourselves, Ed, the job will never be the same again."

Flynn nodded. "You can bet your sweet ass it will never be the same again for either of *us*—not unless we get hold of that little tape recorder."

"What the hell would a couple of thieves want with a tape?"

"You can be sure they won't be delivering it to the commissioner looking to collect a good citizen's award, John. They could easily peddle it to some stinking reporter is what they could do. They'll have no trouble finding a newspaperman who's got a hard-on for the department a yard long."

Hanrahan slowed his pace. "God almighty, Ed. It would make the Knapp hearings look like small potatoes."

"Indeed it would. You see what it means, John? We've got to get hold of these bastards before the Internal Affairs Division does."

"Was Ritter with the IAD, then?"

Flynn dropped his half-smoked cigar into a corner sewer grating and placed two more Tums in his mouth. "Why the hell else would he be wearing a wire? They're on to the whole thing is my guess, and they managed to turn the little rat around. The question now is how much hard proof they've got. There may be very little—that's the reason for the wire. With Ritter dead and no solid evidence in their hands, they may be pleased to forget the whole thing. Sure as hell headlines right now wouldn't do the department any good."

"We play a waiting game, then, Ed?"

Flynn nodded. "Except for hunting down the sneak thieves who killed Ritter. Sure as hell they'll turn out to have sheets the length of your arm and half a dozen felony dismissals from every fucking bleeding-heart judge on Centre Street."

"And if we find them, Ed? Then what?"

"I'm sure they've listened to the recorder. So it's my guess, John, that they'll be shot dead resisting arrest."

Flynn slowed as they entered the dark walkway leading to the Pan Am Building.

"This scum killed a policeman—I for one won't be offering up any Masses for them."

"And the money?"

"This last payment? Gone. Write it off. There's no sense stewing about it. It's what we've built up in our boxes till now that we've got to protect, John."

He chewed another Tums and felt his face growing red.

"I've worked thirty-seven years putting together a little something for myself and my family—and only the last few years with any big money. Most of it is tens and twenties squeezed out over the years before the pile started to amount to something. You know what a grind it is, John. I put in twelve long, hard years riding in the Twenty-fifth, banging every nigger numbers runner on Lenox Avenue for a new hat each week. And all the while making enough collars to work my way up. Plus dipping into the captain's boodle for a few, with some song and dance about people paying poorly that week. That money didn't come easy, John. There's thirty-seven years of hoarding in there, with the fucking inflation eating away at it as fast as it's being filled. Some scum-sucking thieves who see fit to kill a policeman aren't going to blow any whistles on Ed Flynn. They'll not know what hit them, John."

Corliss selected a late-model Buick from the Internal Affairs Division pool. He and the new man rode silently until they were halfway across the Brooklyn Bridge, then Corliss edged into the right lane and slowed the car to a comfortable speed.

"You don't look happy, George," he said.

George lit a cigarette and shrugged. "Hard weekend." He lowered the electric window and tossed out the crumpled cigarette package, then jogged the window several times as he raised it. "You guys go first class all right."

"We can't ride black Plymouths all the time—some of the jobs are undercover. Narcotics sends us over confiscations once in a while. I figured your first day in the unit you could use a treat—maybe make you happier to be aboard."

George said nothing while Corliss steered through the long, sweeping curve at the Brooklyn end of the bridge. As they accelerated onto the expressway, he asked what the assignment was.

"You heard about the detective got killed over the weekend? Bunky Ritter?"

George nodded.

"We've got to question his mother."

"No wife?"

Corliss shook his head. "Bachelor."

"Why the questions?"

"It doesn't smell good. It looks like he was pushed into an elevator shaft. The building where he was found has a trucking company in it owned by organized-crime guys. Their safe was cracked open. The craziest thing was that he was wearing a wire."

"What the hell for?"

"We don't know. He wasn't undercover for the organized-crime unit or Narcotics, and he wasn't with us. Why the hell he would be wired is a mystery."

"Does the mother know he's dead?"

"They were out there this morning."

Corliss concentrated on driving until he got onto Shore Drive.

"You still don't look happy, George. You don't look like a man about to enjoy his time with the IAD."

"It's a job. I'll do my six months, then go back to a precinct."

"But you'll go back with the stigma of six months in the IAD. Any precinct you're assigned to, they'll wonder whether you're good, George. That's what's bugging you. Every guy gets drafted in is unhappy because people will always wonder whether he's good."

George shrugged.

Corliss took a box of Chiclets from his pocket and slid two pieces from the box directly into his mouth. He held the box toward George for a few moments, then laid it on top of the dashboard.

"The job's not so bad for six months. Nobody breaks your balls when you've been drafted in, and they won't trust you enough to put you on anything heavy. You're not going to get staked out to nail some sergeant taking fifty from a construction site. They'll have you investigating drinking-on-duty reports. An off-duty bar fight. Nothing where the guy's going to be bounced—strictly a two-week rip if he's found guilty. And half the time you can gloss your report a little so he's not guilty and save him his two weeks' pay. You get a chance to do a favor here and there."

"What do the full-timers do?"

"We follow up the payoff complaints. Cops taking cash. Lost guns. Stuff like we're on now—cop dies in suspicious circumstances."

"You ever work out of a precinct house, Corliss?"

"Never. Right out of the academy into the IAD."

"You like it?"

"Yeah."

George lit another cigarette.

"What were you doing when they grabbed you for this?" Corliss asked.

"Radio car. I had just finished ten months in an anti-crime unit."

"What made you leave?"

"I just got fed up with it. Seven months riding a Checker cab with my partner. We swapped being the driver and passenger every day. We had one hell of an arrest record, the two of us."

"That's why they drafted you in here, most likely. It also means they couldn't turn up a hint that you ever took a dime."

George nodded. "I've paid for every lunch I ever ate since I left the academy. I didn't come on the force to get rich."

He smoked quietly for a few minutes.

"You can't take the anticrime work too long, though. After the Checker, they put me working alone. Fourteenth Street, a fucking sewer. A week before I quit, I had been in Union Square Park for three days running. Laying out on a bench with a pint of Thunderbird. I had fake scabs glued all over my forehead and an eighth-inch of dirt caked on my ankles and elbows. Three fucking days living in the middle of these skels, watching ten-dollar bags of smack go back and forth and waiting for a good, solid collar. There's eight or nine possibilities—I'm trying to decide which of these animals I want to take out of commission before I blow my cover. I got my eye all this time on a tough little spic with a Pancho Villa mustache. He's carrying a nine-inch kitchen knife in a holder on his calf. A fucking *kitchen* knife! If he puts it straight in your belly, it's going to come out your back. The guy is ready to do some damage with it, too. Twice I watched him pull it in arguments with other skels over bottles of wine."

"It's not worth nailing the P.R. for a deadly weapon?"

George laughed. "You been living in a fucking convent, Corliss? The D.A.'s office wouldn't even bother prosecuting it, the judges would laugh it through the courts. I wanted an assault charge. I could taste the charge I wanted, laying there watching this fucking maggot intimidate the world.

"The third day I'm there, a solid citizen comes through the park with a bag full of groceries in his arms. Thirty-five, maybe. Italian. The spic comes off his bench and asks him for fifty cents. Blocks this guy's way and starts to bulldoze him for the money. The spic finally pushes him, and this guy lets his groceries drop and hits the spic a roundhouse right on the side of his head. Sure enough, the spic pulls this fucking sword off his leg and takes a swipe that actually cut the guy's shirt. I come off the bench like a linebacker and bring him down flat on his belly. Three fucking days I been laying there smelling my own clothes and waiting to lock this cocksucker up. I get my knee on the side of his neck and yank a thirty-two out of a crotch holster and jam the barrel into his cheek so hard I cut up the inside of his mouth against his teeth.

"Meanwhile, the guy he assaulted is busy picking up his groceries. I ask him will he follow through on it and he tells me, thanks a lot, he really appreciates me saving him eighty stitches, but he won't even press charges! He doesn't want to put anyone in jail. This is Mott Street Italian-style. Take care of it yourself or forget it—but whatever happens, you don't call cops."

"You made the collar anyway?"

"Yeah. It was still a decent case, but it would have been stronger with this guy following it up. It took the steam out of me. I was getting stale anyway, but that did it. I figured, let me go direct traffic for a while."

"What happened to the P.R.?"

"Turned out he was Dominican. Fifteen hundred bail. By now he's got himself a new kitchen knife. He'll plea-bargain with them and maybe do ninety days on Rikers."

Corliss shook his head. "It's enough to make you wonder who the enemy is, George."

"I'll tell you, Corliss, it might make *you* wonder—you said you never worked a precinct. I don't wonder. Ninety percent of the people walking the streets in civilian clothes are the fucking enemy. I broke my hump for three days so this guinea can tell me, thanks, but I don't believe in jail. I'm kneeling on a guy just tried to kill him."

He looked out the window for a minute.

"And the other end is the bleeding hearts. They're worse. Just before I volunteered for anticrime, I was coming off an eight-to-four in the Thirteenth. I grabbed a beer on Second Avenue and headed for my car. Twenty-first Street, between First and Second—it's five o'clock—some sixteen-year-old Ubangi looks like he should be playing center for the Knicks comes down the street on a bicycle and yanks a pocketbook off a woman's shoulder. She tried to hang on to it and he pulled her flat on her face into the gutter.

"I was maybe two hundred feet down the block, in street clothes. I just waited until he was near me—the kid must have been up to twenty miles an hour—then I stepped out from between two parked cars and just kicked the side of his bike. Nice and gentle. The brother took a belly whopper across thirty feet of asphalt and wound up headfirst in a pile of dog shit under a parked car.

"By the time I got the pocketbook in my hand and the kid on his feet, this broad is next to me. A forty-five-year-old Manhattan twat with loose black hair halfway to her ass. Some long gray ones scattered in there, too. She looks like she should be running an art gallery up on the East Side. One of her arms is scraped from her wrist to her elbow, and the knees of her pantyhose are totally gone. The fucking *handbag* was worth a hundred and fifty—forget what's inside it. She's *hollering* at me, Corliss. I'm a racist bastard and look what I did to this black child—I didn't have to knock him over. She stood in the middle of the street with both knees and an elbow bleeding—in worse shape than the fucking perpetrator—asking me don't I know this crime was caused by social conditions. Social conditions! She actually used the words. Social conditions and policemen who live outside the city and have the mentality of an occupying army. I wanted to fucking vomit.

"What made it worse was I took a hundred falls as a kid were worse. Really worse. If I cried, my mother would whack me on the back of my head with whatever she had in her hand until I shut up."

"What was the kid doing?"

"He stood there amazed. The kid couldn't believe his ears. He wasn't mad at me for kicking him off his bike. I could see the way he kept catching my eye he had her figured for a loony-toon."

"What happened to him?"

"What happened? He was sixteen. They pushed him through family court for the fifth time. He walked."

George reached over and shook two Chiclets out of the box.

"I ended up at a review-board hearing. This WASP *cunt* brought me up on excessive-force charges. The kid saved me. Is that unreal? They called him in as a witness. The kid shrugged and said he didn't think I used too much force; it was the only way I could stop him. Here's a sixteen-year-old nigger, snatching purses on a bike, had more fucking common sense than this Gramercy Park twat with some stockbroker husband knocking down a hundred thousand a year. It's crazy out there, Corliss. It's fucking crazy."

Corliss found the address halfway along a block of identical two-family brick houses. He pressed the bell twice and waited.

"So this is Bay Ridge," George said.

"You've never been here?"

"I was raised in Inwood. Brooklyn might as well be Timbuktu."

"This part's still nice. Like a small town."

"Yeah—but it's still a little island in the middle of a fucking cesspool." He looked both ways along the street. "Christ, on his salary and no kids he could have had something beautiful out on the island."

She opened the door and looked them over, then turned and began to climb the stairs. "Close the door behind you," she said.

Corliss followed her up the steps, holding his shield out. "We're policemen, Mrs. Ritter."

She spoke without turning. "You're kidding."

They stepped through the glass-paneled door at the head of the stairs into the living room. She sat in a high-backed chair and motioned them toward the couch. The television was playing without sound.

She lit a Camel and coughed. "Can I give you a drink?"

"We're on duty," Corliss said.

She turned to George. "You on duty, too?"

"It's a little early."

"Did you boys know Bunky?"

"We didn't, Mrs. Ritter. But we're both very sorry about Walter."

She stared at Corliss through the haze of cigarette smoke.

"We'd like to ask you a few questions."

She sucked a mouthful of smoke from the cigarette.

"Did he act peculiar the last few weeks or so? Different?"

"What are you talking about?"

"Whether Walter acted differently."

"What the hell does that have to do with some thief pushing him into an elevator shaft?"

Corliss looked pained. "Walter was wearing—"

"Bunky," she said.

"What's that?"

"Bunky. Everyone called him Bunky. Since the third grade. His father and I were the only ones who called him Walter. And the nuns."

Corliss nodded. "Bunky was wearing a tape recorder. Do you have any idea why, Mrs. Ritter?"

"I used to ask him why they called him Bunky. He said it was a nickname, all the kids had one. Then in the fifth grade the principal called me to school. Sister Theresa Agnes. Some new boy had picked a fight with Walter and been hurt enough so his parents came to school to complain. Sister wouldn't believe it. Walter was the politest boy in the school. When she walked into the fifth-grade class and asked if anyone had ever fought with Walter Ritter, everyone stood up. Every last boy. He had beaten them all up at one time or another. Never picked a fight, either. He was the politest boy in the school."

"He was wearing a tape recorder, Mrs. Ritter. Do you have any idea why?"

"How the hell would I know? You're the policeman."

"Did you ever see the recorder, Mrs. Ritter?"

She shook her head.

"Did Walter have a girl friend?"

"No."

Corliss pulled a notebook from his jacket pocket. "Who were some of his friends? Who did he spend his time with?"

She stared at him quietly for a few moments. "No one. He went to church a lot."

"Church!"

She nodded. "Sacred Heart. Most of his free time was spent in church."

Corliss frowned, and looked from her to George, then into his notebook. "Did he gamble, Mrs. Ritter?"

"Gamble? Horses and such? He disapproved of the lottery."

She lit a fresh cigarette and studied Corliss. "What kind of work is it you do in the department?"

"We're with the Internal Affairs Division."

"You investigate other policemen."

Corliss nodded.

She looked toward George.

"I'm a cop." He spoke softly. "I've been assigned to this detail for six months."

She turned to Corliss. "You think Walter was doing something wrong?"

He lowered his voice. "It's possible, Mrs. Ritter. I don't like to say it, but it's possible."

"I think you're crazy."

"I understand your feelings. I hope you're right. But we've got to look into it."

"You don't follow me. I think you're crazy to come talking to me. If I *knew* Walter was up to something, what the hell makes you think I'd give him up?"

They studied one another for a while.

"What the devil would a nice-looking young man like yourself be doing in such a shitty job?"

Corliss reddened. He folded his notebook closed and stood. "We've got to go through your son's room. It won't take ten minutes. Where is it, Mrs. Ritter?"

Her hands trembled while she lit a cigarette. "You can go to hell. You're not poking around this house."

George leaned forward on the couch. "She doesn't—"

Corliss swung around and put his forefinger under George's nose. "Shut up! Just shut up! You'll regret it the rest of your career."

He turned back, still red in the face. "We're going through this place, Mrs. Ritter. Walter may not have been pushed into a shaft by thieves. Whatever he was up to, we're going to find it out. You try to obstruct me and I'll see to it that you get no pension. Not a cent."

She stood up. "A young man was here this morning from the *News*. I sent him away. After you leave, I'll turn this place upside down until it looks like a cyclone hit it. Then I'll call him back with a photographer and let them do a story on how the New York City Police Department treats the mother of a hero."

She stared at him, relaxed now. "My brother is a priest. A nice, old-fashioned parish priest with gray hair. The two of us could do a scene for the six o'clock news that would win an Academy Award." She blew a long puff of smoke past the side of Corliss' head. "Both my boys were tough as a bar of iron. And Walter was the tougher of the two. He didn't get that from his father. Now, do you want to fight, officer? Or do you get the hell out of my house?"

He walked to the door and waited for George.

"I'm sorry, Mrs. Ritter," George said.

"His older brother died in the Battle of the Bulge. Four months before the stinking war was over, he was left behind on the battlefield wounded. They never even found his dog tags. The American Legion put his name up with twenty others on a little honor roll in a park near Myrtle Avenue. It was burned down years ago. A 'gold-star mother,' they called me, and gave me a little silk flag to hang in the window, like it was an honor, while the butcher two blocks away got rich. What a goddamn waste. Now Walter. Another year and we would have been off to Arizona together. I don't know what he might have been doing, but I hope it was something. I hope to hell he didn't die trying to catch a few burglars. What another goddamn waste that would be."

They rode quietly toward Manhattan. As they turned onto the bridge, Corliss spoke. His tone was genuinely apologetic.

"Sorry I got so jumpy with you back there."

"No problem, Corliss. I'm glad I got the chance to see what a collection of first-class hard-ons I'll be working with for the next six months. You don't even sound like a cop, Corliss. When I was talking about Union Square, you said, 'P.R.' Say that in a precinct locker room, the Puerto Rican cops would laugh you out. It's like saying 'Hispanic.' It's what the commissioner or the mayor says in front of a camera for the six o'clock news—where everybody knows they mean spic, but they're not allowed to say it."

He slouched down in the seat and closed his eyes, wanting to bite his tongue. He would have to apologize in the morning. You couldn't work for six months next to someone you'd called a hard-on without giving him an apology.

chapter

XII

Paulie stopped at the front door of the Gallery. He used his reflection to see that his shirt collar lay properly out over his jacket. He centered the tiny gold horn on his chest, then stepped into the dim room. Two customers sat at the far end of the bar, talking to the bartender. Paulie took a stool toward the front.

The bartender took a minute to break away from the conversation. He came down the bar slowly, still talking over his shoulder until he reached Paulie. He recognized the face.

"How are you?"

"Good. A little Black Label on the rocks. Water back." He slid a fifty from his money clip and dropped it on the bar. "You see Frankie Wheels around?"

"Another fifteen minutes he ought to be in. Four, four-thirty he comes in. After work."

He made change and moved back up the bar. Paulie sipped his scotch and pivoted the stool around to face the small front window. He thought about Frankie Wheels.

He would have heard by now that Eddie Grant's trucking company had been knocked over. He would also be pretty sure that Paulie was a part of it. Paulie sipped more scotch. Frankie would be more than pretty sure. The danger now was that Frankie would see a perfect chance to get in solid with Eddie Grant. He was jockeying a tractor trailer through the garment center all day for a living. Ratting to Eddie Grant would get him off the truck. Into a foreman's slot somewhere. Maybe even on the docks, at a longshoreman's pay scale plus a chance to do some robbing here and there.

Paulie spilled some of his water on top of the scotch.

The dead cop was fucking it all up. Without the dead cop, it wouldn't be such a big thing with Eddie Grant—the police wouldn't be climbing all over him. Without the cop, Eddie Grant would say thanks to Frankie, move him into a decent slot for six months, then not even give him a hearing when he got laid off. Frankie knew that, he was raised in the neighborhood. The Mafia loyalty crap might go over big uptown, but people in the neighborhood knew how long Bedbug Eddie's loyalty was good for. But the dead cop made it another story. Frankie would know that.

He swallowed more of the scotch.

Charlie had a point. He sounded a little like a nervous old lady, but he had a point. Any other boss's money, it wouldn't be so bad; the worst might happen is they put you on crutches for six months as a lesson to the neighborhood. With the Bedbug, you didn't know what the hell might happen. The man was definitely a little crazy. Paulie's aunt Rose had grown up next door to Eddie Grant. They had put him in the bin for a year when he was seventeen. She claimed they never should have let him out.

Paulie finished the scotch and wished he had robbed someone else's money.

Frankie came in as the bartender was refilling Paulie's glass. They shook hands.

"Have a drink," Paulie said. He turned to the bartender. "Give Frankie a drink." He put a trace of annoyance into his voice—somehow the bartender was at fault for Frankie being empty-handed.

"Vodka, Frankie?"

He made a sour face. "No vodka, my stomach's no good today. A little green mint, Joey. On the rocks." He dropped a ten on the bar.

Paulie pushed it away. "Your money's no good. Get it here, Joey." He brushed his pile of bills forward. "Have a drink, Joey." He motioned toward the end of the bar. "Give your friends a drink, too."

The bartender poured fresh drinks and called, "*Salud,* Paulie," from the end of the bar. The two customers raised their glasses.

"To your health." Paulie lifted his glass and everyone drank.

Frankie grimaced as he sipped his drink. "I should be drinking Fernet instead of green mint. My stomach's on the bum."

"You should watch your stomach, Frankie. You got to pay attention to what you put in your stomach. You're not careful, you wind up with an ulcer when you're thirty. It'll ruin your life, an ulcer."

Paulie drank down half of his drink. He clapped Frankie lightly on the shoulder. "So how you doing?"

"Good, Paulie. No complaints."

"What's new?"

Frankie shrugged. "Same old grind. I'm still humping that fucking fourteen-wheeler in and out of the garment center from six till three every day. It's no fucking wonder my stomach's always sour."

Paulie patted his shoulder again. "You don't want no ulcer, Frankie. What did you eat today? Do you eat right, Frankie?"

"You kidding, Paulie? I'm careful what I put in my stomach."

"Like what, Frankie? You don't eat that fast-food shit?"

"Hamburgers? No. Ten-thirty every day I grab a container of coffee and a couple of nice fresh jelly doughnuts—ten-thirty the jelly's still warm in the doughnut. If I'm near Tenth Avenue. If I'm across the river, I buy some apple turnovers. They don't make a good jelly doughnut in Jersey. Then for lunch today I had a nice sausage-and-pepper hero with a large bottle of Pepsi and a slice of *abeetz* on Ninth Avenue. There's a *Napolidon* kid there—been there maybe a year—he makes a beautiful pie. A coffee and a Drake's cake for dessert. I quit at three o'clock. I usually grab coffee and a doughnut to hold me till dinner. Today I went light on lunch, so quitting time I had a couple of hot dogs instead of the doughnut. There's one of them Sabrett stands near the garage. With the big umbrella. They use Spanish onions instead of sauerkraut. They put out a hell of a hot dog, Paulie."

Paulie stared at him. "What are you, kidding me, Frankie? Sausages, peppers, quarts of Pepsi, hunks of pizza—that's a light lunch? If I ate what you ate today, I would *die*. Five o'clock my body would groan once and I would fall off this stool and fucking *die*."

He took a long gulp of scotch. Frankie sipped his drink and pressed his fingers lightly against his stomach. Paulie remained quiet. If Frankie didn't bring up the burglary, it meant he had ratted or was about to. They sat quietly for a few minutes.

"What else is new, Frankie?"

He shrugged. "Same old shit, Paulie. I break my ass on the truck all day. I watch TV at night. Friday night I bounce around, Saturday I get laid."

"You got no girl, Frankie?"

He shook his head, no. "I got a cunt up on Fifteenth Street I see Wednesday and Saturday."

"She's nice, Frankie?"

He bobbed his head from side to side. "She's a cunt. Nice, though. She's got a nice way about her." He glanced at his watch and finished his drink. "Jesus, I'm late. My grandmother will have dinner out for me."

Paulie lowered his voice. "You hear about Eddie Grant's place, Frankie? The trucking company?"

He looked puzzled for a minute. "I heard something about a burglary. I never got it straight, Paulie."

"I didn't want you to get the wrong idea, Frankie. You know, we were talking about it—I mean, nothing ever happened, Frankie. I didn't want you to get some crazy idea that I was involved."

"What are you kidding me, Paulie? Come on, I know better than that."

He looked at his watch again and patted Paulie's shoulder. "Let me run. It was nice seeing you, Paulie. Take care." He waved to the bartender. "Joey, *ciao*."

He went through the door quickly, without a final good-bye.

Paulie finished his scotch, left four singles on the bar, and walked up Sixth Avenue slowly. Frankie was about to rat. Or already had. Otherwise he would have wanted money. Thousands. He would have been around days ago looking for Paulie. Anyone shoveled doughnuts, hot dogs, and sausage heroes into his face like Frankie Wheels did was too greedy to let thousands slip away. He thought about calling Charlie, then considered how Charlie would holler at him. The hell with it—it was only his own name that the Bedbug would know. He wouldn't go home for the next few nights. He would stop at the hospital for half an hour to see the old man, then stay in Staten Island at Nino's place for the night. In the morning go to Belmont and try to contact Pete Grillo. Maybe Pete could put in a good word to Bedbug Eddie and settle the whole beef. Pete had to carry some kind of weight with Eddie—he was on his crew.

He hailed a cab for the hospital. Tomorrow he would spend the day at the stables. Somehow it would work out.

chapter

XIII

Charlie held the coffeepot up close to the faucet and let it fill quietly. Diane slept so lightly that the sound of running water sometimes woke her. It would be better if he got in his call to Barney without having to ask her to leave the room for five minutes—that could ruin the rest of the evening. He looked out through the kitchen door to where she was curled up on the couch and wondered whether she was asleep at all. She never napped late in the day, and the way her hand rested lightly on her stomach made him wonder if she was working herself into the role of mother-to-be. Another week, she might be warning him to go easy while they were screwing. He watched her for a bit longer and decided he was wrong. Diane would be washing venetian blinds when her labor pains began.

He picked up the phone. Even if she overheard his conversation with Barney, it wouldn't be the end of the world. She knew he was up to his ears in something illegal from the shoebox full of money in her bedroom closet. Knowing that the Mafia was looking for it might not hurt. She would treat his instructions seriously.

Barney answered on the sixth ring.

"It's me, Barney. Charlie. One more ring I was going to hang up. What do you have up there, a loft?"

"It's a tiny store. Truth is, I could use more room. I was busy fitting an escapement, I must have missed the first couple of rings."

"Look, Barney, I found out more from Paulie. I figured you ought to know." He sensed that Barney was holding his breath. "Are you ready for this?"

"No. But tell me."

"The money belongs to a wise guy. From our neighborhood."

"A heavyweight, Charlie?"

"A fully made Mafioso. Plus, the guy is a total whackadoo."

"Who is he?"

"Eddie Grant. They call him the Bedbug."

"Big shot?"

"Big enough. He runs a crew in Carlucci's family. But nuts, Barney. Truly nuts. You know, the Mafia has its share of honest-to-God crazies. When they hang a name like the Bedbug on one of their own people, you can bet he's a first-rate psycho."

"The kid knew it all the time?"

"All he can think about is his horse. His 'turrow bed.' "

"Is there a chance this Eddie Grant won't wise up, Charlie?"

"I doubt it. Paulie's going to flash money around for sure. I warned him and threatened him, but it won't help. He'll begin spending."

"He can't be that dumb, Charlie."

"He's unconscious is his trouble. Give Paulie a

pocketful of money, there's no stopping him. Barney, you're dealing here with somebody tips tollbooth attendants."

"He what?"

"You got a minute to listen, Barney? It's worth it—you'll know what you're up against with Paulie. The little prick tips toll collectors sometimes. Tollbooth collectors! To impress a girl he's with. He says it's to impress them—for all I know, the maniac does it when he's alone, too. A little eighteen-year-old blonde, could hardly stop snapping her gum long enough to talk, told me how Paulie's the sharpest guy ever took her out. Their first date he's driving her in from Bensonhurst through the Battery Tunnel, he asks does she have a dollar, he'll give it to her later when he breaks a hundred. He's only got a bunch of hundreds and one single, he says. She asks why can't he use the single, the toll's seventy-five cents. He gives her a look like she just ordered spaghetti and meatballs at Ponte's. 'I got to throw this guy a tip,' he tells her.

"She said the attendant's mouth fell open. Paulie gives him a buck, the guy hands him back a quarter, then Paulie pushes a folded single into the guy's hand and gives him a little backhand wave with his fingers. 'Grab yourself a pack of cigarettes,' he says, and breezes through. She said the toll collector was in shock.

"Later on I asked Paulie about it. He gave me a guilty little shrug, like some prince got caught passing dimes to the peasants. 'It impresses these kids from Brooklyn more than a bottle of Dom Perignon. Besides, Charlie, those poor victims got to stand in that little closet breathing car fumes all day. The job's a fucking sentence. You got to throw them a beanie once in a while, no? Makes their day.'

"That's who we're dealing with here, Barney."

"What's this Eddie Grant going to do if he finds out?"

Charlie thought for a few moments. "Hard to figure, Barney. The man is such a fucking psycho, you can't tell. Carlucci might stop him from going overboard— that's our only hope. Otherwise, the Bedbug's got a thing about hacking people up."

"What do you mean, hacking people up? In pieces?"

"Yeah. Seven, eight years ago in the neighborhood, the Bedbug had a terrible beef with a guy they called Carlos Moth Balls. A fucking renegade bandito nobody could control. He threatened the Bedbug. Threatened him! In front of people. Eddie not only whacked him out, he *mailed* pieces of this guy to his family. Tied up each piece nice, in a plastic bag, wrapped them in cartons, and mailed them to his mother, his brothers, and a first cousin. The old lady was in the kitchen over a pot of spaghetti when this special delivery package comes. She had to dry her hands on an apron before she opened it. The guy is fucking gruesome, Barney. He sent her Moth Balls' left arm— it had 'True Love Mom' tattooed on it. The brothers each got a leg. The legs still had his shoes and socks on."

"Holy Christ."

"Barney, the family didn't know what to do with the stuff. Do they take it downstairs and stick it in a garbage can? They finally went ahead and had a funeral for it. At D'Amico's. The casket stayed closed, but the whole neighborhood knew there was only a pair of arms and legs inside it. I heard the oldest brother had to stick a pistol into the priest's mouth to make him do the service; he didn't think the arms and legs were enough for a proper funeral. An old-time greaseball—said he didn't know where the soul was, but for sure it wasn't in the arms or legs.

"I talked to D'Amico over a drink years later. He said it was the weirdest job he ever done. First thing, he couldn't figure out what kind of clothes to put on these limbs. He said they looked all wrong nude, but when he tried them in a suit they looked ridiculous. Then he had a tough time figuring out how to arrange the pieces in the casket. It didn't seem right to just toss them in a pile. He wound up putting each piece where it belonged and folding the hands one on top of the other like he would with a whole body. He even put rosary beads in the fingers. The casket was so light it never really sat right on the pallbearers' shoulders."

Barney whistled softly between his teeth. "And this is the guy whose money we stole."

"Yeah."

"Paulie knew all this?"

"Everybody in the neighborhood knows it."

"This kid is a fucking menace, Charlie."

"That's true. Look, Barney, I don't know what you can do except watch out. Or run. And don't blow your money too fast. There's a half a chance Carlucci will keep a leash on the Bedbug. We may have a shot here. If we have the money to give back, maybe we all just wind up with broken legs."

"That sounds wonderful, Charlie. Meanwhile, we ought to see our parish priests about burying any little hunks of us arrive in the mail." He was quiet for a few moments. "You're sure Paulie will give us up? There's no chance the kid will take the weight? Maybe lie about who was with him?"

"I thought about it, Barney. For about fifteen seconds. He won't be able to stand up. He might like to, but he won't be able. The Bedbug comes near him, Paulie's going to pee in his pants. I mean that, too—the kid's got trouble with his bladder."

He wondered for a minute whether to tell Barney more, then decided to be open with him.

"Barney, I'll tell you the truth. I figure there's a good chance Paulie's going to feed you to them. If it was up to him, I wouldn't even be calling—he doesn't figure we owe you. With him and me there's blood, though. When he's pressed, he might just decide to give them you."

"I been thinking that since you started talking."

Charlie remained quiet.

"I'll do what I can," Barney said. "I can't make promises. Some guy shows up here with an axe on his shoulder asking for names, I can't guarantee I'll stand up. I'll do what I can."

"Thanks."

"I appreciate the call, Charlie. Take care."

They hung up. The water on the stove was boiling. Charlie measured out four scoops of American coffee into the strainer and topped it off with a scoop of espresso, then poured the water into the top pot. He stood facing the stove and listened to the water trickle through.

The worst piece of luck hadn't even been the dead cop, it had turned out to be the blank type on the cop's belly. Something juicy on the tape would have given him a hell of a hand to play with. The three of them had stumbled into the middle of a payoff—no question. The cop hadn't been wandering through Eddie Grant's building at 1:00 A.M. with his own set of front door keys hoping to find prowlers. He was there for the hundred and fifty large sitting in the safe. And the recorder meant that the cop was a plant. They were setting up the Bedbug.

Diane called in from the couch, "Who was that, Charlie?"

He knew from her voice that she hadn't been napping.

"No one you know. You want coffee?"

"No."

He poured a cup for himself and added sugar, then looked in the refrigerator for cream, sure that she had none.

"Diane, can't you once remember to get cream? Even half-and-half. Coffee with milk tastes like shit."

"Was that story true, Charlie?"

"What story?" He took his coffee into the living room and sat on the edge of the ottoman.

"About the Bedbug."

"It's true."

"He had someone cut into pieces?"

"From what I heard, he did it personally. Somewhere out in Sheepshead Bay. Put on a big rubber fisherman's coat and gloves, a pair of hip boots, and whacked Carlos Moth Balls into eight or ten pieces. Parcel-post-size."

"My God."

"You're dealing here with a total psycho. He owns a dog you wouldn't believe. An Italian bulldog, people call it. A kid on Prince Street who worked with dogs told me the real name of the breed is a Neapolitan mastiff. This dog makes an ordinary bulldog look pretty. Snooky, his name is."

"The dog?"

"Yeah. Snooky Yap. The Bedbug named him Snooky. The neighborhood people hung the Yap on him so they know which Snooky people are talking about. The Bedbug trained this dog so it lets anyone into a house or a room—the dog won't make a sound —but nobody leaves without the Bedbug saying it's okay. Any burglar can go in, but never gets out again. He's trapped until the Bedbug gets there. Snooky lays at the door with his eyes closed, his chin stretched out right against the floor, drooling. There's usually a big puddle around his head where he drools. Doesn't move until you want to walk out past him, then he opens his eyes and grumbles. Way down in his chest. You sit down, he closes his eyes again. But try to pass him without the Bedbug being there to give the okay, Snooky goes right through your ankle. He weighs one twenty-five, one thirty. That's what Willie Pep weighed, for Christ's sake. The dog stands up, Diane, his front legs look like two columns for a building. He's got cropped ears and a chest fills up a whole doorway. And he drools. Long lines of saliva, out of both sides of his mouth."

"Is he really vicious?"

"He's vicious. They claim he ate a Chihuahua up on the East Side. In a dog-bath place where Eddie Grant brings him to be washed. This little Chihuahua kept barking at him. Finally the Bedbug lost patience and told Snooky Yap to shut the little fag up. They claim Snooky ate him, right in the waiting room. The lady owned the Chihuahua fainted right there.

"Actually, I think Snooky killed him, but I doubt if he ate him. He could go through a Chihuahua with one hard bite, though. I've watched him outside the social club on Mulberry Street. When the weather's hot he likes to hang out on the sidewalk at night with the wise guys. They give him a little length of two-by-four to chew on. Not a broomstick—a two-by-four! Snooky grabs it and goes to work on it. Doesn't let it loose for a minute, just lays there and crunches on it. It keeps him busy the whole evening. He starts at eight, he's usually through it by midnight. Cuts it right in half.

"I've seen him go through the legs on a couple of barstools in an hour or so, too. At the Blue Goose on

Fourth Street. Eddie Grant went in for supper, brought Snooky with him, and let him chew on a bar-stool while Eddie dug into a sirloin in the next room. The owner, the bartender, the customers—nobody said a word. The place was crowded, too. They sat there with their food in front of them, fascinated, and watched Snooky demolish two barstools. The place sounded like the zoo at lunchtime. When he got through, there was a puddle on the floor from his drooling, you would swear it came from a leaky pipe. The Bedbug and Snooky walked out like nothing had happened."

She reached across for a taste of his coffee. "What do you have to do with Eddie Grant?"

"That's his money in your closet."

"How did you get it?"

"We stole it."

She closed her eyes. "What will he do if he finds out?"

"If he's in the mood, he'll unpack his fisherman's getup for a big night at Sheepshead Bay."

"My God. Will he really do it, Charlie?"

He shook his head. "I don't think so. For one thing, Carlucci would probably stop him. Second, the Bed-bug had a reason to carve up Moth Balls—he wanted to terrorize the two brothers. They were running up and down Carmine Street like a couple of Sicilian speed freaks, threatening vendetta if their kid brother, Carlos, was hurt. They each got that leg in the mail, they shit their pants. They got to the mother's apart-ment she was wailing away at the kitchen table, hug-ging and kissing the arm. It took the two of them to yank it away from her, she wouldn't let go. The big vendetta died right there."

He looked toward the window and thought for a few moments. "The Bedbug really has no reason to chop us up. But you never know—the guy is not all there."

"How could you have taken his money, Charlie?" She shook her head. "No matter how much is there, it doesn't seem worth it."

"I didn't plan it, Diane. Paulie, fucking Paulie, led me into it."

"He's an anchor around your neck, Charlie."

He ignored her.

"And will he catch you for sure?" she asked.

"Yeah, one by one. He'll nail Paulie for sure. And Paulie will feed them this poor victim in the Bronx. Barney. And Barney will give me up."

"There's no way out of it, Charlie?"

He sipped his coffee, and nodded. "There might be. There's two chances here. Paulie's father's best friend, Pete Grillo, is a soldier on Eddie Grant's crew. I don't think it will happen, but Pete might bail us out. Who knows how? The Bedbug might owe him a favor—a hundred things might happen. Pete will do what he can. He doesn't know how to say no to Paulie."

"Has he helped him before?"

"A hundred times. Enough so Paulie counts on it. When Paulie's screwing some neighborhood guy in a two-bit deal, you tell him the guy's going to be pissed, Paulie's favorite line is, 'Let him pull on his prick, we're with Pete!' "

"What's your other chance, Charlie?"

He frowned, still not clear himself about all the details. "I can run." He finished his coffee and went to the kitchen for a refill, talking as he walked. "I can take the fifty thousand and run. Split for New England. A year or two and the whole thing blows over. Meanwhile I've got my country restaurant going."

He filled his cup and returned to the ottoman. He was opening a can of worms, he knew, but sooner or later the idea of his leaving had to come out. Feeding it to her a piece at a time wasn't the worst way to do it.

She watched him sip his coffee and waited for him to continue.

"How are the mime classes coming?" he asked.

"Fine." She said it flatly. He felt her waiting again, and decided not to speak first. After a minute she asked, "What time would you like to eat?"

"You're cooking?"

She nodded.

"You're sure you want to cook? We can eat out."

"You sound frightened."

"Come on, Diane. I figured you might not want to stand and cook on a day off. If you feel like it, that's great. I'm always happier with a home-cooked meal. What are you making?"

"I'll surprise you."

That meant an Italian meal. Another disaster. She was set on proving that she could cook good Italian food. She worked intensely at whatever kind of food she cooked. Her meals came out of the kitchen looking like cookbook photographs, each dish arranged into a perfect color scheme and garnished with tiny carvings of raw vegetables. All of it completely tasteless. She seemed to have no taste buds. Charlie would sometimes close his eyes when she wasn't looking and try to identify a forkful of food from his plate. Only the texture gave him a hint. Even the most elaborate cakes, whorled with buttercream icing, went down without leaving a trace in his mouth. The one time that she had invited Paulie to dinner, he had turned to Charlie with a frown while she was in the kitchen and asked, "What did she do to the food, Charlie? Is this how all these WASPS eat?" He had lifted up a lamb chop on his fork and examined both sides quickly by candlelight. "Where does she *buy* this food, Charlie?"

"What's your restaurant going to be like?" she asked.

He shrugged. "Who knows. That kind of thing never comes out the way you plan it. Right now, my mind's not on it, Diane. I'm thinking a lot more about the Bedbug than my country restaurant."

"Put your mind on it for a minute, Charlie. When you daydream about it, what does it look like?"

"Big. A big country room in one of those old white houses with shutters, with a big pebble parking lot next to it and a fireplace on one wall that you could stand up in. I'll burn real logs, none of that gas-jet crap underneath—big oak logs. Candles on the tables. Really good Neapolitan cooking. Not peasant food. Everybody thinks Neapolitan has to be peasant. Lighter. You won't be able to smell a hint of garlic in the kitchen."

"Is that important?"

"If you're not cooking peasant food. Most Italian restaurants, the asshole they call the chef is some farmer from Calabria got put in the kitchen when he got here because his wrists are thick enough to shake six orders of scallopine in a frying pan all night. He loads up everything with garlic. They chop it. You've got to crack each clove instead. I once seated a party of high Italians, people from Milan or Bologna. They came into the dining room and when we passed the kitchen on our way to their table they sniffed the garlic. They turned around and walked out. I stood there in a crowded dining room with six menus in my hand. I knew when they walked in I had trouble. The men with Borsalino hats and Roman noses—my old man used to say he wished he had that beak full of nickels, he'd be rich. They were right, though. That place had a guy in the kitchen could destroy you with garlic."

"I'd think you would want to be *out* of the restaurant business, Charlie. With a little money you could look for something entirely different."

"Why? It's what I know. Why try to get out of it?"

"There's something low-class about it, Charlie. It isn't substantial. Even when you own a successful place, you're catering to people. It's demeaning."

"That's bullshit. Take a minute sometime and watch rich, cultured people haggle in a store over jewelry. Their fucking eyes glow. There *is* no high-class way to make money except inherit it."

"There are better and worse ways, Charlie, and running a restaurant means you're serving people."

"So what? That's why you're so unhappy waitressing, Diane. When you're waiting tables, you're a servant. If you can't accept that, you shouldn't be doing it. It doesn't have to be demeaning. You serve people. You get paid for it. It's a job. What's the big deal?"

"I'm not a full-time waitress, that's why. I'm an actress."

"If you're earning your living as a waitress, you're a waitress. You work in an easy place, too, Diane. You've never worked with customers who demand service. Real ball-breakers. You bring out one dish lukewarm, it not only goes back to the kitchen, you blew your tip, too. You wind up with a straight ten percent. There's customers out there you don't even know exist. People who spend the whole year bouncing from Miami Beach to Acapulco, the Caribbean. New Year's Eve in Vegas. Hotel people. They want a pint of blood for every hundred they break. The broads are the worst. Wrinkly brown hands with liver spots, but their faces get lifted every five years. They chew up two headwaiters a week."

She decided to let it drop, and went into the kitchen to prepare dinner. Charlie leaned against the kitchen doorjamb with his coffee and watched. One of her large cookbooks was open on the countertop. He leaned over to read it. She was attempting chicken cacciatore. He would manage to keep his mouth shut; whatever help he might give it along the way would be demolished in the final seasoning anyway. She started to carve the chicken.

"Will I be able to work at your restaurant, Charlie?"

"I thought you don't want to be a servant."

She moved close to him and rubbed her hip against his thigh. "Working for you would be different."

"No waitresses. This is going to be a class operation —men only on the floor."

"It's discriminatory."

"It's practical. I'll make you the hat chick. You can have the concession free."

"Do I get to wear a costume?"

"French maid? Black with white trimmings?"

"That's your class operation? What will *you* do there, Charlie? Smoke cigars and get fat?"

"And proposition the hat chick."

He became serious. "I'll manage it. Bang the suppliers on the head once a week, keep the help from stealing too much, seating captain for dinner, expedite the kitchen if the chef gets jammed up."

"In my place I can't remember the last time the manager went into the kitchen. Not while they're working. I think they'd throw him out."

"I've met him, Diane, remember? He's a kid with a suit on. I know how to run a restaurant. A chef walks out on me or his knees buckle when it's busy, I can jump behind the range and put out a hundred dinners. You know how many white dress shirts I've ruined doing that?"

She sliced through the chicken's legs at the first joints—too low for cacciatore.

"The drinks will be perfect, too." Charlie said. "The bartender pours what's ordered. Some asshole wants a Chivas sour, charge him for it but pour Chivas. And whatever the label says is what's going to be in the bottle. No hashing."

"People really hash liquor, Charlie?"

He started to shrug off her question, then decided to elaborate. Give her the kind of story about himself that made her uncomfortable. If he wanted out, he ought to begin working up to it slowly.

"That's one of the nicer things they do. I started in this business behind the bar in bust-out joints on Third Street. Strippers hustling drinks between their numbers. A guy says give the girl a drink, you open a split. Fifteen bucks you whack him for. In those days. If he squawks, you look at him like he was raised on a farm. 'The lady is drinking champagne,' you tell him. Six ounces for fifteen fazools. We had to come in an hour early to make the champagne: white wine and club soda, punch in a cork and shake it a little. The girls used to spit back anyway, then dump the glass the first chance they got. Some of those joints the carpet was so soaked from drinks you could hear it squish when you walked across it."

"You're not going to hash in your restaurant?"

"I've been running away from it for years. It's depressing. But it was good training, the bust-out joints. A cockroach didn't get out of those places without paying a tab."

She broke off the wings below the shoulder joints. Without the shoulders, they were going to get lost in the stew, Charlie thought.

"How could you have worked in those places, Charlie?"

"The bust-out joints weren't the worst. At least I was a kid. Nineteen years old, what the hell is going to bother you? At that age you go through life thinking with your cock. Working with a couple of dozen hookers wasn't so terrible, either. What got to me more was tending bar at Billio's four years ago. I was into my thirties then, and a little down on my luck. When you're sober at four in the morning, it starts to look like the rest of your life is going to be one nickel-and-dime hustle or another.

"Billio's was a joint for off-the-wall drinks. It used to draw a crew of black pimps late at night. One-thirty or so they might have a meet scheduled to deal each other a little coke. Hanging out—telling lies, they used to call it. Every one of them would double-park a custom Caddie or a Continental with the heart-shaped rear window. Pink or chartreuse padding on the outside of the car. Sculptured hood ornaments, maybe some snakeskin upholstery for class. Each one would pull up with his newest little Midwest teenie he grabbed the week before at the Port Authority. They spend a week or so settling the girl in before they put her on the street. These pimps were tough, tough street kids here maybe a year or two from Detroit. They used to sit at the end of the bar with their wide-brim hats and drink concoctions you couldn't dream up. Dead serious, too, when they ordered, with that deep voice, ghetto-tough-guy-style.

" 'Coo vosay and Coca-Cola. Mix dat.'

" 'All out of Courvoisier. Is Remy okay?'

" 'Remy? Man, I can't drink dat shit. Let me try a rum collins instead. With a lot of fruit.'

"Next guy would point to the backbar and ask, 'What you got in dat big yellow bottle?'

" 'Galliano.'

" 'Dat sweet, or bitter?'

" 'Sweet.'

" 'You keep any grapefruit juice?'

" 'Yeah.'

" 'Mix me some grapefruit juice and the stuff in the yellow bottle.'

"It was tougher than taking a food order. Johnnie Red in ginger ale with a slice of orange was the straightest drink they would order. Like a pack of fucking kids loose in a candy store. Then on the second round the bastards would change! The rum collins would ask what was in that little square green bottle. 'Put some of that in orange juice.' Wind up dropping eight or ten bucks apiece and leave a buck thirty total for a tip. And think they were behaving like sports. They just didn't know better. 'Dat's for you, my man,' and push some quarters and dimes across the bar. They play their bad-nigger number to the hilt, these pimps, but meanwhile they don't go for spit."

She stopped sawing at the chicken for a moment and frowned at him in an exaggerated way. "Charlie. Is it so hard to say 'black'? I've asked you a dozen times. That word, 'nigger,' it just grates on me. And it makes you sound dumb, too."

"You don't understand, Diane. These weren't black guys, these were niggers."

"You've really got too much intelligence to be a bigot, Charlie."

"I'm not. I got nothing against blacks. It's niggers I don't like."

"But don't you see, Charlie? Just using that word makes you prejudiced."

"Bullshit. The whole business is a lot more complicated than you give it credit for, Diane. I went through this same argument with Bruce Garrison. He drinks at the Good Times. A nice college guy, works for a big advertising agency. I'll tell you a story, Diane. A couple of years ago Christmas Eve I was at Tony Guarino's house on Spring Street for a holiday drink. While I'm sitting there, he showed me a brand-new three-fifty-seven Magnum he'd just bought. You ever see one? It's a heavy-caliber pistol looks like it's meant to kill an elephant. Chrome-plated. I asked him what he was going to do with it. It's for under the pillow, he tells me. 'Maybe if I'm lucky I'll bag a nigger coming through the window.'

"That's a bigoted remark, no, Diane? It's even worse, it's a racist remark. You're not just using the word 'nigger,' you're talking about shooting one.

"We left the house an hour later to go uptown. Tony keeps his car in a little lot next to his house that maybe parks four cars. We're backing out onto Spring Street and Tony looks up in the rearview mirror and says, 'Stop, stop, stop.' I hear brakes screeching and a few seconds later we get whacked in the rear by a little panel truck. Nobody's hurt. There's headlight glass all over the street. The panel truck is in good shape, but Tony's got five, six hundred dollars' worth of damage on the rear end.

"The guy driving comes off the truck. A black guy. Bombed. Not falling-down drunk, but close to it. Mumbling about how it's not his fault. There's a pint of booze on the floor in the front of his truck. Even drunk the guy knows enough to be nervous. His garage is a few blocks away and he knows he's in a neighborhood don't treat blacks very gently. Ten minutes later a patrol car pulls up, with a sergeant riding it. The sergeant clocks the black guy right away, and says to Tony, 'You were backing out—it looks like your fault. Unless you want to request a drunkometer test on him.'

" 'What if he's drunk?' Tony asks.

" 'Then he's wrong.'

" 'What if I don't ask for a test?'

"The sergeant shrugs. 'I'm not dragging him in on my own. I'll kill Christmas Eve for myself.'

"Tony tells him, 'Let it go. They'll only take the poor fuck's license away.'

"I asked Tony, 'You're going to let him walk?'

" 'It's Christmas Eve, Charlie. The guy had a couple of drinks. Plus, he didn't come up on the sidewalk after me. I was backing out—he ain't a hundred percent wrong, either. What am I going to do, cause this guy's family grief? It's Christmas Eve. He drives for a living. I can't take the guy's living away from him.'

"That was the end of it. The black guy was standing there drunk and mumbling, in the middle of a jackpot, and he skated away clean as a whistle. Every solid-citizen type I know would have told the sergeant to pinch him. My friend Bruce Garrison admitted *he* would have. So how racist can Tony really be? This black guy was better off running into Tony with his three-fifty-seven under his pillow than Bruce Garrison, who told me he sends out CORE Christmas cards every year. It's not such a simple business, Diane."

"What about the person Tony *will* shoot?"

"It'll be someone coming through a window. And that's not so terrible. If you had grown up where I did, you'd look at it differently. You can't afford to be soft if you want to make it in that neighborhood."

He watched her face redden. She controlled her anger by speaking deliberately.

"Soft? Because my name isn't Cookie and I never beat up boys in playgrounds? You've never been in Maine, Charlie. Where I was raised, the men make you and Paulie look like self-indulged little boys whose mothers breast-fed them way past weaning time. Your trouble is that you confuse honesty with weakness. I was raised to think that criminals were people who didn't have the strength to make it honestly."

"You've never been on the streets, Diane. You pull yourself up through the East Side or the Village, you get shit on if you're honest."

"Charlie, you've told me about the streets constantly. Come up to the woods. My grandmother pulls her own teeth. She drinks half a pint of Canadian whiskey and pulls her own teeth. And not because she's too poor or too cheap to pay for it. She thinks a dentist is an indulgence—someone the weak folks need. There's a toughness in Maine, Charlie, that you have no idea of."

He was tempted to pat her on the ass before he spoke; it would be like lighting a firecracker.

"Honesty might work up there, Diane. Wonderful. It takes you about ten feet forward in life on Carmine Street."

"It works anywhere you make it work, Charlie. If you're interested in growing into some kind of human being, someone with a *core,* you've got to develop a sense of integrity about yourself. It's more than not stealing other people's money, it's a feeling of your own personal integrity. I've sat at a bar with you and your friends at two A.M. listening to Sinatra on the jukebox singing 'My Way,' and all of you identifying with that sentimental tripe. It's a hoax, Charlie, and what makes it worse is that you sense it. New England is *filled* with people who, if they do succeed, make Frank Sinatra look like a joke, thinking he did it his way. They would laugh at him, Charlie."

"Maybe Maine's an easier place to do it."

"It is. Charlie, I'm sure it is. But that's a poor excuse. You miss by an inch. The rest of your friends don't—after an hour with them it's easy to see that there's no hope. But you come close. Close enough so that I want to *push* you the last inch away from your damned tribal loyalty to family and friends and to hell with the rest of society. You're so close to climbing out of it, Charlie. Another inch and you could grow into someone special."

"Maybe I don't want to, Diane. You ever think that maybe I see it, that I know I could come out of my pond into your world, but I decide it's not where I want to be? Maybe I'd rather go through life with my tribal loyalty to family and friends. Maybe blood's a better reason to be close than your solid-citizen reasons."

She shook her head. "Paulie uses you, Charlie. Don't you see what you get for your loyalty to family? You cover up for him over and over, and he *uses* you."

"I see it. I allow a little for his weakness. That's what you never learned in the woods—you've got no room for weakness. I know he uses me, I bitch about it all the time. But I don't have a choice." He used his right hand, Italian-style, to emphasize his words. "Paulie is family and he needs a job. I don't have fifty a week to hand him and tell him to go home, then I got to give him a job. Period. Not because it's fair—because he's blood."

She shrugged, and concentrated on the chicken. Charlie poured fresh coffee into his cup and watched her. She was the one who just missed, he thought. By an inch. She felt for people, but thought that the whole racial business could be fixed up if everyone would only call them blacks. And her craziness about waitressing.

After a minute she spoke without looking up. "I'd

like you to give me a straight answer to something, Charlie."

He tensed.

"I don't want to pressure you. Or cling. I want to know where we stand. You talk as though you plan to leave alone."

She looked up at him and waited for an answer.

It would never work unless he really met her half-way, he thought. It would mean changing for her, and he wasn't a twenty-year-old anymore. He wanted an honest restaurant off in the country, where he didn't have to hash liquor after closing, but what she was af-ter was for him to become a total victim. Register and vote—she thought it was terrible that he didn't. Their arguments would drag out for days, too—no throwing a flower pot, then hopping into bed a few hours later. He sipped his coffee. She wasn't the world's greatest lay, for that matter. Plus, her cooking was a disaster. No small thing. Of course he could plan on eating in his restaurant for the rest of his life, but there had to be something seriously wrong with anyone who could destroy good food the way she did.

"What makes you think I might leave alone?"

"That's not an answer, Charlie. *Are* you going to leave by yourself?"

"I haven't figured out what's best for both of us. If there's a good chance the Bedbug will catch up with me, then it's safer to leave you behind."

"Don't worry so much about what's safe for me, Charlie."

"It's not just you, Diane. You're pregnant. I've got to think of that, too."

He ought to just tell her, he thought. They had no contract. He had never made any promises. He would leave her some of the money, for the kid. Ten thou-sand. It could be a nice start for the baby, and it was the right thing to do. She would be cranky about it for a while, but, when she thought it over, ten thousand was a nice start. Meanwhile, he would have a nice fresh start in New England. He moved closer and kissed her forehead. She was leaning against the counter, her hand resting lightly on the chicken.

"Finish your stew, Diane, or we'll never eat. Nobody's going anywhere just yet."

chapter

XIV

Barney got to Hanratty's an hour ahead of the lunch-time customers. He had worked since sunup on a chime problem and gotten nowhere—Charlie's call last night was on his mind. Three of the midmorning heavy hitters were spaced along the bar like sentries, staring up at the television.

"It's a bit early for you, Barney," Ginty said. He set a coaster in front of him.

"A bloody mary. Ice-cold."

Ginty mixed the drink leisurely. Barney took a long gulp, smacked his lips, then finished the drink in one long draught. He pushed the empty glass forward.

Ginty bent for the tomato juice. "Give me a bit of warning if you intend to maintain that pace, Barney. I'll be hard pressed to keep up. It will go easier on the two of us if I bring a little bucket out here and put together a proper-size batch."

Barney sipped the second drink. Ginty hoisted his foot up onto the edge of the sink and lit a cigarette. He looked down the bar. "Like a row of statues, these three. You would guess their necks would be stiff as concrete, looking up at the television for so many hours each day. Why the hell don't they swing their stools around and face the damn screen, Barney? I wonder about it often."

Barney looked. Each of the old men had his body set squarely facing the backbar, his head twisted around and up toward the TV. Barney shrugged.

"They figure they're only going to watch for a few minutes," Ginty said. "That's the conclusion I've come to."

Barney swallowed most of his drink and motioned toward the mixing glass. "You'd better get another one going, Ginty."

The bartender set his cigarette on the edge of the bar and reached for the juice. "All this tomato juice is no good for you, Barney. It's far too much acid. And the Tabasco and Worcestershire will eat holes through the walls of your stomach. Drink the vodka straight, Barney, you're better off. It's easier on the barman, too. All this shaking does my heart no good."

He strained the shakerful into Barney's glass.

"Something's on your mind, Barney."

"The future, Ginty."

Ginty drew on his cigarette. "That's always a depressing business, Barney, if you look far enough ahead."

"I don't need to look very far. I got maybe another five years on my eyes, Ginty. Then the lights go out."

"What will the boy do, Barney?"

He shrugged. "I don't know."

"Is he that bad, Barney. Can he care for himself at all?"

Barney frowned. "Are you kidding, Ginty? Three years ago a young couple rented our upstairs apartment. They're still there. They weren't moved in a week when the girl complained to my wife that our puppy crying at night kept them awake. She said we ought to train him. We don't own a puppy, Ginty. It was Roger. He was seventeen years old. Can he care for himself, Ginty—when a stranger mistakes him for an untrained dog?"

Barney finished two more bloody marys, then switched to vodka on the rocks as the lunch crew gathered. He let Ginty coax him into a roast beef sandwich and french fries. Halfway through lunch, Harvey from the appliance store asked in a low voice, "What happened the other day with the cop on Castle Hill and Westchester, Ginty? Somebody told me a cop collapsed on duty?"

Ginty took a long puff on his cigarette and smiled, then occupied himself washing glasses. The group stopped talking and watched him.

"It's quite a little story," Ginty said. "But I shouldn't be discussing it."

"Come on, Ginty, what happened?"

He dried his hands slowly and lit a fresh cigarette. "Some of it I heard and some of it I saw with me own eyes. It was a cop named Tim O'Hare, the summons man in the Forty-third. I know the man only to nod to."

"The who?"

"The summons man. In the Forty-third. Every precinct has a summons man. Do none of you know that?"

They shook their heads no.

"It's been that way for thirty years and longer. Every cop gives out a reasonable number of summonses, enough to fill a quota, whatever it might be. Ten, perhaps fifteen a day. All parking violations. None of them enjoys ticketing cars. They give out what they have to and very little more. To boost the total for the precinct, though, there's always been one summons man—someone willing to rush like hell and ticket everything in sight. A summons man might dispense a hundred a day. O'Hare writes a hundred thirty a day, I've been told. It's traditional in every precinct to reward the summons man with the eight-to-four tour, Monday through Friday. Never works a weekend, never works a night. A hell of an inducement for a policeman. The summons man wants the shift enough to take on a dirty task. Here in the Forty-third it's Tim O'Hare. Surely you've noticed him, Harvey."

Harvey nodded. "Fat guy with big red cheeks. In his middle thirties. At one minute past eight he's loping along Castle Hill Avenue like a hippo heading for water. The son of a bitch won't look up to give someone directions, he's too busy writing tickets."

"That's him. The lieutenant in the precinct told me that in twenty years he's never seen a summons man like him. He wouldn't interrupt a towing job for a robbery-in-progress call. When the tow trucks blitz the neighborhood, he rides the running board, and even with the belly he's carrying around he hits the street at a trot when they approach an illegally parked vehicle. The man is possessed. In January he towed away Monsignor Burns's car from in front of the rectory, with a clergy sign clipped like a billboard on the sun visor. A brand-new Grand Prix. Took it off to the pound."

Ginty poured himself a cup of coffee.

"He's quick to haul a car off. Like a man with a mission. The monsignor's car didn't get him into trouble, but apparently O'Hare also carted off a couple of the Italians' cars from in front of the Four Aces. One of them came out in time, but O'Hare wouldn't let him go."

"The wheels were up off the ground?"

"No. The tow truck was still backing up. The fellow

raced across the sidewalk, hollering that he would move it. O'Hare never looked up from the bumper. 'Hook it!' he yelled to the driver, and they hoisted it up."

"That's not right. Once the hook's on, that's it. But if you get there before the hook's on, they let you move it. You got to take the ticket, but they let you move it. This guy O'Hare's a prick."

"He's often referred to as that," Ginty said. "At any rate, he made some enemies over at the Four Aces. He stops after lunch each day for two fast highballs at Scanlon's. One of the Italians got over there and managed to slip a horse physic into his drink."

"A what?"

"A horse physic. When a horse is badly constipated, the vet puts a little envelope of this powder into his bag of oats. I'm told the stuff will break up a block of concrete."

"They gave him a *full* envelope?"

"Plus a bit. He's over two hundred, O'Hare is, and the biggest share of it around his waist. Whoever administered the physic felt he needed a generous dose."

"How long does the stuff take to work?"

"It's not slow. Five minutes or so. He left Scanlon's and wrote a few tickets. A dozen customers from the Four Aces gathered on the sidewalk to watch him. He moves at a brisk pace. Halfway to the corner of Castle Hill he began to act peculiar. Fidgety. A minute later he stopped writing tickets and hurried along, bending his knees a bit so he was closer to the sidewalk. At the corner I'm told his eyes were wide and he was looking around in a bit of a panic. He must have decided to make a beeline for the movie house, for he crossed the intersection diagonally. Long, low steps he was taking, like some big, blubbery Groucho Marx. He knew something was terribly wrong, for the

Italians had followed him down the block and were on the corner watching. That's a hell of a busy intersection. He never made it across. Dead center under the el, with cars coming and going around him, the summons man shit his pants."

Ginty sipped his coffee.

"It must have been something terrible. They say it's a wonder the man didn't deposit his lungs there on Westchester Avenue."

"What happened to him?"

"One of the Italians thought it was appropriate to dial nine-eleven with an officer-needs-assistance call. That goes out on the air as a ten-thirteen. It's treated like a nuclear attack—a foot patrolman will commandeer a car to answer it. A dozen radio cars responded in a matter of minutes, parked every which way in the intersection and up on the sidewalk with the doors thrown open and the red lights spinning around on the roofs. Like one of those grand old Hollywood premieres. The cops just watched the summons man crawl to the curb—there were none of them too anxious to assist their brother officer at that moment. One of them was heard to remark that a good pair of fireman's boots is what O'Hare should have been issued."

"What the hell were the Italians doing?"

"Having a fine time on the corner, flashing their pinkie rings around, most of them with drinks in their hands. Announcing loud as barkers at a sideshow to anyone who asked what was going on, 'Cop shit his pants!' "

"Is O'Hare back on the job yet, Ginty?"

"I'm told he's not. The poor bastard is suffering a fit of depression. And he can't afford to delay. There's a young fellow lives out in Smithtown, only in the precinct six months, is trying to become the summons man. Apparently he moonlights evenings as a liquor store salesman. It makes the eight-to-four shift worth a small fortune to him. He's been running up and down the avenue each day trying to break a hundred."

"Will he get the job?"

"He may well. They don't play favorites; it's a competitive slot. The lieutenant says he looks damn good for such a young fellow. The men must think so—they left some big rubber underpants and a pair of fireman's boots in front of his locker yesterday."

The local merchants were gone by 1:30, leaving Barney and the three sentries at the bar. The pensioners now began to appear, one by one, to settle in for the afternoon and follow the soap operas. The day's shots and Schaefer nips would be on credit, against next month's social security check. The room was warm and smoky. Barney had no desire to return to the shop. He sipped his drink and felt himself on the verge of saying more to Ginty than he wanted to. He changed to vodka and tonic and thought again about Charlie's call.

The wise guys would catch up with Paulie, no doubt about it. Anybody who tipped tollbooth attendants wouldn't keep his money in a mattress for long. And sure as hell the kid wasn't going to hand them Charlie; he would cough up Barney for them. Barney was doomed—either the wise guys would nail him or they would feed him to the cops. Either one would want the money, too. With fifty thousand, Nora could get by with Roger for a long time to come. What he needed was a way to protect his money. A place to put it. Telling Nora was out; it wouldn't take someone five minutes to con her into telling where it was. He needed someone to leave it with, someone he could trust to get it to Nora if and when they whacked him out. He looked toward the blurred television screen, then back again to the glass between his hands. Who the hell could be trusted to hold fifty big ones?

"So it's your eyes are worrying you, Barney," Ginty said.

"More than that, Ginty. You wonder sometimes what the hell it's all about. Fifty-eight years old and I'm sitting here hard pressed to come up with one real friend. A friend I could trust completely."

"Ah, Barney, you're feeling sorry for yourself. You've got half a dozen good friends if you think about it."

Barney shook his head. "None. No real friends. Ginty, my own *brother* would screw me if I gave him the chance."

Ginty lifted his apron and hoisted his foot up on the edge of the sink. "I never knew you had a brother, Barney."

"Arthur. Three years older than me. The most selfish son of a bitch ever walked."

"You were not really friends, then?"

"All I ever wanted was to be his friend. He was eleven when he got pinched for stealing coal. We were freezing our asses off in a fourth-floor railroad flat on Ninety-second Street with a toilet in the hall used to freeze up overnight. Those days they didn't fuck around. They sent him off to a reform school upstate. Arthur was a little con man even then—they made him a trustee. Eight months after he got there, they put him in charge of taking five other kids into town to see a dentist. They took off, all six of them. The cops had every one of the other five in three days—they waited at the kids' houses and each one showed right up. Not Arthur. Six fucking weeks this guy hung around our house. He didn't believe it. 'Every twelve-year-old comes home,' he used to say. Seven years later we got a card. Arthur had managed to join the English army somehow, at age nineteen."

"You never knew one another much, Barney."

"Before they sent him away I used to look up to him. The years he was gone Arthur was my hero. I used to daydream about the two of us being together, riding freights out west, sleeping outdoors next to each other. We got to know each other when I was sixteen, seventeen. He deserted after a year in the army and came back to the States. We shared a room together in Philly for a while. He took off one night while I was on the midnight-to-eight shift at Campbell's Soup. Took a beautiful double-breasted suit I had just bought and a new set of luggage. Cleaned the room out. Shoes —everything. He left me shit."

"Is he still alive, Barney?"

"As far as I know. He was in Venezuela the last I heard."

"You've no other family?"

"A kid sister somewhere if she's alive. We lost track of each other thirty years ago."

"It's a bit tough, Barney, having no family. What the hell do you do for the holidays? I've got rooms full of blood relatives right here in the Bronx. Plus a whole tribe back in Ireland. I wouldn't be happy, having no one."

He poured himself a fresh cup of coffee.

"Does your wife have anyone, Barney?"

"Nora? A brother retired from the navy a few years ago. He hasn't been sober since."

Barney chewed an ice cube. "It's crazy, Ginty. The closest friend I ever had was a Puerto Rican kid young enough to be my son. Always in trouble. The poor son of a bitch got stabbed to death in a poolroom on Southern Boulevard. I would have trusted that kid with anything."

Ginty shook his head. "They say there's good and bad in every group, Barney, but these Spanish seem like one hell of a crazy bunch. They're burning the whole fucking borough down."

"Most of the borough could use it, Ginty. They called this kid Joe Loco. He used to tell me he couldn't live long—he was the world's lousiest fighter but not willing to take two cents' worth of shit from anybody. That's a fatal combination. Means you have to reach for something, so every fight goes right down to the wire. 'It's prison or the graveyard, Barney,' he used to say. Kid couldn't change, either. I used to tell him to make an effort—learn to back off an inch. 'I wish I could, Barney,' he would say. 'I try, but it's not my makeup, you know?' He wound up bleeding to death on Southern Boulevard."

"They cut each other up all the time, Barney. When they're not busy igniting some apartment house."

"Latins, Ginty. All those tropical people take fights seriously. Mediterraneans are the same way. They don't brawl. Cold-weather people brawl. Swedes. Irish. Tie a half a bag on and beat hell out of each other for a good time, then take turns buying rounds of drinks. Warm-weather people you don't lay hands on. They don't enjoy a fight—they know when it starts someone's going to be killed or maimed."

"They're quick enough with the hands when it comes to women, Barney. I swear they're busy screwing before they make their First Communion. You'll see a pair of them not a day past twelve years of age leaning against a parked car on Westchester Avenue swapping spits and dry-humping away like it was their own bedroom. The women must grow up with backbones deformed to the shape of a Chevrolet fender."

"What the hell is so terrible, Ginty? These kids might

be better off than us. When I was a kid they were still telling us we would go blind if we jerked off."

"Could that be why your eyes are going on you, Barney?"

Barney laughed.

Francis Cullen came in and Ginty walked down the bar to serve him. Barney guessed that Cullen was paying for his shot and a beer with a pocketful of swag telephone change, and silently wished a bleeding ulcer on him. His fucking corrupt cop son should choke on his fucking lunch, too, Barney thought. He belched slightly from the tonic.

Ginty returned and filled Barney's glass. "This is with Francis."

Barney lifted the glass toward Cullen and sipped from it. "Here's to a bleeding ulcer," he murmured. He emptied the glass quickly.

Ginty filled it and rapped his knuckles twice on the bar to signify that it was with the house. He leaned forward and dropped the professionally warm bartender's tone from his voice. "You know, Barney, keeping that boy of yours at home all these years is no small thing. You and your missus both—you deserve a full measure of credit. It can't be easy."

"Credit for what?"

"For keeping the boy, Barney."

"He's not a boy, Ginty. Roger's an infant. A twenty-year-old infant who's toilet-trained—just about."

"Ah, but you've behaved like parents and kept him a part of the family."

"You think that was smart, Ginty? You know what it cost? It's seventeen years since Nora and me left the house together. Seventeen years. When he was two or three we could still get a baby-sitter—after that it's impossible. We hardly talk to each other, Ginty. I haven't laid a hand on her in fifteen years. It was never right again, with him there. Something is just the matter. We should have got rid of him at the start. We waited till it was too late."

"You don't mean that, Barney. It wouldn't have been right. The Jews can do it, maybe. They certainly waste no time planting their old mothers and fathers into the nursing homes. You wouldn't believe the boardwalk at Long Beach. Perched like some endless row of gulls they are, on a sunny afternoon, a mile of poor old souls staring out at the ocean with their colored maids standing behind the chairs. They must ship off the babies as well if they don't seem suitable. You can bet your ass, Barney, that it's not Irish filling up the nursing homes and the Letchworth Villages."

Barney jerked his thumb toward the front of the bar. "This crew doesn't look much better off, Ginty. Every one of them will cash his next social security check right here and leave most of it in the register."

"Old John O'Connell has to add to it each month."

"So who's to say what's right, Ginty?"

"What if you had it to do over again? That's the test. Serious now. Are you saying you would lock the boy up in some home? Among a bunch of strangers?"

Barney thought for a few moments. "I don't know, Ginty. I just don't know. Most likely I'd do it the same way, but not because I think it's right. I just figured if you got dealt a bad hand, then you sat with it and played it out. I never even stopped to figure it, to tell you the truth—it's just the way it *was*."

"That's my point, Barney. That's exactly my point. It's the way the Irish are. All this nursing-home crap, and homes for retarded, and divorces, and abortions —all the rest of them out there want life to be one grand picnic. *Demand* it, they do. It's got to be every fucking inch of it their way. And if it's not right, then by God it's got to be fixed, whether it means murdering some unborn baby or sentencing their own flesh and blood to something called a 'home,' God love us. They each of them *demand* that life treat them just so. Well, just who the hell do they think they are, that everything should be so easy? They want to answer to no one but themselves."

Barney shrugged. "Maybe you're right, Ginty. Maybe not. We all just go through it our own way. Who the hell can say why?"

"In any case, I'm happy you wouldn't do any different with the boy, Barney."

He walked to the front sinks to catch up on glasses.

Barney exhausted his list of possibilities. He reduced the fifty thousand in increments until it was down to five thousand. There was no one to trust even with that. At thirty-five hundred he decided that Ginty might be trusted, though Barney couldn't remember the two of them ever spending five minutes together without a bar between them. At twenty-five hundred he came up with Anthony, who had been his barber for the past fifteen years. He had been born somewhere in Abruzzi, he had nine grandchildren, he owned a little house in City Island. The surgeons at Misericordia had cut off one of his wife's breasts a year ago. His license to cut hair was propped against the mirror and had his last name typed on it, but Barney had never been able to make it out from the chair.

He resqueezed the wedge of lime into his drink and resisted the temptation to sigh out loud. After fifty-eight years, a local bartender and a barber were the only people he might trust with a few thousand dollars. He had spent forty years with hustlers and small-time thieves—and the problem with thieves, he thought, is that in the end you can't trust most of them.

Thinking back on it now, it wasn't at all clear to him just how he had drifted the way he had. There had never been a single moment at which he was clearly making a choice—to go legitimate or not. Even the dead cop had somehow just happened. Barney wasn't surprised; every guy he met doing time for murder one didn't quite know how it had happened to *him*. All of them had slid into it—and when it was all over and they sat in a cage thinking it out, each of them wished day and night that he could do it over again differently. They reminded Barney of some third-grade kid who had let his dog off the leash and watched it get run over by a car—totally depressed and promising God that it would be *different* if he got another chance. Johnny Santos at Coxsackie said that at night he closed his eyes and *begged* that when he woke up it would be the morning of the day he had killed a transit cop. It hadn't got to Barney yet. He worried more about saving the fifty thousand for Nora than about a murder-one rap or the Mafia.

He leaned back on the barstool and stretched. Maybe things weren't as terrible as he was making them out. They weren't good exactly, but maybe he was overreacting. The wise guys might just take their losses and forget about it. Or Paulie might keep a low profile and they wouldn't nail him. Even if they did, they might not bother coming after Barney. He wasn't from their neighborhood, he wasn't a convenient example to be set for their own people, he wasn't even Italian—why the hell should the Mafia bother him? They might just swallow the fifty-thousand-dollar loss he represented and leave him alone.

Sure—and one of Nora's novenas might suddenly work and Roger would wake up next Sunday morning cured. He started in on a basket of pretzels that he had managed to ignore since eleven o'clock. He thought about Charlie. It had been decent of him to call. The night of the robbery he had been decent, too, half-apologizing about having to take Paulie's side in the diner. The guy might not be exactly trust-worthy, but he wouldn't go out of his way to screw anyone. If anything, he might go a bit out of his way to do a favor. When the wise guys or the cops found Barney, they were going to pressure him to give them Charlie, if they thought there was a third person on the job. Paulie would claim there were only two of them. If Barney agreed to take the weight, stuck to a story of only two people, Charlie would skate away clean. Clean as a whistle—and with his share. For that, Charlie would rightfully owe him. Plenty.

Barney sat for a while longer, and decided that he had no other choice. Age fifty-eight, and a crime partner he had met a few weeks ago was the person he could trust most. If that was what he had to do, then he had better do it. Tomorrow. The money would go inside a trunk and into a storage warehouse down-town. They would issue a duplicate claim check. Charlie could hold one, and Barney could stash away the second. If he did need the money, it would be available.

He ordered a last drink. If that crazy Puerto Rican kid was alive, Barney would have no qualms about him. Charlie Moran wasn't as sure. He wasn't a run-of-the-mill thief, though. There was more there. Enough, Barney hoped, so that Nora and Roger could end their years with a little bit of comfort.

chapter
XV

The traffic light ahead turned yellow. Paulie started to gun the car, then went to the brake instead. It was the last light before the track entrance. He could do without some asshole Nassau cop writing him a ticket at seven in the morning.

He glanced across at the windows of the diner while he waited, and recognized a trainer he had met the week before. A yokel. It made him think of their trainer, Jerry Briglia. Jimmy the cheese man had picked him out. Paulie was convinced that Briglia was jerking them off—grabbing his six bills a month, getting a kickback on the hay bill, and in no rush to get the horse earning money. The horse kicked herself, Briglia claimed. Coming around turns she kicked the inside of her leg. She had to learn not to before she could be raced. Briglia was Italian, born somewhere out in Rockaway. Jimmy the cheese man claimed that half the jockeys and trainers in the business were Italian. Paulie hadn't pressed it, but he would have been happier with a yokel from down south or upstate New York. "What the fuck do Italians know about horses?" he had asked Jimmy. "Except the kind that pull vegetable wagons. How many horses live in Rockaway? You want to fix a race, Jimmy, give me an Italian. But you want to teach a horse how to run, I'll take a yokel. All this hard-on Briglia taught the horse is how to kick herself. What horse kicks herself? Her mother never taught her that, fucking Briglia did."

Now that he could come up with his share of the feed bill on time every month, he would demand more from Briglia. From the first day, Briglia had half-ignored Paulie. He smelled that Paulie was light with the money—maybe asshole Jimmy or Tommy had even said so to him over a drink—and Briglia barely showed any respect. Now Paulie would even that up. Either Briglia had the horse ready for a race in another month, or they dump him.

He saw himself firing Briglia. His partners would be happy to let Paulie do the talking. They would be there, but say nothing. He would do it in a good restaurant, over dinner. Quiet. Wear a suit, order good, and grab the check like an owner. Just tell Briglia that it didn't work out, no hard feelings, but they were going with somebody else.

Briglia would raise his voice—Paulie could hear him now—enough for people at other tables to look their way. That's when Paulie would be at his best. Quiet. Let his face get a little stiff. He would lower his voice and twist his pinkie ring with his thumb. Put his fork down nice and easy and finish what was in his mouth before he talked, then say to Briglia very soft, "What do you think, Briglia, you're dealing with scum bags? You're not dealing here with scum bags, you're dealing with gentlemen." Pat his lips with his napkin. "The truth is, you couldn't clean the fucking store for my horses, Briglia." Nice and quiet. Reach into his pocket and take out a solid roll, then peel off six hundreds and place them next to Briglia's plate. "There's your month's bill. That squares us." Then go inside the roll for a fifty, fold it once, and drop it on top of the C-notes. "Here's cab fare. I never been with a whore I didn't throw fifty for cab fare."

He would put his napkin back in his lap and begin eating again, nice and easy, without looking up. Remember to order something delicate—a scallopine dish that he could cut neatly into small mouthfuls. Even while Briglia was walking out he would stay interested in his food while Jimmy and Tommy watched him. He would have to remember to have crisp bills for Briglia, not new enough to stick together—the fuck might end up with seven fifty instead of six fifty—but crisp, so they came off his roll with a little snap.

The light changed. Paulie stayed beside the white line for the few blocks to the flashing yellow, then took a quick left in front of an oncoming truck into the entrance. He slowed up and acknowledged the guard by raising his hand. The guard stared at him until he stopped completely. He held up his badge, then nodded permission to continue. Another hard-on, Paulie thought. The business was full of them. Two-hundred-a-week guys surrounded by big money and grabbing every chance to shit on anyone wasn't a millionaire. He had recognized Paulie, for sure, but it wasn't a new Coupe de Ville sailing through the gate so the guard would break balls instead of waving him through like an owner. He would have to find an excuse to throw them each a sawbuck. For a sawbuck these Irish beer bellies would stand at attention and salute him every morning.

He drove slowly on the graveled roadways, holding the speedometer under fifteen and taking the long way around, through the early morning activity of the stables. Everyone's pace was comfortable but deliberate, doing work they did every day. At nearly every small intersection he brought the car to a stop to allow a horse to pass. They were led or ridden by exercise boys, headed toward the workout track.

Just before he reached his stable he recognized the exercise girl from an adjacent group of stalls perched on a huge bay gelding. She motioned him past, but he waited and insisted silently that she take the right of way so he could remain at the intersection and admire her ass. It was spread across the top of the horse, divided into two tight globes covered by worn blue jeans. The horse's huge rump accentuated hers. She kept the horse moving at a slow walk down the path. Paulie watched the mounds of flesh of both their asses undulate for a while, then felt embarrassed when he remembered that the horse was a male. He drove on. The groom always insisted she was straight when Paulie asked, but he couldn't believe it. She had to be a dyke to handle those huge horses. A girl might do it physically, but not mentally.

Through his early twenties, Paulie had often thought that he should have been a jockey, until he had met some of them since buying the horse, and watched races closely. "You need a pair of balls the size of *boccies*," he had told his brother Vito. "These little spics come whipping into the stretch doing forty, fifty miles an hour, kneeling up on top of their horses like fucking grasshoppers. They see a crack of daylight between two horses in front, they got to punch right into that little opening. You hesitate, you never win a purse. Takes a pair of *culones* this big, Vito." The exercise girl had to be a dyke to handle those horses.

He pulled off the roadway underneath the large elms at the end of his stable. Jimmy the cheese man was already there. Paulie parked beside his Seville and walked the length of the stable along the enclosed cinder pathway, past the half-dozen stalls to Briglia's. Jimmy was standing in the pathway, smoking a cigarette. The horse stood calmly, her head and neck protruding from the stall, while Terry, the groom, brushed her. Each of her front legs was set into a green plastic garbage pail filled with water. A small whirlpool attachment was clamped to the rim of each pail, creating a flow of water that reminded Paulie of a malted being mixed. The groom had draped a large white bath towel over the horse's neck.

"What the hell is this?" Paulie asked.

"It just started today," Jimmy said. "Briglia wants to toughen up her legs. He says they got to be soaked in saltwater baths every day. After she works out."

"Does she like it?"

The cheese man shrugged.

Paulie called in to the groom. "Terry! Does the horse like standing in garbage cans like this?"

"I don't know."

The horse looked toward Terry and pulled back her upper lip.

"She figures I might have a lump of sugar."

"What the hell is that towel doing on her neck?" Paulie asked.

"That's mine," Terry said.

"But why on her neck?"

"I got no place else to put it. If I hang it on one of the hooks, it gets full of little splinters. They're a bitch when I dry my face."

"Well, she looks fucking ridiculous standing in a couple of garbage cans like that. And the towel makes it worse. As if she's a prizefighter. She looks like a fucking joke instead of a racehorse."

He pulled the towel from her neck and tossed it to

Terry. "Can't you keep her all the way inside the stall when she's standing in the garbage cans? Does she have to be half outside like this?" He looked up and down the row of stalls. "I never saw another horse soaking its legs. Since I been out here I never saw a horse standing in a pair of garbage cans. Jimmy, that fucking Briglia better not be making a fool out of this horse."

Jimmy spread his arms wide. "Jesus, Paulie, she ain't enrolled in a fucking beauty contest. What the hell is the difference how she looks?"

"She looks *dumb,* Jimmy. People want to laugh at her standing there like that. It's embarrassing." He turned toward Terry. "What do you think, Terry? How can the horse have any pride in herself looking like a fucking joke?"

Terry folded his towel and shrugged. "Paulie, the truth is, this horse don't know shit from Shinola. None of them do. You live with them for a while, you learn they're dumb animals. Not too nice, either. You notice half the people work around here limp? They'll go a couple, three years friendly as can be, then out of the blue they kick you across the stall. Only mules are worse. Fellow I knew in the army worked with them all his life said a mule will put in twenty hard years for one real good kick."

Paulie stroked the horse's nose and asked Jimmy, "You see Briglia?"

"He was here five minutes ago. He just went for coffee."

"He ran the horse?"

"Breezed her. She looked good."

"When is he going to race her?"

"Soon, he says."

Paulie shook his head in disgust. "Jimmy, we got to straighten this yo-yo out. We got to give him a date.

He either teaches this horse what she's got to know by then or we dump him."

"What's he going to teach her, Paulie?"

"He's got to teach her how to win a fucking horse race. He ain't going to teach her to read the *Daily Telly*." He jerked his thumb in the direction of the coffee shop. "So far, all this class-A hard-on taught her is how to kick herself."

Jimmy started to protest, but Paulie cut him short. "Her father was a champion, Jimmy. She didn't learn it from *him*."

"Paulie, what do you know about training a horse? You know shit about training a horse. Waiting on tables is what you know about. Making cheese is what I know about. Let's stay with what we know, Paulie."

"You know about making cheese? Not for nothing, Jimmy, but my mother sent me over a hunk of mozzarella last week came from your place was no fucking bargain. Dry, Jimmy. It ain't the first time I noticed it. Your mozzarella's dry sometimes."

"Are you fucking *nuts?* I never made a piece of dry mozzarella in my life. In my life! And my father for forty years never made no dry mozzarella. Nobody in the Village ever bought dry mozzarella from the Garagussos' *latticini*."

Paulie turned toward the groom and spoke softly. "Dry. Like a fucking *bone,* that mozzarella."

He turned back to Jimmy. "Forget it. I was trying to do you a favor. What do I give a fuck if you want to make dry mozzarella? What are we going to do about this prick Briglia is more important."

"I'm going for coffee. That's what I'm going to do, Paulie. Maybe these leg baths will help her. He's going to try blinkers, too. He thinks maybe when she sees other horses next to her she gets nervous and kicks herself."

"We got to give him a date, Jimmy. A definite date."

Jimmy walked along the path. He stopped at the side door of the stable. "You want a coffee, Paulie?"

"No."

He shouted, "Terry, you want a coffee?"

"Light," he answered from inside the stall. "Three sugars."

Pete Grillo came into the far end of the stable while Paulie was stroking the horse's nose. Pete was halfway to the stall before Paulie realized that someone was there. He wore a lightweight lumber jacket and eighty-dollar slacks, stained on the front. From a distance, Paulie recognized his walk first, then his belly; it pushed out from the open jacket, clearing a path for him, thirty pounds too large for the rest of his body but hard as a rock. When Paulie was a kid he had thought of it as a large, smooth stone, solid right through. Pete had always been proud of it. At Paulie's house for Sunday dinner he would open his shirt wide and have Paulie and Vito take turns punching it. Even now he never wore an undershirt, and covered his belly all year round with custom-made silk shirts that fit snugly.

They shook hands.

"What are you doing here, Uncle Pete? I was going to call you."

"Hello, Paulie." Pete clapped his shoulder while they shook hands. "This is your horse?"

"Starry Skies. She's a filly. Beautiful, no, Uncle Pete?"

Pete nodded.

"You should see her when she ain't standing in these garbage cans. My partners got us tied up with some asshole trainer makes her stand in these. I'm going to fire him in a couple of weeks."

"There someplace we can sit and talk, Paulie?"

"You want to go for coffee, Pete? There's a hamburger joint right on the grounds."

He shook his head no. "Someplace private."

Paulie looked around. "There's a bench outside where the grooms wash the horses down. You want to sit on a bench?"

They walked through the wide horses' door out onto the grass. The bench was another fifty feet away, set against the trunk of a thick oak tree.

"It's like the country here, ain't it, Uncle Pete? All the grass and the white stables. I figured the stables would be made out of brick. Maybe plastic, even, but not wood. There's million-dollar horses live in some of these stables and they still make them out of wood."

Pete sat on the bench and lit a cigarette. He watched a groom nearby scrub down a horse who had just been exercised. The warm, soapy water streamed off the horse's body.

"You said you were going to call me, Paulie. What for?"

Paulie shifted a bit on the bench and looked down at the ground. He cracked the knuckles on his left hand. It was important to establish with Pete that he was upset and afraid to own up—that he knew he was all wrong. He started to answer twice, each time holding back, then blurted out, "I'm all jammed up, Uncle Pete. I got myself in a fucking jackpot. You're the only person can maybe help me, Pete." He cracked a knuckle on his right hand.

Pete frowned. He let his voice go soft and husky. Paulie recognized it as his business tone. He had never in his life used it with Paulie.

"What kind of fucking act are you putting on here, Paulie? Your mother still buys this little-boy shit. Don't try to sell it to me."

Paulie pursed his lips in surprise. "I ain't acting, Uncle Pete. The truth. I'm in a jam."

"You're telling *me* you're in a jam? Who in their right fucking mind steals money from Bedbug Eddie Grant? What was going on in your little brain when you done it, Paulie?"

Paulie shook his head. "I needed money for the horse, Uncle Pete. I didn't really think it out."

Pete remained quiet for a few moments.

"So you took the Bedbug's money? Where do you get off to steal money from Eddie Grant? You ain't even a real thief—a full-time thief. You're a waiter. A fucking *waiter*."

"He found out, huh?"

"Of course he found out. Some little rat cocksucker from Bleecker Street—"

"Frankie Wheels."

"That's him. And if it wasn't him, it would be someone else. It's the rattingest fucking neighborhood in the city. Half the mail into box 100 must come from the Village."

"Can you bail me out, Uncle Pete?"

Pete stared at him for a moment. When he spoke, there was no anger in his voice. "Bail you out? You got *me* in it over my head, Paulie. I'm busy treading water here myself."

"You can't put in a good word with Eddie, Uncle Pete? He's your crew boss, no?"

"He's more than that now. The Bedbug took over Carlucci's spot. He's running the Village now, Paulie. Walking around with that maniac dog, Snooky Yap."

Paulie's eyes widened. "Carlucci's through?"

"Out to pasture. He ain't been right for almost a year. I heard he had his wife saving bundles of newspapers and rags to sell to the junkie every month.

Eddie went right over his head to the old man and got permission to replace him."

"Carlucci took it?"

"Peed his pants." Pete nodded, as though confirming his own thoughts. "He's a fucking joke, Paulie. You know Porky Tedesco? Quiet, heavyset guy from Cornelia Street? He's an accountant, or a bookkeeper —something like that. A hundred-percent legitimate guy. Me and Carlucci were gassing up on Houston Street six months ago, this guy pulls up to the pump right next to us. Fast. The way the car pulled in, for a split second it looked just like a setup. Carlucci grabbed inside his coat—I thought, Jesus, the old bastard still walks around with a *pistola*. Then I saw he was grabbing for his heart. He acted like I wasn't even there—he let out a big mouthful of air and, out *loud*, he says, 'Thank God. It's Porky. He don't shoot.' "

Paulie sat quietly and watched the horse being groomed. Pete wasn't angry enough. He was too thoughtful and slow. He was confiding in Paulie, talking to him like a man for the first time ever. Paulie began to be afraid. Since leaving the loft with Charlie and Barney he hadn't been afraid. Now he felt it in his legs. That was always where it hit him first, all around his knees.

Pete continued to talk without looking at him. "I came up with Eddie, Paulie. We go all the way back together. Me and him and his brother Patsy. The three of us got made together. Next to Eddie, Patsy Grantulli was maybe the biggest prick ever got a button. Once he loaned two hundred to a guy from Prince Street, a solid working guy tended bar at a Longchamps. This was money for Christmas presents. The guy was late paying twice, three times—whatever. Patsy got it in his head this guy was making a fool of him. Paulie, he pulled him out of his house, from the dinner table, and he *kicked* him down Prince Street a block and a half to West Broadway. Pulled him out of his *home*. This poor fucking victim crawled down the middle of the gutter while Patsy walked behind him, next to him, circled around him, kicking his ass, his ribs, wherever looked soft. Every once in a while he'd plant one on the side of his head. Made him crawl.

"I watched it, Paulie, from a window. The whole neighborhood had their heads out the windows. The guy's wife stood at the curb screaming. Begging. Johnny Abiello held her back. Patsy would have busted her nose if she ever got close enough to touch him. The guy had a ten-year-old kid followed them out of the house screaming, 'Daddy!'

"At West Broadway, Patsy let him stand up. He still had a big napkin tucked into his collar, through all that. The knees from his pants were gone. Just two big holes. The guy could hardly breathe, a bunch of his ribs were busted. His front teeth were someplace in the gutter. Patsy told him, very careful, he had to bring him twenty a week. If he missed a week for any reason—*any* reason—Patsy would kill him. 'You bring it every Saturday,' he told him, 'until I tell you different. And if you ask me when it's going to stop, if you ever just once *ask,* I promise to do this again. I'll drag you back here and kick you right down the middle of Prince Street while your family watches. You bring twenty a week until I say enough.' "

Pete shook his head slowly, still amazed by it. "It went twelve years, Paulie. For *twelve fucking years,* every week, Patsy Grantulli took a twenty off him. The night Patsy got killed, the guy danced down Prince Street. When the word went on the street that Patsy was dead, this guy came out of his house and *danced,* like you see the Greeks do, right down to

West Broadway. And Patsy didn't have a friend would walk out and give him a smack. His own crew knew what a rat bastard he was. You can't believe how the man was hated, Paulie. You know D'Amico's? The funeral parlor?"

Paulie nodded.

"This guy went to D'Amico and offered him five hundred to let him piss on Patsy's corpse. D'Amico told me this was the fourth guy approached him. He could have made three grand letting people piss on Patsy. He was afraid to take it, Paulie, but I know for a fact that D'Amico done it himself. He stood in the back of his funeral parlor and pissed all over Patsy Grantulli's corpse. He had plenty of reason, too. Eddie's going to wind up the same way—somebody standing over him on an embalming table pissing on his dead body."

Pete lit a cigarette. "Eddie's worse, Paulie. Believe me, he's a bigger scum bag than his brother Patsy was."

"What's he going to do about me, Uncle Pete?"

Pete ignored the question. "I tried to do what I could for you, Paulie. Trouble is, Eddie's had a hard-on for me for years. He moved up fast and I never bowed to him enough—he wanted me to kiss his ass in public. And he held me back, the fuck. For years he gave me the shit end of the stick. Never threw me an extra piece of action when there was something to spread around. Half a dozen times I was entitled to some special machine location somewhere, he said no. Twice I had a beautiful shot to get a little piece of a *babanya* shipment coming in from Vietnam, he put his thumbs down. Would have meant big money for me—fifty, sixty large. The Bedbug grabbed it for himself.

"It got so bad I tried to get out from under. The

guy was choking me. I could have got onto a Brooklyn crew. I went through the whole circuit. Nice. The right way. The Brooklyn crew boss said fine, his bosses said fine. I talked to Carlucci—I never came out and knocked Eddie, just said I would be happier in Brooklyn—Carlucci okayed it. The last guy could veto it was the Bedbug, and he's not supposed to when it's all been done the right way like that. But he did. Wouldn't cut me loose, and old Carlucci too fucking busy tying up newspapers or something to make the Bedbug do the right thing. It was a big mistake, too— it's when Eddie smelled the weakness on Carlucci. Now he's in Carlucci's slot and he's zinging it into me, giving me this."

Paulie's knees got worse. It was going to be more than a threat and an apology. A few minutes earlier Paulie had hoped it would be a slap in public for the benefit of the neighborhood and an apology. He knew now that it was going to be heavier. He started to be nauseous.

"Giving you what, Uncle Pete?"

Pete dropped his cigarette onto the grass and ground it out with his heel. He lifted his foot several times to examine it, and each time ground it further, until it had disappeared completely. His voice dropped so low that Paulie could just make out the words.

"The prick made *me* take this contract."

Paulie suddenly wanted to urinate. The need came over him with no warning, for the first time since he was a ten-year-old. As a boy it would happen when he was terrified, and several times he had lost control and peed his pants, which caused the kids to form a circle around him and point, screaming, "Paulie peed his pants!" until he cried and punched out blindly, and got beat up by someone bigger.

"He wants me dead, Uncle Pete?"

Pete shook his head slowly. Paulie had to lean closer to hear his words. "He don't want you dead, Paulie. I'll tell you just what he wants and you listen close and behave like a man. Don't sit here and whine like a boy-ass. If you won't say who was with you, he wants you killed, Paulie. He wants to do his famous Bedbug act and hack you up into pieces."

"He'll really *do* it, Pete?"

"Hack you into pieces? He'll do that part of it personally. And make me sit down with him to a steak pizzaiola and a bottle of wine right after it. Somebody dying gives Eddie an appetite. I'm not lying, Paulie— he wants your head in a plastic bag and left in front of your mother's door. He said so. He said so in front of five underbosses and me. He wouldn't back down now even if he wanted to—he's busy being the Sicilian Don. There's no use thinking about clamming up, Paulie. The fuck would love it."

"I can't rat, Pete. I ain't built that way. I can't rat on a friend."

"You'll rat if it means your head. This ain't Carlucci you're dealing with, Paulie. Eddie wants to be another Genghis Khan. Listen close, because I mean every word I say. Eddie Grant will kill you, then he'll cut your head off with an axe. He said so."

"If I say who was there, Pete? That'll square me?"

He shook his head, no.

"He's going to bust my legs, Uncle Pete?"

He shook his head again, and spoke slowly. "You lose your right thumb, Paulie. The maniac says Carlucci got too easy the last few years, the whole neighborhood needs a lesson. He say two broken legs are bullshit—when the casts come off, it's all forgotten. He wants something will last for years."

Paulie looked at his hand for a half minute. "He ain't going to really do it, Pete? Not my *thumb!*"

"Paulie, the man is a fucking psycho."

"My *thumb,* Uncle Pete! You know what it is to have no thumb? I'm a *waiter.* You know what kind of place I can work with no thumb? A fucking diner. A hash house. I can't make a hundred bucks a week with no thumb. A decent restaurant won't hire me. Pete, it means a shit living for the rest of my life."

"He knows that, Paulie."

"So how can he do it, Pete? What kind of fucking animal is he?"

Pete watched the groom brush the horse. "This is his first decision as a boss. He talks about going greaseball-style, getting a lot of discipline and respect back. The man is going to terrorize the neighborhood, watch. 'We do this *a la siciliano,*' he said. Those were his words about settling with you. On top of that, the man is bona fide crazy. The Bedbug *likes* to hack up people. Paulie, there are cellars on Mulberry Street he dug into twenty years ago and put people in. I know hit guys, they'll choke you with their bare hands, are nervous around Eddie Grant. Believe me, if he hadn't been a wise guy, if he had never been made, he would be one of those whacks you see in the *Daily News* hacks up people and writes on the walls with lipstick. On top of everything else, he's got this hard-on for me that's a foot long, and here's his chance to put it in my ass. It lets everybody know I don't have the weight to save you."

"Pete, you got to do *something* for me. You're my *goombah.* I been calling you uncle since I could talk. You got a button, Pete—that's got to count enough to save my thumb."

"I got news for you, Paulie. It's getting so the button means shit. Except for some greaseballs come over barefoot from Palermo, they got trouble getting good young guys aboard now. And they're almost handing out buttons for stealing a set of hubcaps. It's no bargain. The feds decided a long time ago—they can't beat you in court, they're going to make life miserable for you. Every wise guy's funeral they're there, whispering to the brothers or the kids: 'That scum bag should rot in hell.' They want you to lose your temper and take a swing—they whack you for assault. At Tony T's funeral I heard this crew-cut WASP kid on the steps of Saint Anthony's lean over while the casket was coming down the steps and tell Tony's brother Vincent, 'Your brother would have crawled over his dead sister's body to fuck his mother.' Vincent gritted his teeth and kept going. Who needs it?"

"Pete, it got to count for something. With Eddie Grant, you can make it count enough to save my thumb."

"It saved your hand, Paulie. I made a plea with the underbosses there. That he owed it to me. He said, 'His fucking *hand* is what I would take for stealing my money except the boy is like family to you, Pete. It's only out of respect for you that I'm leaving the boy his right hand.' Then he went into his new Don-Jeech-the-Sicilian routine. How my loyalty had to be first to my brothers—a pile of shit would have drowned us all in five more minutes.

"I wanted to vomit. I couldn't listen no more, knowing what a fucking he was giving me with all this brotherhood crap. At my age, Paulie, I ain't supposed to get shit on like this. I interrupted him—I asked him, 'We going to cut our fingers here, Eddie, and swap blood around the table like kids in the backyard?' His face drained, Paulie. I seen it before. It drained like somebody pulled a plug out of his neck. Another word from me and I would never have walked out of that social club. He would have whacked me out on the spot and put me down in the cellar."

He looked at Paulie. "I did what I could."

"He's making me a cripple, this fuck. It ain't a man's punishment, Pete."

Pete nodded. "There's another part to it, Paulie. He says you got to wait tables at the social club every Thursday night."

Paulie clenched his teeth, then wanted to cry. He sat quietly for a few minutes, afraid to try talking. Then he said, "The kids from Spring Street do that job, Pete. It's a big thing for somebody fourteen, fifteen. Nobody over fifteen ever had that job. It pays a sawbuck for the night. He's going to make *me* do it?"

Pete nodded.

"It's not even a waiter's job, Pete, it's bringing espresso to them while they sit out on the sidewalk with the chairs tilted back to the window. Running to Arturo's for an *abeetz,* or going for a raw sirloin for Snooky Yap."

"It's a couple of hours a week, Paulie. You learn to swallow it and that's it."

"Swallow it? Pete, you're at the club on Thursdays sometimes. They snap their fingers for their espresso. People tuck a dollar into the kid's shirt pocket. And Eddie Grant's the worst of all—he makes waiters twist the lemon peel into his coffee. I'm going to be standing there trying to twist a peel with only four fingers while that fuck watches me and tucks a sawbuck in my pocket at the end of the night? His fucking kids should die from cancer, Pete. I'll make novenas that his kids get leukemia."

"The novenas will be jammed, Paulie."

"How long do I have to do this, Pete?"

Pete hesitated. "Till he tells you different. You ain't

ever to ask him how long—you get there every Thursday night till he tells you enough."

Paulie groaned. "That means years, Pete. That's not four or five times to embarrass me for the neighborhood. He means years. He wants to crush me, Pete. For what? I took *money* from him. I didn't rape his daughter. I didn't spit in his face. I took *money*. It don't call for this, Pete."

Pete nodded. "The man is bona fide crazy, Paulie. It's why they call him the Bedbug."

The urge to urinate grew stronger. Paulie stood. "I got to take a leak."

He walked past the horse and groom to the side of the stable and pressed close against the wall, his back to the roadway. Pete sat quietly on the bench and smoked.

Paulie was calmer when he sat down again. "How did this *happen,* Pete? I went to rob some money. Not even a lot of money—thirty, forty large. The kind of money Eddie Grant would hardly miss. All of a sudden there's a fucking bundle in the safe don't belong there, and a cop laying in the elevator shaft. The rest of my life is ruined. I'm being made a fucking slave for Eddie Grant. That's what it comes down to. I never figured any of it. How the hell did *I* end up in this?"

Pete nodded at him. "Paulie, my first holdup I was seventeen. Robberies, assaults, I done them all, but never a stickup. This was a liquor store. I ran right into John Q. Citizen. This fucking mope buying himself a quart of booze decides to grab my arm. A one-in-a-million shot. I closed my eyes and yanked on the trigger. It hit him somewhere around his stomach. He lived, this fucking dodo, but I left the joint shaking. We were sure he was dead. They burned you back then, too. No bullshit, no long stories—you knocked off a solid citizen like that, they sat you down in the chair

at Sing Sing and fucking fried you. For a week, while
the mope was in Bellevue on critical, I sat up nights
in a daze, Paulie. Same thing—how the hell did it
happen to me? I went on a simple stickup and some
hard-on attacks me with his bare hands. That's like
getting hit by lightning. Why me?"

"What would you do in my shoes, Pete?"

"If I was you in your shoes, Paulie? Or if I was *me*
in your shoes? It's two different things. When I was
pushing thirty I wasn't waiting tables, I had already
whacked out a couple of guys here and there. A long
time before, I had decided to take what I want and
fuck it."

He stared toward the stable and thought for a minute, rubbing his stomach absently with short, vertical
strokes.

"If it was *me* in this spot at your age, I'd sacrifice
my thumb to the Bedbug—that would square me later
with the other bosses. But the first cup of espresso I
carried to the fuck would have a spoonful of lye in it.
I'd croak that cocksucker right in the middle of the
social club and let the chips fall." He squeezed Paulie's
shoulder. "I don't recommend it though, Paulie. I
wouldn't be able to do it different. It's why guys end
up with buttons. And I tell you, it ain't a very happy
way to live anyway."

"What do *I* do, Pete? I'm not you. I can't put lye in
Eddie Grant's coffee. But I got to get even. He's making me a rat, and a cripple. He's making me a fucking
slave, Pete."

"You don't get even, Paulie, you swallow whatever
shit the Bedbug shovels into your mouth. You can't
have it both ways. You can't be a waiter and a tough
guy both."

They sat beside one another quietly, watching the

groom put the finishing touches on the horse and prepare to lead him to his stall.

"What happens to anyone was with me, Pete?"

"They from the neighborhood, Paulie?" He didn't wait for an answer. "Anybody from the neighborhood he's going to take their hand. He said so. He tapped the table right in front of him and told us, 'Their right hands get brought to me here. I want to *see* the hands that robbed my money laying on this table.' This is a banana case, Paulie. If they're not from the neighborhood, who knows? Drop them on a dump in Staten Island maybe."

"What about the money, Pete?"

"What did you bag?"

"Fifty large. That's what my end came to."

Pete thought for a few moments. "Get me thirty-two, thirty-three, to bring back to him. You say you blew the rest. The maniac will hardly count it, he only wants hunks of people's bodies on his table." He shook his head in disgust. "There's none of us going to make a lot of money with this guy. It'll be what brings him down."

"Pete, when do I lose my thumb?"

"Today. He wants it brought back to him." Pete looked away. "He sent two gorillas along. I made them stay in the car."

Paulie looked toward the end of the stable. Pete's car was out of sight. He had to urinate again but was ashamed for Pete to see his fright He thought about Charlie, and remembered him standing next to the bed in his room, asking, 'How could you do it?'

"Pete, I can't give this guy up if it means his hand. He didn't even know it was the Bedbug's money. I lied to him. It's like a total fucking I'll be giving this guy if I rat on him and he loses his *hand,* Pete."

"Paulie, you're not in criminal court here. There's

nobody to plea-bargain with. Eddie Grant is God here. He says the guy's hand, it's his hand. End of story." He looked at Paulie. "You brought a guy along and you didn't tell him what he was robbing, Paulie?"

"He wouldn't of gone if I told him."

"He's a friend?"

Paulie nodded.

"You got to decide for yourself. I never told no one to rat or not to rat. You want to stand up, Eddie's going to whack you out. You rat, and your friend loses his hand."

Paulie looked around. It crossed his mind that he might run, just leap up from the bench and run. He would pee his pants while he was doing it, he thought. He turned back to Pete.

"There was a third guy, Pete. I'll give him up and say it was just the two of us. Some old Irish hard-on from the Bronx. I don't owe him nothing."

Pete spread his hands in a gesture of resignation. "It's a gamble. You got to decide for yourself. You figure you owe your friend? Then you give up the Irishman and shoot crap with your life. Maybe Eddie won't find out. You want a guarantee that you'll stay alive? Cough up your buddy."

"What would you do, Pete?"

"What's the difference?"

Paulie wet his lips. "The Irishman is named Barney. Fixes clocks. On Castle Hill Avenue in the Bronx. An old guy, an old-time thief."

Pete stood. "You saying it was just the two of you, Paulie?"

He nodded.

Pete squeezed his shoulder. "Paulie, don't fucking whine to these two gorillas. Nothing ever hurts like you think it will. You'll go numb. You twist your belt around your wrist and get to the local emergency room." He took Paulie's cheek between his thumb and index finger and squeezed it hard. "Don't behave like a boy-ass."

He turned his back and walked toward where his car was parked. Paulie stood at the bench and watched him, the red jacket flapping as he walked, distinct against the white wood planks of the stable. The groom had finished with the horse and was leading him toward the open double doors, a shiny brown colt who seemed to prance toward his stall, snorting puffs of gray vapor into the cold air. Paulie breathed hard, suddenly wanting to let himself cry. He didn't deserve it. Just before Pete reached the end of the stable, Paulie called, "Uncle Pete!"

He turned.

"Charlie Moran, Pete. From the Village. He works at the Good Times."

"There were three?" Pete asked.

Paulie shouted, "Yes."

"Charlie Moran?" Pete called. "He's the half-Irish kid from Carmine Street?"

"Yeah, Pete. He works at the Good Times. The night manager."

Pete stood perfectly still, silhouetted against the white barn, only his open lumber jacket flapping gently in the wind. Just loud enough to be heard, he called, "He's related, no, Paulie? Ain't he the kid, his mother's related to your aunt Josie's people? He's family, no, Paulie?"

"Yeah. That's him, Pete."

Pete seemed to be about to say something, then turned and moved again toward his car, hard and fast.

Paulie stared at his back, then turned and hurried toward the barn to urinate again.

chapter

XVI

Barney gripped a tiny brass screw in a pair of tweezers and tried for the third time to thread it into the works of a ship's clock. It slipped free even before he had it near its mounting hole. He started to fish for it at the bottom of the case, and heard the front door open and close. Old Francis Cullen stood there, half-stewed. Barney glanced at his watch. It was almost noon.

Cullen leaned against the front counter and waited, his eyelids drooping. He held the large ring of telephone keys in his hand.

"What is it?" Barney asked.

Cullen's jaw worked up and down several times. A series of growls came out.

"I can't make out a word you're saying. What the hell do you want?"

Cullen held the key ring near Barney's face and shook it. For an instant Barney thought he was returning it, then Cullen held one key away from the rest. It was broken—fractured at the deepest groove

197

from having been turned hard before it was fully inserted in the lock. Cullen apparently wanted it repaired or replaced. Barney felt his face flush.

"You've got some pair of balls walking in here. There's no lifetime guarantees come with those keys. They break—they break. Too fucking bad."

He turned and walked back into the shop. Cullen came around the counter and followed him, tugging at Barney's sleeve. Barney scrutinized the works of the ship's clock and tried to ignore him.

"How the hell did they ever bounce you off the force?" he said, while he searched in the clock for the screw. "You've got the perfect cop mentality—take, take, take, it's all fucking coming to you. You should have made inspector, Cullen."

Two more minutes he might hit him, Barney knew. Bust the old bastard's nose and throw him out onto the sidewalk. Cullen calmed down after a minute. He looked around the room, bleary-eyed, until he spotted the open door to the cubbyhole bathroom in the corner, then walked to it and unzipped his fly. He didn't lift the toilet seat. Barney watched him urinate, knowing he would have to clean off the seat when Cullen was gone. He dropped the pair of tweezers beside the clock and stood up.

"Fucking shanty Irish sot!" he called toward the bathroom, then turned and walked to the front of the store. He should hold his temper for a few minutes, he knew. Hold on for a few minutes until Cullen left, then forget about him. He was standing at the window and staring out, listening to Cullen urinate, when the car rolled slowly into the bus stop in front of the store. His stomach tightened. There were four men in it. The front passenger scanned the signs above the storefronts and homed in on Barney's shop. The car stopped.

Barney moved deliberately. He reached across the counter for his coat, pulled it on, and stepped out the front door. The curbside doors of the car opened and two heavyset men in suits approached him. He looked straight ahead and started to walk toward Westchester Avenue. One of them stepped partially in front of him. Barney looked surprised.

"I'm looking for a Barney Rush."

"You mean Barney the clock man?" He jerked his thumb over his shoulder. "He's in the shop." He extended his left wrist out from under his coat and tapped his watch several times. "Three different people couldn't fix it. He got it running perfect. With a few drinks in him, too. Best goddamn watch man in the Bronx."

He started to walk, and paused after a few steps to call over his shoulder: "He might be a minute, he's taking a leak in the back right now."

He continued to walk, holding his pace steady, his heart pounding. Almost a block to the avenue, he thought, then turn the corner and move like hell for another block. There would be a cab at the stand. Those were cops. Tough, fat, red-faced, old-time, Irish, hard-on cops. He counted to himself to maintain a steady pace. The thing to do was to get his money out of storage, and get out of New York fast. Chicago, he thought. He could get lost nicely in Chicago. Use as little of the money as possible, see how hard they were looking, then squirrel it away again. Back into storage, and maybe get another claim check into Charlie Moran's hands if it still seemed the best way to go. Right now he needed that money with him in Chicago.

He turned the corner and half-jogged toward the cabstand. The cops would still be standing at the counter, he thought, waiting for Francis Cullen to piss away his morning's beer chasers. They'd have a long wait—and Francis, with his speech impediment, would have a long while explaining that he wasn't Barney Rush.

The private phone on Ed Flynn's desk rang. It was John Hanrahan.

"It's me, Ed. Can you leave the office?"

"Yes."

"I'll ring you on the other line, then?"

"Give me five minutes."

He hung up and took his topcoat from the closet. The patrolman at the secretary's desk glanced up. Flynn said, "Twenty minutes, George, if anyone needs me," then paced in front of the elevators impatiently and chewed several Tums. He would go through hundreds more in the next few weeks, he knew. With Bunky Ritter dead, there was no bagman to send off to the Italians. It meant dealing directly with Eddie Grant until things settled. He found it tough enough to figure out Italians who were sane—with their handshakes twice a minute and a toast to everyone's health each time they sipped a drink. Making sense of this maniac Eddie Grant and his guinea bulldog would be next to impossible. Their phone conversation last night still left him uncertain. Why the hell had Grant made him a gift of this burglar in the Bronx?

The elevator was crowded with a group of chiefs from Virginia on a training program, joking loudly about using the evening to study the prostitute problem along Lexington Avenue. Flynn listened to their banter and decided that they might be more difficult to make sense of than the Italians. Outside, a stiff wind blew across the plaza. He turned his back to it and walked down the ramp onto Park Row. Two blocks north he stopped at an outdoor pay phone and waited a few minutes, his head and shoulders inside the shelter, until it rang.

"Is that you, Ed?"

"Yes."

Hanrahan sounded exasperated. "We can't get a thing out of him, Ed."

"Who the hell is he?"

"Barney Rush. I looked at a rap sheet early this morning. A broken-down safe man, put in five years at Coxsackie in the forties for robbery one. Fifty-eight years old. Looks more like sixty-eight. With some kind of speech impediment, as well. It's a wonder the old bastard can still open a box of corn flakes, much less a safe."

"He was in the loft?"

"Of course."

"Does he know about the tape on Ritter?"

"I'd swear not, Ed. We've worked on him for nine hours now, with no letup. Plays absolutely dumb about it all."

"Who's with you?"

"Do you know Meehan? A lieutenant in the First. Him, and old Tom Garber."

"They're not feeling sorry for him, John? This is no time to be soft."

"Jesus Christ, Ed, their necks are out as far as ours. And both of them did tours of Harlem in the old days —they're not amateurs. Meehan must have lost three pounds, he worked up such a sweat swinging a little length of heater hose he found in the trunk of his car. Stopped for a quick shower earlier. He told me he had forgot what the job had been like before the bleeding hearts had us standing like schoolteachers and reciting lists of rights to common criminals."

"You say he's fifty-eight, John. How damned hard can you be trying?"

Hanrahan became annoyed. "Ed, the man's not got a rib left intact, and I can't imagine his kidneys ever functioning properly again. If we were to rush him into Bellevue this minute it would be six months before he might be out of a wheelchair. There's none of us forgetting that this scumsucking thief killed a policeman. He just won't give us a squeal. What we're working on up here now is two hundred pounds of meat, not much more. Meehan thought for hours that the speech impediment was an act. He didn't improve it any with his little piece of heater hose."

"Where do you have him, John?"

"A motel room. It's a little place near the Whitestone Bridge."

"You've covered yourselves well, John?"

"There's nothing to worry about. A bottle of whiskey is what I neglected to bring along. I had forgot what a thirst you can work up on these bastards. Tell me, Ed, why the hell did the guineas give us this one?"

"I've asked that myself a dozen times since last night."

"It means they don't know about the recorder is my guess."

"That's my conclusion, too, John. They've caught one of the others already, Grant told me."

"Jesus, a hell of a lot faster than the department would have, too."

"The very same thought occurred to me, John, with all the fancy reorganizations every six months. The one they got hold of coughed up the other two. One of them they want. They intend to cut the fucker's *hand* off. 'We already took a thumb off the other one,' Grant told me. Like a little group of Arab sheiks, they are, sitting over on Mulberry Street. The rest of

America doesn't exist for them. Public executions they'll be holding next."

"It's why they've got some law and order in Little Italy, though, Ed. It's the only neighborhood in the city old ladies can walk around at night. You know, when they catch a nigger wearing sneakers in a hallway on Mulberry Street, he gets hauled up to the roof and thrown five stories into the street. No questions, no explanations. There's a lesson there for the rest of us."

" 'You can have the Irish,' Grant told me. 'Keep it in the family.' He's giving him to us as a favor is my guess. Thinks we want to make a collar."

"What do we do now, Ed?"

"Does it pay to put in a few more hours on him, John?"

"Ed, one of our hearts will give out before this old cocksucker breaks. The only thing he's mumbled is some madness about stealing telephones. The man is no longer very coherent."

"He's that far gone, John?"

Hanrahan lowered his voice to a tone he might use in church. "We've got him on his back in the bathtub. He's vomiting up enough blood so we'd never be able to clean up the room. Nearly choking on it, too, the old bastard, croaking away about his telephones."

Flynn thought for a few moments, then said decisively, "Write him off, then, John."

"How?"

"Do you have to ask? You're in a fine, deserted section up there."

"Tom Garber says no."

Flynn felt his face heat up. "Is Tom Garber prepared to throw his career, his good name, and his family's happiness down the drain? And the rest of us with him? For some common thief? Let him do what has to be done, then make a novena if he needs comforting."

"He says no, Ed. And he means it. He says he would sooner sit out his retirement in a cell than be the one who actually does away with this guy. This isn't some nigger rapist, is what Garber told me. He's one of our own."

Flynn raised his voice above the roar of an oil truck turning south onto Park Row. "What in God's name does the silly old bastard suggest?"

"He says give him back to the guineas."

Flynn waited until the noise of the truck subsided. "That's not the worst idea in the world either, John. They're better at it than we are."

"Can you do it?"

"I think so. I'll get to Grant now, if I can. He ought to have someone up there as soon as it's dark. I'll let him know about the tape, too. There's a fine chance he can get something out of the other two thieves."

Flynn thought for a few moments. "Will Garber go along with it, John?"

"He'll go along with anything we dream up, just so his own hands stay clean."

"How will you transfer him?"

"It's the Manor Motel. On Hutchinson River Parkway, just past Saint Joseph's—the old school for the deaf. Room one thirty-six. Let me know an exact time that they'll make the pickup. The three of us will sit outside in our car. I'll leave the room unlocked. None of us is about to deal face-to-face with a couple of guinea hit men."

Hanrahan was quiet for a minute. Then: "I never thought it would come to this, Ed."

"Nor did I, John. But here we are. We either do what must be done, or behave like old Tom Garber up there. There'll be time enough later to sit over a glass and think it all out."

"It's a good full glass I could do with now. I'll get back to you in an hour, Ed, if you'll know by then what time the Italians will be here."

"I'll know."

Flynn pulled off the expressway and parked in front of a small bar on the service road. He dropped in perhaps once a month, to wait out a particularly heavy traffic jam or to talk with John Hanrahan over a good phone. The bartender never remembered him from one time to the next. He ordered a bottle of beer and finished half of it before going to the phone booth. Hanrahan answered on the first ring.

"John? It's me. Did it go all right?"

"Yes."

"Call me back, John."

"You're at your homeward-bound stop?"

"Yes."

"I'll get back to you in a few minutes."

Flynn kept the receiver to his ear and held down the lever with his index finger. He visualized Hanrahan gulping down whatever was in his glass, then pulling on his coat and mumbling something to Helen on his way down the two flagstone steps. He would huff and puff his way through a few quiet blocks of Queens Village to a public telephone. When the phone rang, Flynn released the lever immediately.

"You're late getting home," Hanrahan said.

"I had a pile of paper work was about to bury me. Believe me, John, you're better off in the field. I'm earning every cent of my pension in this slot."

"It went smoothly enough, Ed. The Italians were right on time."

"I spoke to Grant since. The three of you delivered them a corpse."

"Jesus, Mary, and Joseph."

"Well, I wouldn't lose a wink of sleep if I were you, John."

Hanrahan remained quiet.

"You're not going to let it get to you, John?"

Hanrahan let out a long, audible sigh. Flynn was sure now that he had been sitting in front of his TV sucking on a bottle of gin.

"Eddie, let's not kid ourselves. We never thought it would come to this. Tom Garber had a point—it wasn't some nigger rapist laying nude in the tub with blood gurgling in his throat every time he mumbled about his telephones. It was one of our own. The man was an everyday thief."

"Who pushed a policeman into an elevator shaft."

Hanrahan sighed. "Who the hell knows how it happened."

"If they hadn't been there, John—committing a crime—Ritter would be alive today."

"You can say exactly the same thing of Ritter, Ed."

They remained quiet for a minute.

"It's not the end of the world, John. You're thirty years on the job. Long before the hearings, too. Surely it's not the first time you've gone a bit too far with a billy or a piece of hose."

"I was working, though, Ed. It was in the line of duty. Questioning someone properly in the rear of a station house, not off in some motel room. It's happened, all right, but I was earning my month's pay. I was doing it for the public, not for myself."

"You'll get over it, John. It will look a lot better to you in the morning. I only wish we were free to tell Bunky Ritter's poor old mother that one of the maggots who killed her son has gotten his proper punishment. It would be a bit of a comfort to her."

"Meanwhile I'm not feeling good about it. Did you tell Grant about the recorder?"

"I did. And I wonder now if it wasn't a mistake to tell him. Carried on like a man possessed. John, he screamed things he would do to Ritter if he were alive—they made me shudder."

"He sounds crazy."

"He's also a man afraid, John."

"You're kidding."

"I'm not. I can smell fear. Even a hint of it. Over a phone, too. You never get a whiff of it off these guinea racketeers, not for a second. It's just missing, like some kind of vitamin deficiency. It's the only way they can be Mafia. But I get it from Grant. The man lives in terror, like some of the raving ones that need three patrolmen to deliver them to Bellevue. I don't like dealing with this fellow, John. I was comfortable with old Carlucci—he was a decent sort. Not this one, though."

"He's actually going to chop a hand off, Ed?"

"When they get hold of him, he is. And it won't be long, he claims. John, the man let out a little laugh when he said it, reminded me of a giggle I heard in nineteen forty-three at Sing Sing, from a little punk cop-killer was being strapped into the chair. It's an eerie feeling he leaves you with, this Grant."

There was a long silence, then Hanrahan asked softly, "What the hell do we do next?"

"Not a thing. It doesn't look so terrible to me, John. No question it's the thief still at large has got the tape Ritter was wearing. According to Grant, they'll have him confined safely inside their social club in a matter of days. Ready for their little hand-cutting ceremony. The man sounds like he plans to have it bronzed and put on his mantelpiece."

"And what about the Internal Affairs people?"

"Whatever they've got can't be too much—they would have made a move already. They may have just turned Ritter around, John. This could have been his first tape. If they've got very little, they'll be as happy to drop the whole thing as we'll be. A few of us might have to go out on early retirement. It wouldn't bother me at all, the job has become so stinking these days."

"I hope you're right, Ed. I'm going back upstairs to my chair and my glass. I won't sleep too soundly, thinking of old Barney Rush laying in that tub."

"With all due respects, John, leave me out of any little prayers you might be offering up for him. I'm sure the world is just a little better off with that particular piece of garbage gone. What I *will* join you in is a little prayer to Saint Jude that the Italians get hold of that third son of a bitch still walking the streets. We'll all sleep a bit more soundly then."

chapter
XVII

Charlie opened his eyes and looked at the ceiling for a few moments, then turned his head and saw that he was alone. He relaxed. For two days running he had woken up with a desperado snoring beside him, and no recollection of picking her up. He sat up on the edge of the bed and massaged his eyes softly, then looked at the night table for his watch. It was still in pawn. Later, on his way to Diane's, he would stop at Edelweiss's and redeem it. He picked up the phone and dialed room service.

"What time is it?" he asked.

"It's ten-fifteen, sir."

"This is 3720. Send me up an order of poached eggs. A large orange juice. Toast, coffee. And a bloody mary—vodka on the side, in a shot glass."

He lit a cigarette and walked to the window. Directly across First Avenue was the U.N. Building. Several out-of-town buses were lined up at the curb. He watched two cars turn off First Avenue and pause at the front gate, then move slowly past the guards.

Yesterday, in the sauna on the twenty-sixth floor, a squat, pitch-black African sitting on the boards across from him had been amazed that Charlie had lived his entire life in New York and had never been inside the U.N.

"You know nothing of the institution?" he had asked.

"Just that they don't pay their parking tickets."

The African had smiled.

Charlie finished shaving as his breakfast arrived. He left the bloody mary untouched—the shower had cleared his head. It was as good a time as any to make a break from the morning-through-night drinking pattern he had fallen into. The whole day could be a fresh start. He drank his third cup of coffee beside the window and decided that just after noon was the best time to get to Diane's. She would positively be at work. By tonight he would be in Boston, ready to scout around New England, with forty thousand in green to plunk down on a place. Money the seller wouldn't have to account for.

He would feel a hell of a lot more comfortable, being out of New York. Vito had told him the word was all over the neighborhood—Charlie was going to lose his right hand. That meant the Bedbug wouldn't change his mind. It gave him chills.

He would leave whatever clothes were at his place. It wasn't worth the risk of going back to his apartment. Diane would be angry that he had run out, but she would get over it fast enough, and the ten thousand he was leaving for her and the baby was enough to make up for it. It was the only thing to do. He would hate her within six months, together in New England. It was time to start looking out for himself.

He had an hour to kill before leaving. A few laps in the pool would fit in nicely, and get him started on a health program he could continue in New England —gym workouts and some swimming every day. He took out his bathing suit, and thought again that leaving her ten thousand was more than fair. His conscience was clear.

As he turned the key in Diane's door, he remembered that he hadn't stopped for the watch. He had rung the phone a dozen times before leaving the hotel to be sure she was at work. She must be steaming, he thought, not having heard from him for three days. There would be a note on the table, opening with "You don't give a shit about anyone but yourself," then the suffering-female number, finally that he should call her at work immediately. She would underline "immediately," and write "Love" at the bottom. It was in the center of the table, with the sugarbowl set on top of it. He read it quickly.

Dear Charlie,

This is not easy for me. I haven't left the apartment for two days now, pacing up and down, looking out the window, waiting for you to come back. Worried sick that you are lying dead somewhere or have just decided to leave me. I haven't been able to eat, I have literally been nauseous. And I've cried a lot. Maybe from being pregnant.

It has given me time to think of what my life will be like, living with you. The truth is, Charlie, that you don't care enough about people's feelings. You won't be happy to hear that, but it's true. You have lied to me a hundred times, and you barely try to hide the lies. It never occurs to you how low and unimportant it makes me feel to be deceived so obviously.

I only see things getting worse after the baby is born. You already resent it that I'm pregnant. You don't even bother to see your own two children, Charlie. There is something wrong with that. You can't just go through life with so little feeling for anyone else.

Our baby needs a good start. I don't believe she or he can ever look forward to much help from you. So I don't feel guilty about taking the shoebox full of money for the baby. She or he deserves it. I have left you five thousand dollars.

You haven't been good for me in any way, Charlie. From the little I know about other women in your life, I don't believe you have been good for any of them. To borrow one of your Carmine Street expressions, Charlie, the truth is that you have treated me like a piece of shit. If I let you, you'll treat my baby like a piece of shit, too. Not because there is any real malice in you, just because it takes some effort not to.

I told you a week ago that you miss by an inch. I still believe that. I don't want to go through life with someone I can never trust. My baby needs a father who works at some honest job, has enough self-respect so he doesn't steal anything that isn't nailed down, and feels enough a part of what goes on around him to go to the polls and vote. I wish she could be brought up with some of the fierce family loyalty you claim to believe in so much. I recognize the security it must give a child, but if the price is a total disregard of everyone else in society, then it isn't worth it. It strikes me as heading back toward the caves.

With forty-five thousand dollars, the baby will

have a decent chance in life. It should be a comfort to you to know that. Somehow, I doubt
that it will be.

                                    Diane

He laid down the note and went into the bedroom.
Hesitantly, holding his breath, knowing he would find
that his money was gone. The dresser drawers were
pulled out and empty. Some of the smaller prints had
been taken off the walls. A handful of empty wire
hangers were bunched together at one end of the
closet rod. He reached up to the shelf and took down
the shoebox. The top hadn't been replaced. There
was a single bundle of hundreds held by a rubber
band. He riffled through it to see that they were all
hundreds, but didn't bother to count the bills; there
looked to be about fifty of them.

He sat on the edge of the bed and squeezed the
bundle of bills in his hand. How the *hell* could she
have picked up and left? What kind of yo-yo did she
expect to find out there who would take her in pregnant? He went back to the table and picked up the
note, started to read it, then crumpled it in his fist and
threw it at the living-room lamp. It fell short.

He was broke again. Five grand might get him
started in Boston in a one-man sliced-pizza operation, if the owner would take paper. Open window.
Sixteen hours a day, six days a week. Greaseball-
style. Washing flour off his body in the shower every
night. And worrying anytime a Caddie parked
within a hundred feet that someone had clocked him
and told the Bedbug. It was a fucking sentence.

He pictured her sitting on the edge of the bed with
the shoebox beside her, tucking the stacks of bills
into her pocketbook, lifting the last stack of five thou-

sand and turning it in her hand, then dropping it back in the shoebox for him. He clenched his right hand into a fist and swung a body punch, emitting a grunt as his fist connected with the caned back of a dining-room chair. The caning was old and brittle. His fist went through it to the shoulder and lifted the chair off the floor before it could fall over backward. It dangled from his bicep. He held his arm outstretched and watched the chair sway for a few moments, then let it drop to the floor.

Ten years ago, he thought, he would have hit the wall, and broken or dislocated a knuckle. Now his hand didn't hurt at all. Ten years ago, though, girls weren't walking out on him. He pushed the chair aside with his foot and turned his head up toward the ceiling. "Jesus *Christ*," he whispered loudly. "But what the fuck did I *do* to rate this?"

He went to the kitchen cabinet and took down a bottle of scotch. When he opened the refrigerator for ice cubes, he saw a small container of light cream on the top shelf. He wondered for a moment whether it was there as a gift, then decided that she must have bought it for him before she decided to leave. He sat on the couch and finished a second scotch, then picked up the note, smoothed it out, and read it again.

She didn't even sound ashamed to be stealing his money and sneaking away. He had treated her well, too, everything considered. A hell of a lot better than he had treated Cookie, and Cookie had wanted him even after he walked out. Even the lousy five thousand she had left showed how selfish she was. He had been about to leave ten. As a gift. She had left half that amount for him, and it was his money. He wondered for a minute whether there had been another guy lurking around, and decided there hadn't. There would be soon, though. Someone would come along and smell forty-five thousand and that would be it. All her crap about the baby needing the money would be forgotten and some twenty-two-year-old actor with hair to his shoulders and intense blue eyes would beat her for the money. For a moment he saw himself choking the long-hair, banging the bastard's head against a wood floor, with Diane screaming in the background and loose hundreds scattered all around them. He sipped his scotch.

The doorbell rang. Three short blasts. He froze. It rang again. He walked softly across the carpeted floor to the door and listened. When he heard footsteps going away, he would open the peephole. The bell rang again and a voice whispered loudly, "Charlie. It's me, Charlie."

It was Paulie.

"I know you're in there, Charlie."

He opened the door.

Paulie grinned. His exaggerated, sheepish grin that he used when he was caught setting the wall clock ahead ten minutes so he would get through work early. He stepped into the apartment and walked ahead of Charlie into the room.

"I was watching from across the street. I seen you come in. I figured you'd show up here sooner or later."

His right hand was bandaged. Charlie motioned toward it with his head. "I heard about your thumb."

"That fuck. His kids should get stomach cancer. The last thing I do before I fall asleep at night, I lay in bed and pray that his kids get cancer. Out loud. I use their names. Nunzio should get stomach cancer. Tommy should get stomach cancer. Each kid."

"I heard the maniac wants my hand."

Paulie looked down and nodded. "I couldn't help it, Charlie. He sent my uncle Pete. They grabbed me out at Belmont." He looked at Charlie. "I was just so fucking scared, Charlie. The Bedbug would have put me in the ground if I didn't give you up."

Charlie shrugged. "It's done. I hear he's got you waiting tables at the social club."

"The fuck. I'm going to spit in his espresso, Charlie. It'll take me another week maybe to get up the nerve, but I'll put a fucking lunger right into the bottom of his espresso cup."

"He got back your share, Paulie?"

Paulie nodded. "All but a couple of thousand. I held out maybe six grand."

"Any word about Barney?"

"You didn't hear, Charlie?"

"What?"

"*Morto.* They whacked the poor fuck out. The *cops* done it."

Paulie noticed the chair on the floor. He picked it up and examined the torn caning for a moment before setting it beside the table. "You do this, Charlie?"

"What cops, Paulie? How do you know the cops done it?"

"My uncle Pete told me. The cops worked Barney over something terrible. Not in a station house, neither. In some hotel room up in the Bronx. Eddie Grant sent two guys up there—they were supposed to whack out Barney after the cops were through with him. He was already dead—these asshole cops didn't know when to let up. One of the guys went up there was Lenny Razor Blades. Pete says he bitched for a week what a wasted trip it was, all the way to the Bronx for nothing."

"What the hell were they knocking Barney around for?"

"That's what don't add up, Charlie. Unless they were pissed off because that cop dived into the elevator shaft. Or they were after his money."

Paulie thought for a few moments. "I wonder what the old bastard did with his share?"

"He left it for his kid. He had that retarded kid."

"He told you that?"

"He asked me to make sure the kid gets it."

"What the fuck is a retard going to do with fifty large? Somebody's just going to take it away from him. That money is rightfully ours, Charlie. You and me deserve that money."

"*We* deserve it? How do you figure that, Paulie?"

Paulie held his bandaged hand in front of Charlie's face. "I lost my fucking thumb! Charlie, I feel like they cut my *cock* off. The only people I ever knew had no thumbs were dishwashers. I've already been fired from the Good Times. And you're worse off— chances are you'll lose a whole hand. What are you going to do with no hand, Charlie? You going to get a fucking hook? You going to seat people in a classy restaurant and hand them menus with a hook? Maybe you can get it chromed, Charlie. Look, there were three of us. One of us got knocked off—then the two of us left are supposed to split his share. You seriously going to hand fifty thou to some Irish retard? He's going to drool on it trying to say thank you. He sure as shit ain't going to go out and party with it."

"Drop it, Paulie. You got no fucking face? First you turn me and Barney in. Then——"

"Charlie!" Paulie spread his arms wide.

"Yeah, I know. You were scared. Scared or not, though, Paulie, let's face facts. You acted like a fucking stool pigeon. I can't hold it against you too much, Paulie, but let's not make believe it didn't happen. You ratted. Plain and simple. You could have given them Barney—even he figured you would. But I'm family. Neither one of us figured you would throw me in, too, Paulie."

"That Irish hard-on would have given you up anyway, Charlie. It wouldn't of made no difference."

"He wouldn't have given me up. He didn't. The poor fuck died first. We made a deal, Paulie—he wouldn't give me up, and I gave my word that his wife would get his share for the kid. What neither of us figured was that *you* would rat on me, Paulie."

Paulie shook his head in disappointment. He lowered his voice. "I'm surprised at you, Charlie. They *forced* it out of me. They put a gun in my mouth, Charlie. I can still feel the barrel on my teeth. Like a chunk of ice. That's what it took for me to give you up."

"They forced you, they forced you. I can't get too mad at you. But Barney went right down the tube and he didn't rat. He held up his end of the deal, and those bastards must have lit matches under his toenails. I'll hold up my end. So forget about us grabbing his fifty thousand."

"It wasn't like we were taking it from *him*, Charlie. I wouldn't take it off *him*. I figured somebody's going to rob it off the retard. They'll give him a little rattle to play with, he'll hand them the fifty large. I figured it was better if it went to us than to strangers. Besides, Charlie, you can be a sport, you got your fifty thousand. I got shit. I got a lousy ten thousand. And no thumb."

"I thought you only held on to six?"

Paulie shrugged. "Six thousand, ten thousand—I didn't count every twenty-dollar bill in the pile."

"Paulie, if you say ten, it means you wound up with twenty minimum. And I don't have my fifty, I got a lousy five grand left. Diane split with forty-five thousand of my money. She left me a note."

"Charlie, you're *kidding!*"

"There's the note."

"Why?"

"Why? Because she's an ungrateful cunt, that's why. You treat them a little bit nice, they shit all over you."

"I'll tell you, though, Charlie, she would have put you in the ground with her cooking, that broad. No doubt about it, you would have *died* sooner or later. I never saw anything like it. Maybe you got off cheap."

"I was going to *give* her ten thousand. Like a fucking gift. I was ready to leave her ten grand. Instead, she beat me for my money."

"What are you going to do, Charlie?"

"I don't know. From the minute we went on this score, it's been nothing but headaches. And now I wind up with a lousy five thousand."

"Plus, you might lose your hand. Don't forget that."

He looked at Paulie. "Thanks for reminding me."

"You might as well face it, Charlie. It don't help to hide it." He was quiet for a few moments. "And you're still going to behave like an asshole and hand fifty large to the retard?"

"Just forget that, Paulie. I can steal from almost anybody, but not from Barney's retarded kid. Not after promising him."

Paulie shook his head vigorously. "The retard's going to get robbed, Charlie. Some thieves are going to rob him. You grab that fifty, you ain't robbing the retard, you're robbing the thieves who are going to rob the retard. Think about it, Charlie."

"I got to shave in the morning, Paulie. Forget it. It's like stealing quarters from a March of Dimes card."

"That ain't so terrible either. A couple of times I been short of cab fare I glommed a deuce off one of them cards in the restaurant. Nothing happens."

"What do you mean, nothing happens?"

"You know, no curse comes on you. You stand there pulling quarters off the card with the little kid in the wheelchair looking up at you, you worry that somebody in your family might get polio. It don't happen. And I'll tell you, Charlie, nothing's going to happen if we keep the retard's money."

"The money goes to Barney's wife. Case closed."

Charlie poured another drink for himself.

"I thought WASPS were honest, Charlie. They're not supposed to rob. My mother, my aunts, they may not be so crazy when they say stick with an Italian girl."

Charlie shrugged. "You want a drink, Paulie?"

"Too early."

Charlie sipped the scotch and sat back on the couch. He rested his head against the wall. "What brings you around, Paulie?"

"I feel terrible, Charlie. I'm no fucking stool pigeon. They just squeezed me so hard I couldn't help it. *Superman* would of broke, Charlie. Superman couldn't of stood up."

"I told you, forget it. Water under the bridge, Paulie."

Paulie leaned forward on the chair. Charlie recognized that he was about to be sincere.

"I feel like a scum bag since five minutes after it happened, Charlie. If the Bedbug nails you and and takes your hand, I won't be able to look at myself. I want to make it up a little, Charlie."

Charlie stretched out his arm and waved his palm toward Paulie's face. "No!"

"I'm serious, Charlie."

"So am I! Don't make anything up to me. Just leave everything like it is, Paulie. I can't afford any of your favors."

"This is for free, Charlie. This is to make up for your hand. I ain't going to charge you for it."

"I'll pass. Let me call it quits with my hand."

Paulie shrugged. "It's up to you. What are you going to do now, Charlie?"

"I don't know. I got to get out of New York. That's why I came for my money. But what the hell am I going to do with five grand? Five grand won't get me into any kind of action. I can't even look for a decent job—any contacts I got are people would sooner or later hear that the Bedbug was looking for me. I'm in a fucking corner here."

"Take my advice, Charlie. Grab the retard's money."

"Jesus, I'm tempted. But I just got to draw the line somewhere. I been hustling since I'm a kid, but you're not careful you wind up stealing quarters out of tin cups. I'm thirty-five. I haven't done anybody a lot of good—Diane even said that in her note. This is where I got to draw the line, Paulie."

"Suit yourself. If it was me, I'd grab it. You lose a little sleep, but it don't last, Charlie. A week or two goes by, you'll sleep like a baby again."

"What are you going to do, Paulie?"

"I'm going out to the track. Starry Skies runs in the seventh today. That's why I came by, Charlie, to tell you. It's a chance to make a bundle."

"That's the favor you were talking about?"

"Don't laugh, Charlie. The horse has busted loose all of a sudden. No joke. The jock who breezes her has been pulling her in a little so the clockers won't ruin our odds. Even the trainer says so, Charlie. The *trainer* is putting three, four thousand on her today. We got her way over-classed in this race. Seventy-five hundred maiden claiming. She's running against garbage."

"What will she go off at?"

"They got her twenty-to-one on the morning line.

By the time Jimmy the cheese man and Tommy get down five grand apiece, Briglia, the hard-on, goes for his three or four and I spring for ten large, she'll go off eight-, maybe ten-to-one. Even then, I already placed ten thou with the books on Mott Street instead of at the windows so I don't wreck the odds."

"You're going for twenty?"

"The whole works. This is my shot. I could wind up here with a quarter of a million bucks, Charlie."

"What if, God forbid, she doesn't win?"

"She's up against garbage, Charlie."

"I almost forgot—this horse has the champion gene."

"She does. You can laugh, Charlie, but she's got the gene. It's in her."

They sat quietly for a few minutes. Charlie drank his scotch slowly. He wondered where Diane was now, and pictured her walking through an airport terminal somewhere, followed by a porter wheeling bags. The money would be in her handbag, hanging from her right shoulder. Christ, some fifteen-year-old purse snatcher would make the score of his life if he grabbed that. And it would serve her right. He topped off his drink with more scotch. This thing with the horse might not be a hundred percent madness, either. If the horse was running good, she was running good. You couldn't argue with a stopwatch.

"You say the trainer's going for three or four grand on this horse, Paulie?"

"Briglia. And this is a guy don't go for spit, Charlie."

"Who's riding her?"

"Laplanta. We're putting down five hundred for him. He'll bust his hump for that kind of a shot."

"You didn't pay the shylocks, Paulie?"

He waved his hand. "I'll pay those vultures after

the race. It's like throwing away money, paying them now. It just eats into my winnings."

Paulie looked at his watch and stood up. "I better move. Look, Charlie, there was nothing in it for me, putting you on to this. Your five grand would have just cut the odds down a little more. I figured I could make it up to you a little."

Charlie thought for a few moments, and saw himself pounding out dough at an open-window pizza stand. He stood up. "Fuck it. Now ain't the time to pinch pennies. This horse better have the champion gene in her, Paulie."

Paulie slapped his arm. He poured a splash of scotch into Charlie's glass, lifted it in a silent toast, and swallowed the liquor quickly. "Wait till you see her run. She's beautiful, Charlie."

"Two minutes. I have a claim check for Barney's wife I got to put in the mail. I'll feel better when Barney's money is away from me. Let me just write out an envelope."

"Charlie, you sure we shouldn't put a little of the retard's money on Starry Skies for him? Not for us, Charlie. For the retard. The winnings go right to him."

Charlie smiled, and walked to the kitchen for an envelope and a stamp. "It's nice of you to worry about him, Paulie, but he'll have to manage on the fifty thousand."

Paulie shrugged. "I was just trying to do the right thing. Let's go."

chapter
XVIII

The light went from yellow to red while Paulie was still half a block short of the intersection. He cruised through it and took a right onto Linden Boulevard.

"Look at these private houses. All coloreds—the whole neighborhood. You'd never guess it, Charlie, would you? Nice little brick houses. The weather gets warm, they're out in their little yards cooking hamburgers like anybody else."

He began to whistle softly, tunes that Charlie couldn't recognize, while they rode the mile or so to the track parking lot.

"How's your old man, Paulie? I never asked you."

"He's good. They cut him open, they done whatever they had to do with the ulcer, and they sewed him up again. All neat and clean. He's puffing a pack of cigarettes a day—he never even lost his cough. And trying to con me into sneaking up a bowl of calamari in hot sauce. Wants to know why the hell did he let the Jews open him up if he can't eat hot sauce. He's good, Charlie."

Paulie pulled into the parking lot.

"You figure she'll go off at ten-to-one, Paulie?"

"Say eight or nine."

It would bring him back something like forty thousand—what would be in his pocket now if he had run to New England and left ten behind for Diane.

"You counting your winnings, Charlie?"

"I'm not counting any winnings until they're in my hand."

"You were counting, Charlie. I could hear the bills snapping all the way over here. A thousand. Two thou. Three thou. Four—"

"Okay. Maybe I was counting a little."

Paulie continued to count aloud as he drove across the parking lot to the valet-service area. "Nineteen thou. Twenty thou. Telephone numbers, Charlie, these are fucking telephone numbers we're talking about here."

He drove fast, in a beeline toward the clubhouse, cutting diagonally across the yellow-striped traffic lanes and parking spots. Charlie braced his hand against the dashboard.

"God forbid somebody pulls out of a space."

"Nobody's pulling out of nowhere. All these chumps are inside losing their money." He pointed to his left. "Look at the little round towers, Charlie. Like the gun towers in those old prison pictures on 'The Late Show.' They got TV cameras in them, to watch the horses coming around the curves where the stewards can't see them. These New York tracks, you try to pull a scam, forget about it. They cover every inch. Like people hunting for a lost contact lens, these stewards. You get out to them jerkwater little tracks, you're on a fucking picnic with the yokels. Change markings on a horse, box in a favorite—they do everything out there but print twenties. One race a day, the jocks decide whose turn it is to pick up a purse. They got a swindle going out of town, it's enough to make you drool."

Paulie left the car with an attendant and tipped him a dollar. They went up into the clubhouse. The fifth race was just going off. Charlie heard the crowd noise build up suddenly—the horses would be coming out of the first turn.

"Packed today," Paulie said. "There was a big stakes race today. We waited to get her on a card with a big stakes race on it. The handles are bigger that way. The odds hold up better."

He looked around.

"Classy, no, Charlie? It's the only way to see a race, from the clubhouse. You stay over there in the grandstand, every garbage can walking the streets is standing next to you scratching his crotch. You wind up with crabs, you hang out in the grandstand."

"You call this class? Paulie, all these lamps are fake Tiffanys, seventy-five a pop on the Bowery. They're plastic, the same shit they got hanging in the Good Times. They make the grandstand so bad, the clubhouse looks good next to it. This is like a big factory."

"You're too picky, Charlie. You don't enjoy anyplace."

"You've never been to Churchill Downs, Paulie. There's a fucking track. Whitewashed wood. The place is real. Anything here looks like wood, guaranteed it's Formica. Look at what they call a bar, for Christ's sake. Who the hell would drink at it? It's a little factory production line, like at the airports. Half the liquor comes out of hoses. And they put those little meters on everything. Next year you'll be dropping quarters into a machine for your martini. In a paper cup.

"Look at the goddamn litter, Paulie. There's a ton of ripped-up paper on the floor. You might as well be in the OTB on Fourteenth Street. Check out the people, for Christ's sake. Just look at this fucking collection."

"They're worse in the grandstand. You catch crabs in the grandstand."

"They're bad enough here. All these guys with two and three days of beard on them—you can bet they didn't bother hopping into the shower this morning either. Do you believe it, Paulie? Half of them don't even walk outside to watch the race, they just look at the replay on the TV screens."

"Maybe they're ascared of the fresh air—these are city guys. Believe me, Charlie, the grandstand's worse. You wind up next to degenerate gamblers there go maybe a week without changing their underwears. You look at their faces, you'd swear you're on the charity ward at Saint Vincent's. There's nobody healthy over there. Bathrobes and slippers is what they need for that whole crew in the grandstand. You got it nice here, you're still not satisfied, Charlie. It's a real fucking curse you carry around."

He tugged lightly at Charlie's sleeve and moved off to his left. "Let's get a program. We'll get some binoculars, too. It's a waste up here without a pair of binoculars."

He had his driver's license out of his wallet by the time he reached the tiny counter. He put it down along with a five-dollar bill and took two pairs of binoculars and two programs.

"Let's grab ourselves some nice, fat cigars, too, Charlie. I'm a fucking owner, no? We're entitled to act like a couple of sports." He hurried over to the small tobacco counter and took four of the best cigars she had—big, dark, dollar-and-a-quarter Macanudos.

He tucked two of them into Charlie's shirt pocket.

Charlie motioned up over his left shoulder, toward the section of roofed-over private boxes. "You don't have a box, Paulie?"

"Next year. They cost a fortune, those boxes. They're filled up with state racing commission guys, OTB big shots, track officials. People taking a gallop on the taxpayers. All the victims carrying lunchpails on the IRT at six in the morning are picking up the freight for those boxes. I got to lay out green. Next year I can afford it. I'll get my own binoculars, too, with my initials on them. No more of this renting shit."

They walked out onto the concrete apron and found an open spot. Charlie lit a cigar, then adjusted the binoculars by focusing in on the furlong markers. Paulie stood beside him and opened the *Racing Form*. He spread it wide, and frowned as he read it.

"Look, Charlie. Starry Skies in the seventh. They got her name in the papers." He moved his lips while he read each few words first to himself, then repeated them aloud to Charlie. "They got her name in big letters. Starry Skies. Owner, Garagusso Stables." He looked up from the paper. "Fucking Jimmy the cheese man—he come up front with most of the money, so he stuck his name on the deal. It's fucking ridiculous—Garagusso Stables. It's got no class. Thank God the maniac didn't decide to call us the Bel Paese Barn."

He returned to the *Form* and frowned again. "*TR.*—that means trainer. Briglia, J. 'Hard-on,' they should print next to his name. Fucking dunce teaches horses how to kick themselves. *BR.*—that means breeder. Twilight Time Farms, N.Y. Means she was folded in New York."

Charlie lowered the binoculars. "She was what?"

"Folded. In New York. When a horse is born, they don't say she was born—she was folded. Don't ask me why. Anyway, Starry Skies was folded in New York."

He went back to the paper. "*F.*—That means filly. They call girl horses fillies. You see a *G.*, Charlie, that's a gelding. That means they whacked the poor horses's dick off. Can you just see that, Charlie? Whacko! It's gone." He shuddered, then frowned intensely. "Just think what—"

"Paulie, *please*. Spare me. You went through this number the night we robbed the loft. About the fags on the docks on West Street."

"It don't bother you, Charlie? Guys losing their dicks? Even fags. Even horses, Charlie, it makes me shiver."

"Go back to reading the program, Paulie. You're doing great."

"It says here, 'by Stoordzy.'" He looked up and leaned closer to Charlie. "By Stoordzy my ass. Stoordzy is her fake father. He was some fucking *lemone* in his day. You read his charts, this victim Stoordzy's got to wind up on a supermarket shelf inside a bunch of dog food cans. They put her real father's name on this program, Charlie, Starry Skies goes off at maybe three-to-five. And somebody claims her, to boot."

"Who taught you to read all those hieroglyphics like that?"

Paulie looked down modestly. "I been practicing. Tommy Botondo showed me. I don't know where he learned."

He opened the paper again. "Look at this, Charlie. Her latest workout it says *H.* That means handily—the exercise boy ran her nice. Five furlongs, one-o-five and three-fifths. Shit time. He should be in the movies, that kid. Handily. He never even let her breeze good he was holding her back so tight. And the clockers never picked it up."

He tapped the page several times with his hand. "Look at this pile of garbage she's up against. There'll be a flock of fucking sea gulls following them around the track. We're going to make money here today, Charlie. In my fucking *bones* I feel it."

"What race, Paulie?"

"The seventh. Post time is four-thirty. Probable. It's been on my mind all week."

"How are we betting her, Paulie?"

"What do you mean?"

"We going right across the board?"

Paulie slapped the *Racing Form* against his thigh. "Across the board my ass. You bet her to win, Charlie, or do me a favor and keep your money. I didn't bring you here to jinx her with place and show bets."

"Jinx her? Have a heart. Paulie, maybe she's got the champion gene, but let's spread our money across the board. Just in case, Paulie."

"I knew it. I fucking *knew* it. Once in your life, Charlie, don't hedge. Lay your money on the line and roll the dice for a big one. It's hard luck to hedge. You'll ruin her race, Charlie, and you'll fuck up my bet, too. Bet her to win, Charlie, or don't bet her at all."

Charlie pressed the palms of his hands together. "Paulie, have mercy. Show a little mercy. I'm going for five large here. The only money I've got in the world. Let me throw a thousand on place and show. God forbid she runs second, I don't wind up broke. For insurance, Paulie."

Paulie squinted, and waved the *Racing Form* from side to side in front of Charlie's face. "There ain't no insurance allowed. You want insurance, buy a policy off Metropolitan. You want to make money with my horse, you don't louse her up with a bunch of shit insurance bets."

"Serious, Paulie. This is money I can't lose. I'd like for you to say, 'Bet her your way.' But if you don't, another minute I'll tell you to fuck off and I'll put my money across the board."

Paulie stared into Charlie's face, forgetting his usual little affectations. "I *am* serious. Charlie, you know better. You bet enough to know. Do the right thing here, Charlie. If it wasn't for me, you wouldn't be making the bet. If you're betting my tip, you bet it my way. That's the rule, Charlie. Unless I don't care. But if I'm scared of a jinx—and, Charlie, I fucking *know* a place bet is going to jinx her—then you don't jinx me. If you're scared, hold your money. But you ain't allowed to fuck up my bet. You can walk off and bet her across the board, but it ain't the right thing to do, Charlie, and you know it."

Charlie closed his eyes and shook his head slowly several times, then let out a long sigh. He raised the binoculars again and continued to focus each eyepiece. Paulie folded the *Racing Form* under his arm and opened the narrow official program. He frowned again and moved his lips as he read everything twice— first silently, then aloud.

"Seventh race. Starry Skies is in post position three. They tell you what the jockey wears, Charlie. The colors. So you know one horse from the other while they're running."

He held the program closer. "Orange. Pink yoke. Green 'G.' Pink blocks on sleeves. Orange cap, pink visor and pompom." He shook his head in disgust. "Do you fucking believe that getup, Charlie? I argued with the cheese man three fucking days, it didn't do no good. A big green 'G,' for Garagusso Stables. I told him with those fucking colors he should forget the

'G,' and have a big P.R.K. for Puerto Rican Kitchen. He's got the poor jock looking like some queen off Christopher Street. All he's missing is a pair of high heels."

"Paulie, forget the colors. Forget Jimmy the cheese man's 'G.' Is this fucking horse going to *win*? Are we going to make money here today? That's what counts, Paulie, not whether the jockey looks like a fag or not. How fast can this horse run?"

"How fast! What are you, pulling on your prick, Charlie? You laugh about the champion gene, but she's got it." He closed the fingers of his left hand into a loose fist and moved it back and forth quickly as though masturbating. "That groom who jerked off her father, he wasn't just winding up his watch, Charlie. Starry Skies could set a track record here today. Take my word for it."

"We don't need a track record. We need her to run a little bit faster than all the other horses."

"Garbage. She's running against garbage."

"I don't care who she's running against. What if she comes up shy by a tenth of a second, Paulie? Just enough so she runs second. Or maybe a whole second shy, so she winds up third. Let's drop a couple of big ones on her to show. We'll still make money, Paulie."

Paulie closed his eyes and shook his head from side to side.

Charlie spoke slowly. "You're putting me on the cross here. Let me bet this horse my way. Paulie, don't crucify me."

Paulie kept his eyes closed tightly. "You're going to bet her my way, Charlie. I ain't going to let you wreck my shot. If that's crucifying you, then too fucking bad. Cross your feet, I only got three nails."

They bet first at the hundred-dollar window on

the main level of the clubhouse, then at the two windows, tucked away in a semiprivate alcove on the upper level. Paulie stood behind Charlie to be sure his entire five thousand was bet to win. The clerk counted out the money and barely looked up. At the next window, Paulie ordered a hundred win tickets, and pulled two tightly bound packets of hundreds from his inside pockets. He slid them through. The clerk raised his eyebrows, then pressed the buttons of his keyboard. Paulie lit his cigar, moving the match in a tiny circle and drawing deeply, then examined the tip before applying the match again while the machine issued the tickets. He divided them into roughly equal stacks and pushed them down into the side pockets of his jacket. They went downstairs and walked outdoors again.

"We going to watch the horses walk the circle?"

Paulie shook his head. "I don't want to run into Briglia. After the race, we'll go. I ain't even dressed right, Charlie, for an owner."

"What the hell does that have to do with it? Let's walk over and see the horse."

"I'm nervous, Charlie. I'm only going to make the horse nervous, too. We'll see her after she wins."

Paulie drew on his cigar and waited calmly for the race to begin.

Charlie felt his teeth clench as he waited for the start. He zeroed in with the binoculars as best he could on the number three gate. It sprang open suddenly. The horse jumped through the little circles of light, then Charlie jerked the glasses forward too quickly and found himself ahead of the horses. They were approaching the first furlong marker before he steadied enough to pick them up again. Starry Skies was running third. Coming into the first turn she was moving into second, but a horse was coming up from behind faster than everyone else.

She held her own into the second turn, then moved ahead, neck and neck with the horse coming up from behind. The two of them inched into the number two position and held it past the second turn. They came into the top of the stretch still running neck and neck, half a length behind the leader. Charlie heard the crowd around him begin to shout. A voice off to his left kept calling, "Hopatki! Run, Hopatki!" Starry Skies and Hopatki stayed together as they overtook the front-runner. For half a furlong the three of them were in a perfectly dead heat, then Starry Skies and Hopatki inched ahead together. It was going to be a fast time and a close finish. The crowd pushed forward, pressed closer to the rail than usual. The sound built up as a low rumble, rolling out of the clubhouse and grandstand, across the apron toward the two horses kicking up clumps of dirt on the track.

"Get her up there. Get her up."

It was Paulie's voice, low and pleading and insistent. Charlie heard it clearly through the roar around him. He let the binoculars fall against his belly and felt the strap pull across the back of his neck. His throat was too constricted for him to yell.

Starry Skies and Hopatki stayed together and pulled away from the front-runner on the outside. A few hundred feet from the finish line, they took the lead by half a length, the two of them running in step as though yoked together, their sides nearly touching. Starry Skies was closest to the rail, her jockey holding the whip in his left hand but not having to use it. Hopatki's jockey was whipping her right rump with sharp, deliberate strokes. They fell into a rhythm. Their bodies seemed cemented together; only their necks and heads snaked forward and back, first Hopatki's neck outstretched to give her half-a-head lead, then Starry Skies' head creeping forward while Hopatki's drifted back.

Charlie tightened his stomach. It was more a dance than a race. They ran in step, only their heads rippling into different positions. Whichever position the rhythm happened to freeze them into at the finish line would decide who won—it would have nothing to do with who ran faster.

The crowd noise grew louder. Charlie realized that he was up on his toes. Beside him, Paulie's cries for the horse to run subsided into a long, pleading "Starry," that he repeated slowly. His head was turned away from the race. Charlie stretched up as the horses crossed the finish line. He couldn't be sure because of the angle, but it looked like Hopatki by a head.

Half a minute later the numbers went up on the board. Starry Skies ran second. Charlie exhaled slowly and stared at Paulie. His throat was so dry that his voice cracked as he spoke.

"I knew it. I knew it while I watched the machine spit out those win tickets. Fortunes I don't tell, Paulie. Only fucking *fortunes* I don't tell."

Paulie's face was white. It occured to Charlie that he was more upset now than when they had discovered the dead cop sprawled at the bottom of the elevator shaft. Paulie pressed his hands against his chest, his left hand clenched into a fist, his bandaged right hand stiff and bulky, then rolled his eyes toward the sky.

"Christ. But only *Christ* knows how I suffer."

Charlie waited a minute, until Paulie seemed relaxed again. "What do we do now, Paulie? We didn't jinx the horse with place bets, but all our money's gone. I just blew my little pizzeria in Boston. What do we do now?"

Paulie raised his eyebrows and bobbed his chin

forward and back an inch, in a gesture of resignation. "We better look for Briglia. That hard-on bet her across the board for sure—he never in his life bet like a fucking man. Guaranteed he's got a pocket full of money. I'll loan five hundred off him, Charlie. It'll give us a night on the town at least—no?"

chapter

XIX

The expressway opened up after a construction bottle-neck near the Van Wyck. Paulie squeezed in behind a trailer truck in the outside lane and tailgated at a steady pace, pressing the brake with his left foot whenever the truck slowed down. He reached forward and turned on the radio. Charlie turned it off, then waved away an offer of gum a few minutes later. Paulie unwrapped three pieces and chewed them loudly. The sweet odor filled the car for a few minutes. Charlie wondered if it was bubble gum.

As they approached Manhattan, the crowded gray tombstones of Calvary Cemetery appeared. Charlie stared at them through the closed window.

"They squeeze them in there with a shoehorn," Paulie said. "It makes me think of the subway. Those have to be Jews or Protestants in there, no, Charlie? The Catholics don't pack you in that tight."

Charlie watched the tombstones recede as Paulie accelerated to pass a van. He couldn't distinguish any rows; each stone seemed to be huddled in at any convenient angle. They reminded him of the crowded gray buildings around Wall Street. He spoke very softly.

"You know what I would be sitting on now if I had bet her to place, Paulie? Even across the board, it wouldn't be a disaster."

"Don't, Charlie. Don't start that shit."

Charlie nodded at the closed side window. "You're right. You're right. If. Every year of my life is a list of *ifs*. This is the year for if I didn't listen to Paulie—if the cop hadn't barged in—if Diane hadn't run out on me—if I had bet the horse to place. Busy year."

"Jesus Christ, Charlie, you think like this all your life it's a wonder you bother getting out of the bathtub in the morning. You ought to just sit there and slit your wrists." He thought quietly for a few minutes, staring ahead, but with this mind not on driving. "I'll tell you, though, Charlie, she ran beautiful. But perfect. She never kicked herself, neither. You watch her coming into the stretch? She looked like one of those paintings in the Jockey Club the way she came out of that turn in front of the pack. It looked like all her feet were off the ground at one time. Her head was stretched out like she wanted to *eat* the finish line. With the jock kneeling right up on top of her. He never had to touch her with the whip, Charlie."

"I'm glad she looked so pretty, Paulie. It almost makes all the money we blew worth it. And thank God the jock didn't have to whip her—it would've ruined my day."

Paulie glanced across at Charlie, then looked ahead and pursed his lips in disapproval. "You ain't being fair, Charlie. She ran her fucking heart out—the jock even said so. She put every last ounce in it. You got to love her for that."

They slowed for the toll plaza. Paulie paid the toll

and rolled slowly into the mouth of the tunnel, beside a tank truck.

"You didn't tip him," Charlie said. "Poor son of a bitch stands in that tiny booth all day. You didn't throw him anything."

"Fuck him. What am I, Santa Claus?" He accelerated to move ahead of the tank truck's exhaust.

"What the hell are either one of us going to do, Paulie?"

Paulie looked surprised. "I figured we would have a few drinks. What else are we going to do?"

"I don't mean this afternoon. What the hell are we going to do long-range?"

"Jesus, Charlie, your whole fucking life is long-range. When do you get to enjoy anything?"

"I can't even get out of the city now. I don't have enough to get out and start fresh someplace else."

"We'll stop at Rocco's. A couple of drinks, you'll feel better, Charlie."

"What's the matter with you? I'll be in Rocco's ten minutes, somebody's going to make me and give the Bedbug a call. Let's go someplace we won't bump into people we know."

They came out into the twilight. Paulie swung across to the uptown exit, then took a right onto Third. "We'll go to Sheridan's. Seventy-fourth or -fifth. It's one of them East Side scenes. Business guys, some loose girls. There's nobody from the neighborhood there."

He reached forward and turned on the radio. This time Charlie let it play.

Half a block past the bar, Paulie swung into a parking place.

"It's a hydrant," Charlie said.

"You'll never find anything else in this neighborhood."

"It's twenty-five dollars, Paulie."

"It's worth every cent. We could drive around for half an hour hunting. Thank God it's here."

Paulie checked his hair in the rearview mirror while Charlie waited on the sidewalk. They entered the bar through a side door on Seventy-fourth and took stools away from the service end, where a liquor salesman was taking an order from the bartender. Halfway down the bar, two middle-aged businessmen, left over from lunch, their attaché cases standing partly in the aisle, were trying to convince one another of something important, each one in turn grasping the other's forearm to interrupt and make a point. Near them, a young lawyer or accountant who had gotten away from his office early was reading an afternoon paper and sipping his first martini of the day. The bartender motioned with his hand that he would be down to serve them in a minute. Charlie watched two waitresses setting up their stations for the dinner shot, wiping the tops of ketchup bottles, filling salt and pepper shakers, and adding to the stacks of sugar packets.

"Jesus Christ, they still dress them in miniskirts up here."

Paulie nodded approvingly. "Nice, ain't it, Charlie? Half the restaurants in the Village, the waitresses look like a gang of construction workers got laid off for the cold weather. It's all this liberation shit."

"You don't think they need liberating, Paulie? You're not on the side of the feminists?"

"I didn't mind at first, Charlie. When they gave up the bras. I got nothing against that. But then they went too far. Now you can't tell the dykes from the straights. That's who's cashing in on all this shit, the dykes. They poison these broads against guys so they can strap their dildoes on and go to work. These miniskirts look fine. You know when you look at them that there's a pussy inside."

The bartender finally left the service end and walked toward them slowly. He stopped to refill the salesmen's drinks, then again to empty an ashtray.

"You think this hard-on's going to get around to serving us?" Charlie asked.

"Don't rush him. This is an East Side superstar you're dealing with here. Somebody sees him rushing for a customer, he blows his whole image."

When the bartender reached them, Paulie ordered a bottle of Dom Perignon. Charlie looked at him in disbelief. "You celebrating something? You got something to celebrate, Paulie?"

"It'll cheer us up maybe, Charlie."

"Cheer us up? A bottle of champagne is supposed to cheer me up?"

"You want to sit here all night depressed? We can behave like a couple of sports, or like a couple of fucking garbage cans. Maybe you like being depressed, Charlie. I don't. If I don't cheer up a little, I'll fucking die."

"Not champagne, though. I'll choke on champagne."

They settled on Remy. The bartender set two large snifters on the bar. Paulie pointed at them before he started pouring. "These things are for fags. We look like a couple of fucking fags to you?"

The bartender hesitated, unsure whether he was supposed to laugh or not. He held the bottle in midair.

Paulie brought the fingers of his unbandaged hand together, palm up, and shook it slowly near the bartender's face in the classic Italian plea for understanding. "Give us a break and bring over a couple of pony glasses. Let me drink my brandy tough-guy-style. What's your name, bartender?"

"Todd."

"Todd, you don't learn to tell the difference between a couple of fags and a couple of tough guys, you'll never make it in New York. They'll ship you back to Texas."

While the bartender went for the ponies, Paulie turned to Charlie. "You don't break these superstars in right, they'll behave like hard-ons all night. You can't give them no confidence."

The bartender filled two pony glasses. Paulie said, "Very good," then raised the glass toward Charlie. "To better days."

They sipped the brandy.

"You come here much?" Charlie asked.

"Once in a while when I'm bouncing on the East Side. It's okay at night. Gets some stewardesses, secretaries. Twats from the neighborhood."

After a few minutes of watching the waitresses, Charlie turned back to Paulie. "How the hell are you going to meet shylock payments?"

"I don't even want to think about it, Charlie."

"You're going to have to think about it."

"Not now I don't. Not till Saturday. My next payment ain't due till Saturday afternoon."

"That's three days away, Paulie."

"That's what I'm saying. I got three days before I start worrying. You want me to ruin the rest of the week for myself?"

"You don't even have a job."

Paulie gulped the brandy in his glass and beckoned to the bartender. "Nobody's ever going to accuse you of being happy-go-lucky, Charlie. Why don't we make believe for a while that Starry Skies ran first. We're each sitting here on a hundred large. Let's talk about all the pussy we could be looking forward to for the next year."

Charlie finished his drink and watched the bartender fill their glasses. He would relax for a while if he could. He slowly tuned Paulie out, nodding from time to time. As he drank he felt his face grow flushed.

The bar filled up gradually over the next few hours. Charlie looked quickly from face to face, wondering what troubles any of them might have. It was two deep now, a young crowd of East Side locals and people in from Queens, some out-of-town businessmen in dark suits cruising the singles bars, and a cluster of loud Irish-American office workers celebrating one of the girls' birthday. The jukebox had either been turned up or the brandies were making his hearing more acute.

"You ever wish you could go back to square one, Paulie? Make everything the way it was a month ago and start fresh?"

"Maybe six mornings every week since the fourth grade."

"It doesn't drive you nuts?"

"You get used to it. If it ain't one thing, it's another. Things work out, Charlie."

"How the hell can you say that? You're missing a fucking thumb. How the hell can you say things work out?"

Paulie brought his palms together in a position of prayer and looked toward the ceiling. "But, Jesus *Christ*, this guy isn't going to let up on me." He turned toward Charlie. "You trying to make me cry? Is that what you want, Charlie? You want me to lay my head on the bar and cry like a fucking baby?"

"I don't want you to cry. Just face reality. Things *don't* work out. Not when you're minus a thumb and I'm going to be minus a whole fucking hand. Take my word for it—anybody sane, they don't say things are working out when the Bedbug is whacking hunks of their arms off. Face the facts, Paulie."

Charlie caught the bartender's attention and had him pour another round. He counted the bills on the bar. Paulie had put down a fifty when they walked in; what was left meant they were starting on their sixth round. That explained why his ears and cheeks felt hot. He visualized again the one-man pizzeria in New England that he had thought about earlier. Before the race it had seemed like a sentence. Now he saw it as warm and cozy, with steamy windows on a bitter, snowy day and a wave of dry heat rising from the oven each time a pie went in or out. He could smell tomato sauce simmering under the hood of a stove and the dryness of white flour dust in his nostrils.

It would have been a healthy life for a while, he decided. It would have been good for him for a year or two, pounding out dough, on his feet eighteen hours a day, hoisting hundred-pound sacks of flour around the place. No time for heavy drinking. Nice, mindless, peasant labor for long hours, better than a four-hundred-dollar-a-year gym membership. Six months, he would be like a rock. Collapse on a bed every night into a tired, total sleep, spread-eagled on his back. With a head clear as a piece of crystal each morning after a shower and half a cup of breakfast cappuccino made with scalded milk on the kitchen stove. He should have hung on to the five thousand.

"What are you thinking about, Charlie?"

"My five big ones."

Paulie shook his head slowly. "I thought it was a good deal, Charlie. I figured you could make it all back."

"I don't know what the hell to do, Paulie. There's no way I'm going to be able to locate Diane. Where the hell would I start looking? Without that money I'm fucked."

"Something's got to turn up."

"I treated her good, too. I didn't walk around abusing her. I never raised my hand to her. I should have treated Cookie half as good. *Half.* She would have been happy as a clam."

"You can't do that, Charlie. You ought to know better. You don't abuse them once in a while, they're going to shit on you. I don't mean all the time—you can't walk around morning till night whacking them on the side of the head like some old greaseball. But once in a while. You got to terrorize them once in a while just to keep them in line."

Charlie sipped his brandy. "How many times she *provoked* me, I still never gave her a smack? We were at a party at Arthur's house last year, she had a couple of drinks and I catch her making a pitch for Little Ralphy. The coke dealer. That fucking maniac. She would have had me in some swindle with that whackadoo. A ten-year-old could clock Little Ralphy for a space case."

Paulie shook his head unhappily. "You made some mistake there. That's when you whack them with a backhand. Maybe two. Not out in the middle of the living room like some animal. Nice, in the bedroom. You call them in the bedroom alone. Ba-*boom*—what do I look like, some asshole? Ba-*boom*—another one— what is this, some kind of *joke?* Get on your coat. Fast. And I don't want you saying goodnight to anybody, you understand?"

He swirled his half-glass of brandy gently, then swallowed it. "That's just to keep them humble, Charlie. When you don't let them say goodnight to nobody, they walk out looking down at the floor. You know how the girls used to do in church? When they walked up for Communion? Same thing." He motioned for another round. "She would have tried to give you some shit in the elevator. Once they're away from everybody, they try for some sympathy. You can't pay attention. Listen, you tell them, you behave like a cunt, you get treated like a cunt. Then you take them home.

"I'll tell you, Charlie, I never had a girl leave me for giving her a smack. Open-hand—I'm not talking about busting their noses. As long as they deserve it, they don't leave. Right home, into bed." He moved his fist up and down in a pumping motion. "Slip them the old *sauseech,* they'll stand in the kitchen and cook you pasta for a week. And whistle."

"Maybe. But you can always go out to eat pasta. Four dollars a bowl, they'll even cook it for you *al dente.* And you don't have to smack anybody."

"You don't smack them for the pasta, Charlie. I never said that. You smack them for whatever they got to be smacked for. The pasta's extra."

"Doesn't seem like a great way to live."

"Your way's better, Charlie. Except the broad puts on her lipstick some morning and walks with your fifty grand."

Charlie shrugged. "Maybe you're right."

He suddenly visualized Diane doing her yoga exercises on the living-room floor, straight up in a shoulder stand, her toes pointed toward the ceiling. His anger turned to sadness for a moment. Her stomach would swell up soon if she went through with having the baby. She wouldn't be able to find work waitressing. And where the hell would she start over with a whole new group of friends? She really hadn't wanted to leave him. If he had just said he wanted her along, she would have stuck with him through anything. It occurred to him that she might come back, the whole thing might overwhelm her, then he realized that she wouldn't. Her talk about how tough they were in Maine was true—he had known it even while she was telling him. She would manage, and have the baby, and keep on managing. What the hell made having a baby so important to her he wondered.

"Let's eat something," Paulie said. "I'm starved."

"You got an appetite?"

"I'm not supposed to eat? You want me to wear black for a week, too?"

Paulie caught a waitress's attention and ordered a cheeseburger. "Eat something, Charlie. It'll absorb some of the acid in your stomach."

"I can't eat. And I don't have stomach acid."

"You do, Charlie. You're burning up inside, and you're pissed at me. I see it on your face. When you can't watch somebody eat, it means you're pissed at them."

"I'm pissed off at myself. And at Diane. The only gripe I got with you, Paulie, is on the original score. You should have told me it was the Bedbug's money. You weren't honest."

"This is maybe the tenth time you're telling me that, Charlie. You make it sound like you were a hundred percent honest with me and Barney."

They looked at one another quietly. Charlie heard the jukebox and the loud hum of bar conversation behind him. He spoke softly. "Where wasn't I a hundred percent honest, Paulie?"

"It ain't the most important thing in the world. But that dead cop was wearing a tape. That's what they were probably working on Barney for, the tape. You're the one went down in that shaft, Charlie. You took the tape off that cop and you never told me or Barney."

They were quiet again for a few moments, then Paulie shrugged. "I don't hold it against you, Charlie. We ain't saints."

Charlie nodded. "There was a tape. I should have said something."

The bartender filled their glasses and gathered Paulie's bills into a neat pile.

"How did you hear about it?" Charlie asked.

"My uncle Pete. He didn't even know about it when he grabbed me out at Belmont, he found out later. From people on his crew. You know how the wise guys gossip. They're worse than the old ladies on Carmine Street."

"What the hell does the Bedbug want with it? There's nothing on it."

"He must be nervous. Until Carlucci got pushed out, Eddie Grant was the guy used to make the payments to this dead cop."

"How do you know that?"

"Pete. Eddie Grant and the cop used to meet at the Fishouse. Turns out that cop was the biggest bagman ever."

Charlie sat back on the stool. Maybe the tape wasn't useless. With no money to run with, he would lose his hand for sure. The tape was the only thing he had going for him.

"It might be my way out, Paulie, that tape. If the Bedbug wants that tape, then he's worried there's something on it can hang him."

"But there ain't."

"I just might bluff my way through with it. It could save my hand."

"Maybe you ought to wait till the drinks wear off, Charlie."

"The drinks have nothing to do with it. It's a shot. It's the only shot I got."

"Charlie, you're talking about bluffing the Bedbug. The fucking *Bedbug*. I see the guy up close, I got to fight off the shakes. For real. Last Thursday night was the first time I waited on him. The demitasse wants to shake on the saucer every time I go to his table. I steady it with my other hand just before I get to him. And then I don't look at his face. I look straight into the Bedbug's face, I swear my balls go cold."

Charlie barely listened. "I either wait around to have my hand chopped off, or I take a shot. What would I do if there *was* something on the tape could hang him? You bet your ass I'd use it."

He thought for a few moments. "That's the key, Paulie. What would I do if there *was* something on the tape?"

The bartender came over with the brandy bottle. Charlie covered his glass with his hand. Paulie nodded, and the bartender filled his glass.

"What I'd do, Paulie, is to get the tape into somebody's hands where it was safe, and tell them it should go to the D.A.'s office if anything happens to me. That's the only thing would make sense. Then I would let the Bedbug know and try to make a deal for myself."

"How? That's the thing. How? You going to walk up to him on Mulberry Street and tell him to his face? Look the Bedbug right in the eyes and *threaten* him? To his face? I'll tell you, Charlie, mention the D.A.— *mention* him, if you could get it out without stuttering— the maniac would choke you on the spot. In the middle of Mulberry Street in broad daylight he'd choke you to death and leave you laying on the sidewalk. Blue. And nobody in the neighborhood would see nothing."

"Mulberry Street *is* the way to do it, Paulie. Right in his own social club. Face-to-face. It's the only way he'd believe I had something on him. Walk in there like fucking J. Edgar Hoover. Ice-cold sober. It'd take a pair of steel balls, Paulie. *Steel.* But I could bluff that cocksucker down."

Paulie poured half of his drink into Charlie's glass. "Have a drink. You look serious."

"I am serious. It's my hand otherwise. I can't give up my hand, Paulie. I mean, I *can't*. I'm thirty-five, and I'm going nowhere fast. If I let him take my hand, it's like throwing in the towel. I'm washed up with one hand. I'd rather take this shot."

"Could you do it, Charlie? It's one thing to bullshit at a bar, but could you do it?"

He stared into Paulie's face absently for a few moments. "I don't know." He sipped the half-glass of brandy. "I'm going to try it, though. I'm not going to sneak around corners for the next few months waiting for Eddie Grant's gorillas to catch up with me. They'll stretch me out on a bench and hack my hand off while I scream like some fucking alley cat."

Paulie shuddered. He spoke softly. "You don't have to tell me, Charlie."

"The secret is to walk in there like I had the atom bomb in my back pocket. If I fucking flinch, the Bedbug will put me in the ground. If I walk right into the club like I just bought the joint, he's got to figure I got something up my sleeve."

"You'll really do it, Charlie?"

"Tomorrow. He's there tomorrow night?"

Paulie nodded. "It's Thursday. He's always there on Thursday. That's the night I got to wait on the maniac."

"Then that's the night I face down Eddie Grant."

He waved for the bartender. "One last drink. For luck."

chapter

XX

Charlie fingered across the rack of hangers in the closet and lifted off two shirts, both still covered with plastic from the cleaners. She had left his closet intact. He draped them on the bed and stepped back. The chocolate brown was the more expensive— an eighty-dollar custom-made, no pockets, bone buttons—but he would look like he was on his way to a high-rolling weekend in Vegas instead of a sit-down with Eddie Grant. He hung it back in the closet and unbuttoned the beige from the hanger. Open neck, under his dark brown suit, it would look just serious enough. He squatted, and dug around the closet floor for his wing tips. He started to blow away the dust with short puffs of breath, then stopped. There would be plenty of time to stop at the shoemaker's on Twenty-third for a shine.

The clothes would probably make no difference, but it was worth the trouble to get every last thing going for him. He had to walk a careful line. Sharp, sure of himself, but serious. Nothing too soft. And not too

251

sharp, either; Eddie Grant would find it easier to back down to a solid citizen, someone a little bit square, than to someone coming on like half a wise guy. Even a hint of a threat from one of his own kind, the Bedbug would reach across the table and strangle whoever it was. With a dozen eyewitnesses there.

He walked out of the shoemaker's just after eight and crossed in the middle of the block to the barber shop. He settled into the first chair and asked for hot towels and a shave. When the chair was tilted nearly horizontal and the foot support raised, he closed his eyes.

The barber lathered his face for a long time, working the warm soap into his beard with his fingertips. He shaved him slowly, with a light, deliberate hand. Charlie opened his eyes to watch the first towel come out of the steamer, then consciously relaxed as the barber arranged it into a careful mound on his face and patted it down gently. The heat penetrated through to the bones in his face.

After a few minutes he heard the door open and close near him. A gust of cold wind swept across the shop. The customer said hello and took the second chair. He had just come from a workout at the McBurney "Y," the Business Executives' Club, he pointed out. First half an hour with the weights and the rowing machine, then fifteen laps in the pool. There was an inflection in his voice that Charlie took for Puerto Rican. Educated, but with a hint in his pronunciation of a street-kid childhood that he didn't want to give up completely.

"The usual style, Mr. Garcia?"

"Old-fashioned, uptight. Looks good in court, Bruno. Juries like lawyers who look like ex-marines."

Charlie heard the regular metallic snipping of the scissors.

"You go to the jury a lot, Mr. Garcia?"

He laughed. "About once a year, tops. If there's no way to avoid it. F. Lee Bailey fights cases. Bennett Williams. Everybody else pleads their clients. Small-time criminal lawyers, Bruno, we're negotiators. I bargain all day with assistant D.A.s. We sit and haggle like merchants in the Fulton Fish Market. When we stand up and shake hands, the client takes his class-D felony and does twenty-two months."

"From the way things are going out there, I don't see you running short of business for a while."

Garcia laughed. "It won't get any better. I spend all day dealing with criminals and I still almost got taken off Monday night. On the subway. I never ride the goddamned thing, but when I left the gym Monday I stood fifteen minutes at Seventh Avenue without getting a cab. I walked to Sixth, waited a few minutes more, then just started walking across Twenty-third to keep warm, watching for a cab. I finally see I'm at Broadway and I decide the hell with it, I'll catch the subway for Queens. Ten o'clock. There were five or six people in the car, solid citizens on their way home, and two bad Puerto Rican kids. Twenty, twenty-one maybe. But talking sign language. Grunting a little and going like hell with their hands. Who the hell suspects a couple of deaf-and-dumb kids? I relaxed and read a *News* I had picked up."

"They weren't deaf and dumb?"

"Not after we pulled out of the Lexington Avenue station. You're under the river then. They were standing over me with a knife before I knew what was happening. I was furious. Not even scared—furious. All I could think was that these two kids saw the suit and tie and the briefcase and took me for a turkey. I was *raised* on a Hundred and Fourth Street, and these two had me down for a nice, middle-class turkey from Queens.

"I had thirty lousy dollars in my pocket. The right thing to do was to swallow hard and hand them the money, then finish reading the sports page. I couldn't do it. Something in me wouldn't let me do it. I fell right into street Spanish. 'You two *pussies* better know how to use that knife, 'cause after the dust settles there's going to be one motherfucking mess in this car.' I never even set down my newspaper, just stared over it at them. 'Now you move your ass down the car and find some old lady to hit on. Fucking *maricones*.' I put my head right back into my paper.

"They walked away. My heart was beating like hell. I should have been dead, but they walked away. All for thirty lousy dollars. And I should know better— these are my clients every day of the week. They have a run-in one morning with their methadone counselor, so that night they push a knife into someone's belly and it's homicide instead of robbery one.

"Anyway, we pulled into Queens Plaza and they got off. My hands were shaking, but God *damn*—I felt good! First time since I was eighteen that I didn't give a fiddler's fuck about getting hurt, or my wife being a widow, or whether my insurance was up-to-date. I was eighteen again, with nothing to protect. I went home and screwed for an hour, I felt so good."

The barber changed towels on Charlie's face. He wished that he could relax completely. Another hour or so he would be sitting down with the Bedbug. He wondered what Diane was doing at the moment. Watching television in a room somewhere, unless she had already found a small apartment, sitting back in the corner of a couch with her feet tucked under her, eating a frozen yogurt. In another hour she would switch to the floor for twenty minutes of the cross-legged yoga position, back perfectly straight, chin lifted a bit, her hands resting on her knees, palms up. Maybe after the baby was born she would come back. Most of the forty-five thousand would still be there, too—Diane wasn't one to spend fast and furious. Sooner or later it would bother her that the baby wasn't with his father. That's when she would come back. Maybe.

Every few minutes the barber lifted the towel from his face and applied a fresh one from the steamer. Charlie kept his eyes closed and tried to rehearse for his meeting with Eddie Grant. He couldn't. There was no way of knowing how the Bedbug would react. It was a one-in-three shot that he would listen to Charlie state his case, then put on his coat, walk to the door, and pause just long enough to call back over his shoulder, as though it were an afterthought, "Put that cocksucker in the ground."

That would do it. One of the gorillas would choke him to death at the table before Eddie Grant got to the corner of Spring Street. They would carry him out in a box a few hours later and leave him in the trunk of a car in the long-term parking lot at Kennedy. Paulie, too, would go in the ground if that happened. He would be an eyewitness, the only one in the room without a button. They would jam him in next to Charlie. And his uncle Pete wouldn't even have an argument.

Or his luck could change. It was long overdue. He might pull the whole bluff and save his hand. It would put him right back to square one—no money, no prospects—but he would be in one piece. If Paulie were out of the picture, clear of the whole thing, Charlie would feel better. Paulie was like a little jinx, running around with his own brand of craziness, making everyone laugh but leaving behind a straight, thin path of total destruction, like the tornadoes in the Midwest they showed sometimes on the eleven o'clock news.

He thought about Barney's money. It was sitting quietly in a storage warehouse, in the same denominations that his own had been, most of it tightly bound stacks of hundreds. Nicely worn money that had been handled carefully all its life, the way hundreds were, with no grease stains or torn corners. The whole pile would fit neatly into the shoebox that Diane had emptied. He could leave the barbershop, forget about Eddie Grant, and head for New England like a gentleman to look for his restaurant. Maybe go up by train, where he could sit down to breakfast served on a white tablecloth and watch the countryside go by while he poured a second cup of coffee from a little silver pot. All he would have to do is spend the next few years trying not to think of Barney's retarded kid drooling somewhere in the Bronx.

The barber lifted the last towel from his face, massaged in a palmful of witch hazel, and patted his skin dry. Charlie checked himself in the mirror after he put on his suit jacket, then again after he put on his overcoat. When he stepped outside, his face felt warm, even in the cold wind that pushed against him steadily while he walked to Seventh Avenue. Twice he started to cross the street to a bar near the corner for one quick scotch, but each time pushed himself on, afraid to reach for even a small crutch.

The corner of Seventh Avenue felt like a wind tunnel. He stepped out into the street, just past the line of parked cars, his collar pulled up over his ears. He let three empty cabs pass. Each of them had the filthy exterior that Charlie knew meant a passenger seat with broken springs that would collapse under him.

He would be riding in a dark cubbyhole with his ass at floor level and his knees jammed against a grimy partition, rattling along on shock absorbers that bottomed out on every pothole. When he saw a polished cab cruising the west side of the avenue, he hailed it. The inside was spotless, with cardboard signs posted all around warning passengers not to smoke—driver allergic. The signs had been lettered with different-color marker pens. Every ashtray was neatly taped shut with strips of aluminum duct tape.

"Mulberry Street," Charlie said. "Go across Canal, then uptown." He sat back and relaxed.

The driver missed the light at Eleventh Street. While he waited, Charlie looked out at St. Vincent's. The hospital had always been a part of his life. While he was living with Cookie they had rushed into the emergency room on a snowy night carrying Vincent wrapped in a blanket, a fish bone stuck in his throat, his face a deep shade of purple and puffed to nearly twice its normal size. A Filipino resident had done a tracheotomy on the spot, cutting into the boy's throat while Charlie and Cookie stood beside him. They had waited then outside the emergency room, standing in the corridor for a long time, hugging one another tightly. Cookie's knees had shaken, but for some reason she wouldn't sit down. She had given Charlie as much support as he had given her.

He had been back at the hospital a few years later, sitting with his mother for a few hours every day of the week while she died of stomach cancer. It had taken three months for it to eat away so much of her that she couldn't live. He still remembered the sweet perfume dispensed in the room to cover the odor of the cancer. It had nauseated him every day he sat with her.

Long before that, on a sweltering August night when he was twelve, during a game of ring-a-levio on Carmine Street, he had charged the den and been kicked under the chin in the pileup. His tongue was caught in his teeth and he'd bitten it nearly off. He was half-carried, half-pushed into the emergency room by a group of kids who somehow managed to flag down a car on Houston Street. A surgeon had sewn it together again, and it had healed without leaving a hint of a speech impediment. If it had been just a little different, they said, he would have gone through life honking, straining his facial muscles to be understood. It was how he visualized Barney's retarded kid, when he thought of him.

The light turned green. The driver started moving again along Seventh Avenue. It occurred to Charlie that if the Bedbug decided to chop his hand off, it would be St. Vincent's he would rush to. That was still a possibility, losing his hand. The Bedbug could hear him out and not get pissed enough to kill him, but decide to carry out the original sentence. His hand.

He wanted to smoke. Here he was, five minutes away from going head-to-head with the Bedbug, and he was sitting like a victim, intimidated by a bunch of hand-lettered signs hung up by a fat cabbie from Queens. He lit a cigarette and dropped the burned match on the floor. As the small cloud of smoke found its way through the holes in the plastic safety barrier, the driver looked up into the rearview mirror, then turned quickly to see the cigarette for himself.

"Hey, put that out!" he called back.

Charlie took a long drag on the cigarette, inhaled, then directed the stream of smoke directly at the pattern of holes behind the driver's head. "Go pull on your prick. What are you running here, a cab or a fucking elevator?"

"I'm allergic, mister. It's no good for my lungs."

"That's bullshit. You don't like the smoke, open your window. I don't believe you're allergic, anyway. All these signs are bullshit."

"They're not. You want the truth, mister, you're a pretty inconsiderate son of a bitch."

"Go to work in a paint factory." Charlie puffed slowly. "Maybe write a couple of 'pleases' on your signs. You're allergic to cigarettes, I'm allergic to signs that say don't."

The driver accelerated. He coughed several times, but kept his window closed. Charlie smoked quietly until the cigarette was finished.

"You want me to untape one of these ashtrays, or you want me to stamp this out on your nice new carpet? You got some pair of balls, taping up ashtrays."

They were crossing Houston Street as Charlie spoke. The car swerved several times for half a block, as though a drunk were driving, then screeched to a stop along an empty stretch of curb on the left. The driver switched on the interior lights and swung around as far as possible in his seat to face Charlie through the partition. His face was red.

"That carpet is left over from my living room. My living room! That's Bigelow shag, seventeen-fifty a yard wholesale. My wife picked that carpet, mister. You grind out your butt on that rug, it's like you walked into my living room and ground out your butt there. That's how I'm going to treat it." He poked his index finger at Charlie for emphasis. It pressed against the plastic with enough force to flatten and turn white. "This is my *home* you're shitting in now. Not my cab—my home."

Charlie thought for a moment about dropping the butt out the window—why provoke a fight over nonsense? He decided instead to work himself up further for the meeting with Eddie Grant. He raised the butt to eye level, then opened his fingers wide and let it drop to the floor. He ground it with a hard, twisting motion of his shoe, without looking away from the driver's face.

"There. I just shit on your living-room shag. You get out of that door and try to do something about it, you fat fuck, they'll find you laying on this sidewalk tomorrow morning. Now take me to Mulberry Street, and be fucking happy I don't smoke cigars."

The driver turned slowly and started the cab moving again. "That was rotten," he said over his shoulder softly. "That was a pretty rotten thing to do."

Charlie started to feel sorry for him, but knew it was the wrong mood to get himself into. He put it out of his mind for the few minutes it took to go across Canal Street and up Mulberry. The driver coughed several times. He was coughing when they pulled up at the social club. Charlie got out and stood beside the driver's window to pay him. Looking down at the driver's sagging jowls and listening to his little cough, he suddenly did feel sorry. He had just come out from being babied with hot towels—the driver hadn't even shaved that day. Charlie took his change and pushed a five back into the driver's hand. "Sorry. I'm just in a lousy mood."

He turned and walked between two parked cars to the curb. Halfway across the sidewalk he heard the driver call, "Hey!"

He turned. The cab was beginning to inch along. The driver had his window down. His head was half out of it, turned toward Charlie. He waved the five at him. "Schmuck!" he called. "I ain't allergic to tobacco. Two packs a day I smoked, until last month. Schmuck!"

The outside of the social club hadn't changed since Charlie could remember. The two store windows had always been painted black. The door pane was covered by a curtain pulled tight across top and bottom rods. The door was recessed from the street, leaving a pocket just big enough for a man to pull a chair out into on summer nights without blocking the doorway. Charlie always thought of the place as it looked in summertime: the door cracked open for air, a few wise guys with folding chairs out on the sidewalk, each with a huge belly covered by a sleeveless undershirt. Snooky Yap, the bulldog, sitting with them, chewing on his two-by-four. Now there was no sign of life. He set his overcoat collar flat and knocked on the glass door pane twice. Someone pulled back the curtain and stared at him for a few moments, then opened the door. Charlie took a deep breath and stepped inside.

It had been nearly two years since he had been in the room, to see Carlucci about his breakup with Cookie. It hadn't changed. There was still a haze of smoke. A single line of fluorescent fixtures on the ceiling gave off a yellowish light. The floor was bare, worn wood, sagging noticeably in the center and littered with cigarette butts. The whole room looked tired. Half a dozen red Formica tables salvaged from some luncheonette were set around at random. On his right, two tables had been pushed together for a six-man card game. Charlie recognized Tony Centro, a soldier still in his mid-twenties who was already made, and moving up so fast that everyone in the neighborhood had their eye on him. The only other player he knew was Paulie's uncle, Pete Grillo. Pete glanced up from his cards and looked right through Charlie, then lowered his head again.

The Bedbug was at a table on the left, hunched forward in a conversation with Nunzi Nun Nun, who ran errands for him and drove his car. The gorilla who had opened the door waited until Charlie had looked over the room, then he raised his eyebrows in a silent question.

"I got to see Eddie Grant," Charlie said. "I'll sit here until he finishes with Nunzi."

He folded his coat once and draped it across the back of a chair, then sat on the chair beside it. The strong odor of freshly ground espresso beans filled the room. He looked toward the back. There was Paulie, standing in his medium-high heels at a kitchen stove set against the rear wall, his back to the room, brewing a batch of espresso. A bare light bulb hung from the ceiling directly over the stove. A large, open pot of water was boiling on a front burner. Paulie turned down the flame, waited until the boiling stopped, then emptied a bag full of ground coffee directly into the water. He stirred it for a few minutes with a tall wooden spoon, blackened over the years from coffee, then stretched two clean cotton dish towels across an empty pot and filtered the gallon or so of coffee through it slowly.

It occurred to Charlie that Paulie knew he was here to bluff. Paulie could have bailed himself out of a lot of hot water earlier today if he had decided to tell the Bedbug. Charlie lit a cigarette and stared at Paulie's back. When the last of the coffee was poured onto the towels, Paulie set down the empty pot and turned toward the room. He was careful not to look directly at Charlie.

One of the cardplayers got up and crossed the room. He stood behind Eddie Grant's chair and leaned forward, his hand on Grant's shoulder, to whisper in his ear. After a few moments the Bedbug looked directly at Charlie, then half-turned his head to ask the cardplayer something. Grant nodded, and turned again to Nunzi. Charlie became aware of his own heartbeat. He wanted a cigarette but was afraid his hands would shake.

The Bedbug was meatier than Charlie remembered, with more flesh on his cheeks and a thicker neck. He had the chunky bone structure of an old-time middleweight: short and thick, thirty pounds too heavy now, but all of it well distributed. Even from across the room Charlie could see the halfway droop of his left eye where he had been butted forty years ago in a six-round preliminary at St. Nick's. He was balding fast, developing a horseshoe around a huge dome, but all the hair left was combed flat back at a three-quarter angle, not a strand pulled forward to cover the baldness. His suit jacket hung open. His shirt was white-on-white, heavily starched, open at the collar, no tie—old-time poolroom-style. He sat hunched forward, his forearms resting on the table, hands crossed in front of him, his hard, heavy fingers intertwined. No pinkie ring. Charlie could visualize the fingers wrapped tight around an axe handle.

The Bedbug uncrossed his hands, pulled a pack of cigarettes from his breast pocket, and lit one before Nunzi could fish a book of matches from his pocket. Charlie couldn't make out the brand; he would bet they were unfiltered—Camels or Luckies. It should be a cigar, Charlie thought. His build, his hands, his whole size called for a cigar. His face would dwarf a good-sized cigar stub.

The Bedbug looked up from the table and glanced around the room. His eyes met Charlie's for a moment, then continued to circle the room. The corners of his mouth turned down, permanently unhappy and hurt, Charlie thought, as though he had just swallowed a bad clam. He said something to Nunzi, who got up and joined the cardplayers, then he stared into Charlie's eyes for a minute. Charlie stared back. He tried for a blank look on his face, no hostility, but no fear, focusing his gaze a foot or so behind the Bedbug's head. The

Bedbug beckoned to him, as though he were signaling a waiter. His right hand came up from the table to eye level, then his index finger moved sharply once, summoning him to the table.

Charlie stood up and walked across the room. The cardplayers continued their game. No one looked up, but Charlie sensed their attention. A lump formed in his throat. As he approached the table, he used a trick his father had taught him years ago for when he felt intimidated: He pictured the Bedbug squatting on a toilet bowl, his pants crumpled down around his ankles, hunched forward, forearms on knees, the veins of his neck bulged out and red from straining. The lump in Charlie's throat dissolved. He lowered himself onto the chair slowly, as though preparing to relax over a cup of coffee after a long day, then shifted the chair to face the Bedbug squarely. They looked at one another for a minute, then the Bedbug spoke softly.

"You brought back my money?"

Charlie shook his head. "I don't have your money."

"You're Charlie Moran?"

He nodded.

"Then you're one of the scum bags took my money. You brought it back?"

Charlie shook his head. "I took the cop's money, not yours. One hour later—if we had gone in there one hour later—the cop would have already had the money. We robbed him, not you. The money's gone, anyway."

The Bedbug shook his head slowly. "It don't matter, one way or the other. The whole neighborhood knows you went into my pocket. It's like in a family. A kid steals off the father—if he ain't stopped, pretty soon he's hocking the silverware. You showed no respect at all. Not just for me, but for the neighborhood. This kind of thing, it ruins the neighborhood if it ain't nipped right in the bud. You were brought up here, no?"

"On Carmine Street."

"Close enough. Then you should know. All of us, we got to look out for each other if we're going to keep it nice. We owe the neighborhood some respect. People start robbing Eddie Grant, it's like a total breakdown. Everything goes upside down. Pretty soon people don't know what's right or what's wrong anymore. Before you know it, you got niggers moving in the neighborhood."

He rubbed his forehead several times, as though he were tired.

"I got to keep everybody's respect. For their own good. I try to get it out of love. That's how I would like to get it. But if I can't get their respect out of love, then I'm forced to get it out of fear."

He waited a few moments for his words to sink in, then motioned toward Charlie with his chin. "You're not Italian."

"Half."

He shrugged. "Your mother was Italian?"

"Yeah."

"Not Sicilian, though."

"Napolidon."

"Ah." He looked away from Charlie and pursed his lips in thought. The drooping eyelid seemed to droop more.

"What the hell *brings* you here? You didn't hear that I called for your hand? At this table. I sat where I'm sitting now and I called for your right hand."

Charlie nodded. "I heard."

"So then what the hell are you doing here? They told me you were sitting waiting to see me, I figured you brought back my money to try and save your hand. Now you tell me you don't have my money. Are you fucking *stunadz,* or what? You got a brain in your fucking head, right now you're supposed to be in California somewhere hiding. Like the rats the government sets up. What the hell brought you here?"

Charlie glanced from side to side, as though worried that someone might overhear. He leaned forward and spoke softly. "What brought me here is a tape. A little tape recording that I took off the cop's belly."

He watched the Bedbug's face. It stayed absolutely still. Too still, Charlie thought. He was working at it.

"What do I give a fuck about some tape? What you took off the cop, you took off the cop."

He knew about the tape, Charlie decided.

"That little tape will put you away. A jury listens to that tape and they'll lock you up. The cop had you bugged."

"What are you talking about?"

"He was wired. The tape he had strapped to his belly had you on it. That tape can hang you. By the balls." Charlie reached halfway across the table and tugged upward with his fist at the empty air several times. "By the balls."

The Bedbug frowned. He stared at Charlie for a few moments, then let the frown disappear slowly. His eyes widened. "You're here to threaten me? You walked in here to *threaten* me?"

Charlie forced himself not to swallow. "You're fucking right I'm here to threaten you. I got you by the balls, Eddie. You chop off my hand, you sit in a fucking cage for the next twenty years or so. You'll croak in jail."

The Bedbug stared across the table at Charlie. His eyelids drooped slightly and he pursed his lips. "The last guy talked to me anything *close* to the way you're talking was some creep from the Village. From your neighborhood. Carlos somebody. I parcel-posted the little scum bag home."

"Carlos Moth Balls didn't have a tape sitting in a safe-deposit box could put you away for twenty."

"That was his name, Moth Balls. Carlos Moth Balls. A regular little scum bag. Something about you reminds me a little of him. The voice, maybe. He come on like a tough guy, too. He turned out not to be so tough. He was almost tender—like a nice piece of veal off a cow's been fed milk all its life. Like you use for scallopine. White and tender."

He started to laugh, but it became a cough immediately. It came from deep in his chest and after a minute turned to heavy wheezing. He reached into his shirt pocket for a cigarette. While he lit it, Charlie breathed deeply several times, letting the air out silently through his nose. The Bedbug blew a stream of smoke across the table.

"We'll finish this talk in the back room. Where there's some privacy. Me and you and Snooky." He looked past Charlie to the front door and said, "Hey, Snooky." His voice was barely audible. The dog opened his eyes and stared across the room. "Come here," the Bedbug mumbled.

The dog pushed himself up to a standing position. He stood still for a few moments, drooling a long ribbon of saliva from one side of his mouth, then lumbered across the room and stood beside the Bedbug's chair. He panted slightly from the exertion. The Bedbug stood up and walked through the open door into the back room. Charlie followed, with Snooky Yap walking beside him. The cardplayers looked up from their game and glanced at Charlie. As he passed the stove, Paulie looked directly at him for the first time. He was stirring the pot of espresso absently. His face held a combination of dread and excitement that reminded Charlie of a third-grader watching his partner in some kid's crime being taken down to the principal's office.

There was a single round table in the center of the room with seven or eight folding chairs opened around it. The Bedbug motioned to one and said, "Sit," then sat himself down on the chair opposite. Snooky Yap stopped just inside the door and moved out of the aisle, then lowered himself. He stretched out his front paws, rested his chin on them, then exhaled a long sigh through his lips and let his eyes close. The Bedbug dropped his cigarette on the floor and ground it out, then lit a fresh one.

"Now what's with this—this tape you're talking about?"

"I took a little tape off the cop. You're on it. I ain't going to sit still for losing my hand. You take my hand, Eddie, and the tape goes right to the D.A.'s office."

"I just might take your fucking head instead of your hand."

"Then it goes to the D.A. tomorrow. That tape is with somebody who's waiting to see I'm okay."

The Bedbug exhaled a long sigh. It reminded Charlie of the sound Snooky Yap had let out a minute earlier. He spoke in a deliberately soft, hoarse voice.

"Listen to me. I tell you this for your own good. You're behaving like a *mamaluta. Cabeesh?* Out of control, like one of them elephants comes charging out of the jungle and runs through a little town smashing up all the niggers' huts, trampling on the niggers' kids. The elephant has to be stopped—he's a threat to everybody. It don't matter why he's doing it, either. This elephant might not be a scum bag—the poor bastard might have a toothache he can't do nothing about. You're behaving like that, threatening the whole neighborhood. Talking about the D.A. You come in our club here, you don't behave like a guest, you don't show the club some respect, you behave like a real scum bag. You're half

Irish, so I make some allowance for it, but that don't excuse you either."

He motioned with his hand to indicate everything around him. "The last few years there's no discipline at all. You see it everywhere. The whole fucking world is upside down. Years ago people snatched some rich kid for ransom, now every whackadoo with a piece in his pocket grabs off a whole fucking airplane if he feels like it. Kids in school are beating up the fucking teachers. Half the fucking city, people can't walk the streets at night without some nigger whacking them over the head for their money. The last few years things are running down in the neighborhood, too. Carlucci let it happen. If this was Carlucci's money you robbed, he would of made your legs get busted. He thought that looked good for the neighborhood, some guy hopping around on a cast for a couple of months. It means shit, busted legs. People bust their fucking legs these days skiing on a weekend. Carlucci let his house get out of order."

He closed his eyes for a moment.

"I got my work cut out for me, straightening up after Carlucci. You're a good place to start. I already took your partner's thumb—the neighborhood sees I'm serious. Now they see you on the streets with no hand, people are going to start shaping up. I don't even have nothing against you—you look like a nice, clean-cut boy. You tried to rob me, it didn't come off. Things don't always work out. But now you come in here talking about the D.A., sounding like some Irish hard-on instead of a kid raised in the Village. Now you force me to not like you."

Charlie wondered whether he had forgotten the tape entirely.

"You got a lot of balls for a waiter. You're a waiter,

no? Like that little prick of a partner you got out there."

"I'm a manager."

The Bedbug shrugged. "You got some pair of balls. First you rob my money. Now you threaten me. You made *some* fucking mistake for yourself, walking in here. You figured a little tape would back me down?" He placed his fingertips under his chin, the back of his hand toward Charlie, and flicked his hand outward, brushing his fingernails against his chin. "I give *this* for your tape."

He was working himself up.

"I got where I am by backing down to any scum-bag waiter walks through the door? You think I'd be sitting here today if I spent time worrying about twelve assholes on a grand jury might listen to the D.A. play a tape for them? I *piss* on your tape." His face became red. He extended his hand over the table and imitated a gardener playing a hose over a flower bed. "I *piss* on it. You either go out of here in a sack, scum bag, or you give me the tape and you walk out. Without your hand. You still lose a hand." He leaned toward Charlie. "I promised myself—I'll wipe my ass with your hand."

Charlie wanted to swallow.

"I'm going to give you a few minutes to think. I'll take some fresh air and let you think about what's best for you. You go get the tape and bring it back, you only lose a hand. You keep on behaving like a scum bag and you go into the ground."

He stood up and walked past Charlie without looking back. Charlie turned and watched him continue through the front room to the door. As soon as it closed behind him, Paulie walked into the back room.

"What happened, Charlie?"

"I got five minutes to decide whether he gets my hand or he buries me. He gave me a choice."

"He still wants your hand, Charlie?"

"To wipe his ass with. He says he promised himself."

"What are you going to do, Charlie?"

He shrugged. "Nothing I *can* do, now. Even if I tried to give him the tape now, all I got is a blank. He'll believe I'm holding out the real tape. I've fucking had it, Paulie. I took a shot and I crapped out."

Paulie stood quietly for a few moments, then walked out of the room slowly. He hesitated in the doorway. "I'm sorry, Charlie. About this whole *mishkadenze* I got you into. I'm sorry."

Charlie shrugged again. "I'm not twelve years old, Paulie."

He closed his eyes and thought. There was no sense in going for the tape, and there was no sense trying to explain. Either way he was dead. His only shots now were to bluff it out or to run for it. He looked through the doorway to the front of the club. One of the gorillas was sitting near the door. He wouldn't get across the sidewalk to the street. He closed his eyes again. His only shot was to stick with the bluff. With a pair of balls like *boccies*. He thought of the Puerto Rican lawyer in the barbershop.

The Bedbug came in a few minutes later and sat across from Charlie. His eyelids drooped.

"I hope you decided to do the right thing here." He spoke in the tone of a father giving good advice. "We'll have a coffee, it's good for you. You drink brown coffee, or black?"

"Black."

He called, "Paulie, two espresso," then paused only a few seconds, not long enough for Paulie to reach the door. "Where's that fucking kid?" he called. "Where is he?"

Paulie hurried into the doorway. "You call me, Eddie?"

"You waiting tables like you're supposed to do, or you watching a card game?"

"I was watching that the pot don't boil, Eddie."

"Bring us two espresso."

Charlie watched the Bedbug light a cigarette.

"You got balls. You got a big pair of balls for a waiter. I don't get too mad at that. My patience got a limit, too, though."

He stared at Charlie intensely for a few moments. When he spoke, the hoarseness in his voice made Charlie lean forward to hear.

"Listen to me. You're living in a fucking dreamworld. I let people step on my toes the way you're trying to do here, I would of been driving a truck a long time ago."

Charlie nodded unconsciously.

Paulie came through the doorway quickly, his bandaged hand balancing a small round tray. He seemed nervous. He had to set the tray on their table before lifting off the small glasses of espresso. "Three sugars, Eddie?" he asked.

The Bedbug nodded.

Paulie measured out heaping little spoonfuls into the glass.

"Lemon," the Bedbug said, without looking at Paulie.

Charlie helped himself to two sugars while Paulie struggled with the peel, using only his left hand. The Bedbug raised his glass and inclined it slightly toward Charlie. "To your health."

"*Salud.*"

The Bedbug drank down half the glass in a series of long sips, then set it down. A few seconds had passed—Charlie was still sipping his coffee—when his face changed. He was about to say something, but seemed to change his mind. At first it was a look of surprise. His eyes grew wide and his mouth opened. He came up off the chair so quickly that he knocked it over. Both his hands clutched at his chest. He stared wide-eyed at Paulie, who had backed against the wall, holding a waiter's towel in his good hand. The Bedbug let out a bellow that filled the club, then turned and charged through the door and across the front room. He pulled the front door open and ran out onto Mulberry Street, still bellowing. The cardplayers followed him out. Pete Grillo poked his head through the doorway into the back room. He stared at Paulie.

"Lye," Paulie said. "I filled his fucking espresso with lye." He held out his bandaged hand. "That cocksucker took my thumb. He was going to whack out my cousin Charlie. Now let him fucking *die*. He got a bellyful of lye."

Pete looked over at the Bedbug's glass. "How much did he drink?"

"Plenty," Paulie said. "You know how he gulps his coffee down. Red hot, the way he likes it, so the fuck never caught a taste of it. He drank more coffee than what's left in the cup."

"How much lye you put in?"

"Two teaspoons. Two fucking heaping teaspoons."

Pete moved his head slightly from side to side, weighing it out. "He'll never make Saint Vincent's," he said. "Two *big* teaspoons, Paulie?"

"Heaping. Like a kid spooning out sugar. I couldn't fit no more on the spoon."

Pete whistled, and glanced again at the glass. "The

Bedbug ain't going to make Houston Street." He turned and hurried to the front door.

Charlie stared at Paulie. "How could you *do* it? You just killed Eddie Grant. Bedbug Eddie Grant. You *killed* him."

"I figured I owed you, Charlie. I got you into it. I didn't want to see you go down."

"You owed me? Paulie, he would've caved in. I know it, Paulie. I had him bluffed."

Paulie waved his hand in disgust. "Fuck him. I never met nobody deserved it more. That rat bastard's going to crawl across Houston Street. You know that, Charlie? People swallow lye like that, they *crawl*. They fed Patsy Ricci lye in the Lido on Mott Street for ratting—he crawled the last few blocks to his house."

He held up his bandaged hand. "We poisoned the Bedbug, Charlie. And it's just what the cocksucker deserved."

"*You* poisoned the Bedbug, Paulie. You would have been better off taking a shot at the president."

"Fuck him. Let's get out of here, Charlie. Fast. There's no sense standing here talking. We'll go somewhere and we'll think this thing out."

Charlie moved toward the doorway ahead of Paulie. He heard a low, rumbling sound, like a far-off subway train. He started to turn, then realized it was Snooky Yap. They stopped. The dog sidled a few feet across the floor into the open doorway, trailing his string of saliva from the side of his mouth. He barely lifted his chain off the floor while he moved. He settled in the exact center of the doorway and pulled back his upper lip to expose his teeth, then growled louder. Charlie moved one step closer, and stopped. The dog pushed himself up to a sitting position and set his front legs into a wide, bowlegged stance.

"But is this fucking Snooky Yap pigeon-toed?" Paulie said. "I don't know how the hell he walks. If he ain't tripping over his own fucking big feet, he's slipping and sliding around in that puddle of spit follows him wherever he goes."

"What do we do?"

"We ain't going to get past him, Charlie. He's a bear trap, this fuck. Snooky plants himself in a doorway and drools, nobody gets through unless Eddie Grant gives the okay."

"You got any more lye?"

"It don't matter, Charlie. Snooky don't drink espresso."

"Jesus Christ, I don't mean feed it to him. Maybe throw a little at him, he'll take off."

"It's outside. It wouldn't budge him anyway."

The dog stopped growling but kept his lips pulled back to expose his teeth.

"We're going to be trapped in here forever by this slob, Charlie. Like a couple of fucking mice. We could starve before this mutt lets us loose."

"You got any bright ideas?"

Paulie stared at the dog for a minute. "We just knocked off a big-shot Mafioso, Charlie. Sure as shit we ain't going to fold up for some *Napolidon* bulldog."

He moved past Charlie and knelt in front of the dog, lowering his head so their eyes were level. The dog growled again and extended his neck a few inches forward. Paulie spoke in a low voice.

"Go drool somewhere else, Snooky. You don't move out of this doorway, I'm going to tear your fucking head off."

The dog raised himself to a full standing position. Paulie pivoted his body and swung a roundhouse left, open-handed, the way Charlie remembered nuns swinging at kids in a classroom. His hand rebounded off the side of Snooky's head with a loud clap. The dog's eyes opened wide. He stared at Paulie for an instant, then lowered his head and backed up a few steps. Paulie raised his hand as if to hit him backhanded. "Beat it! Fucking punk."

Snooky turned and moved sideways toward the front door, watching Paulie out of one eye. At the door he turned fully and hurried out onto the street.

"I should have clocked him for a phony a month ago. You see the way he dogged it, Charlie? And he had the whole joint bulldozed. Even all the wise guys."

They walked out onto Mulberry Street. Pete Grillo approached from the uptown direction, his big, hard stomach protruding.

"The Bedbug went down on Broadway and Houston. Nobody on his crew was giving him too much help, either."

"What about us, Uncle Pete? They're going to hold me and Charlie responsible?"

"Every wise guy in the city will have a quiet drink tonight to celebrate. Nobody trusted the fucking maniac. There was nobody made any money with him, either."

He looked into Paulie's face and shook his head slowly from side to side. "But you can't kill a made guy and stay alive, Paulino. You know that. Unless you walk in on him in bed with your wife. Or he fucks your thirteen-year-old daughter. Anything else, you got to die, Paulie. That's the rules. Maybe it's not fair, but that's the way it is. It just ain't allowed, to kill a made guy."

"So what happens, Pete?"

"Run. Run like a thief. Both of you."

Charlie stared at him for a moment, then asked, "Run where? Where the hell do we go and stand a chance?"

Pete looked away.

"Nowhere," Charlie said. "There's nowhere to go."

Pete spread his hands and looked from Charlie to Paulie. "Take your best shot. What else can I tell you?"

They turned and walked the few blocks to Canal Street without talking, then crossed against the light to the congested Chinatown side of the street. Families of Orientals were shopping in the early night, the women bent across the outdoor stands, testing fruits and vegetables with their fingers. Open crates of whole fish packed in shaved ice blocked off the inner half of the sidewalk, forcing people to rub past one another in two single lanes of traffic. A young Chinese couple had parked a Volkswagen van at the curb, its side door open fully to present a huge glass tank filled with live carp swimming slowly near the bottom. A second van parked behind it offered live turtles. Everybody seemed to be talking. Charlie listened to the babble of singsong Chinese, haggling and laughing. They continued down Mulberry to the park and slowed their pace as they entered it, both of them glancing up for a few moments at the tall stone wall of the Tombs. The park was deserted.

"I would have been better off letting the maniac take my hand."

"You think they'll really come after us, Charlie?"

"Of course they'll come after us—what's the matter with you? We're dead, Paulie. Dead. It's like a doctor just found cancer on us and gave us three, four months. It's that sure."

"You always see the worst side of things. Maybe they'll forget about us, Charlie. A couple of months go by and maybe they'll forget all about us."

Charlie closed his eyes for a few steps.

"So where do we head for, Charlie?"

"You mean, where do I go and where do you go."

Paulie stopped and spread his arms wide. He frowned in an exaggerated way. "You're kidding, Charlie. I thought we were partners. We're cousins, Charlie. I was bailing you out back there. Maybe I was wrong, but I done that for you. I knocked off fucking Eddie Grant for you, Charlie."

"But every time I get hooked up with you it's trouble. It always turns out you meant well, but you walk around causing disasters."

They walked quietly past the playground area.

"Another thing. Something doesn't smell just right, Paulie. Suddenly you're looking out for me so hard that you feed lye to Eddie Grant."

Paulie stopped, so Charlie had to turn to face him. Behind him, the Tombs blocked out the sky.

"Family, Charlie. There's blood. I took you on the burglary without giving you the whole story—I was a thousand percent wrong. You think I don't know that, Charlie? Then I gave you up. At Belmont. Superman couldn't have stood up. Still, I gave you up. You think I don't know that, either? And then the horse. I wasn't out of order there, Charlie. You didn't have to bet her. Still, I felt bad. I couldn't watch Eddie Grant kill you, Charlie. Just your hand, I wouldn't have got up the nerve. But after everything else, I couldn't watch you *die*, Charlie."

He shook his head slowly, disappointed. "When I go all out for you to make it up—I pull out all the stops— you're going to tell me something don't smell right?"

They stood quietly while two children rode past on tricycles in the darkness. Then Charlie reached forward and pinched Paulie's cheek, tugging on it. "Come on, hard-on. Somebody's got to look out for you."

They walked again.

"Where are we going?" Paulie asked.

"Pete said to take our best shot. Our best shot is Oregon, or Washington. Maybe Alaska."

"Alaska! What the hell kind of action is there in Alaska? And it's *cold* there, Charlie. We'll freeze our asses off in Alaska."

"You figure Vegas makes more sense, Paulie?"

"It beats Alaska. There's some action in Vegas. It's warm in Vegas."

"And there's two million wise guys, too. I'm heading for the Northwest. You want to come, fine."

Paulie frowned for a minute, then nodded. "Maybe you're right. There can't be no wise guys in Alaska. There can't even be any espresso in Alaska."

He walked a little faster. "Thank God we ain't broke, anyway."

Charlie swung sideways to look at him. "We ain't broke? What the hell are you talking about? You got money in your pocket you're not telling me about?"

Paulie smiled. "I got no money, Charlie. But you do. You still got the retard's money."

"I mailed that claim check to Barney's wife on our way to the track. You were with me."

"You palmed it, Charlie. You went to the mailbox, but you never dropped the envelope in. I clocked you, but I didn't say nothing."

Charlie clenched his teeth and lifted his head toward the sky. "I *knew* it smelled wrong. You would have let me lose my hand back there—for sure I would have gone along with keeping Barney's money then. It's when Eddie Grant was ready to kill me that you panicked. You saw the fifty large going up in smoke and you reached for the lye."

"Charlie! That's fucking insulting, what you're saying. Give me a little credit. I saved your *life*, Charlie. Your *life*." He grasped Charlie's bicep with his left hand and held his bandaged right hand between their faces. "You're alive, Charlie, and you got your hand. My fucking thumb is gone forever."

He seemed to choke on the last few words, then he calmed down and released Charlie's arm. "It's all fucking water under the bridge now anyway. You didn't rob the retard's money when Barney mailed you the key. You done the right thing once. Once is enough. You still had five thou then. We're up against the wall now. We're in a corner. A second time makes you an asshole. The *pope* does the right thing always. You going to be the pope of Greenwich Village, Charlie? They can write it on your gravestone—Charlie Moran, the pope of Greenwich Village. He did the right thing always."

"Barney's kid deserves that money, Paulie. It's like saying a Hail Mary for keeping my hand. And we're fucking doomed, anyway, let's face it. This is my chance not to be a total scum bag my whole life."

Paulie clutched his arm again. "Being a scum bag ain't the worst thing in the world, Charlie. Being poor is worse."

"The poor fuck Barney had nobody in the world to turn to but me. He smelled something right in me, Paulie. The same way Diane did."

"And she said you miss by an inch. You told me so."

"This is my chance not to, Paulie."

"Forget your chance not to. Missing by an inch ain't so bad—most people miss by a mile. What the hell is it you're missing anyway? After thirty-five years you want to start being a victim? We're from Carmine Street, Charlie—we can't start behaving like a couple of WASPS from Maine. Next you'll be voting. She wanted that, too, you told me."

"She did."

"It'll give us a start, Charlie. Even in Alaska, we could use a start. You could mail the retard his money after we're settled in. It's not like we'd be keeping the money for good. It's our start. We replace what we use in a couple of months and mail it to the retard."

Charlie closed his eyes, and remembered that his watch was still in hock. There was that whole little suitcase of hundreds waiting in a storage warehouse. The two of them didn't really have more than a couple of months anyway.

"Fuck it," he said. "It won't hurt the kid to wait another couple of months, no, Paulie? Meanwhile, something's got to turn up. What am I going to do next, vote?"

They walked west, past the deserted municipal buildings of Worth Street, neither of them in a hurry. A steady wind carried a sheet of newspaper along the sidewalk and wrapped it momentarily around Charlie's legs. He hunched his shoulders and leaned forward. Paulie pulled up his collar and turned around completely to walk backward into the wind, just ahead of Charlie, bouncing lightly on the balls of his feet with short steps, his arms pumping slightly at his sides.

"We'll grab a cab uptown on Centre Street, Charlie."

Charlie watched him move, like a fighter doing road work, and wondered if he was humming. It was possible.

"You look happy, Paulie."

"I ain't happy. But things could be a lot worse. They're looking up, Charlie. Things are looking up for us."

Charlie moved faster to keep up. "They're looking great, Paulie. We got maybe three whole months to live. Meanwhile, we're on our way to rob a retarded kid. Things are looking up all right."

Paulie had moved too far ahead to hear him. He slowed until they were beside one another again. "What did you say, Charlie?"

Charlie remained silent for several paces, then clapped Paulie's shoulder lightly. "I said you're right, Paulie. Things are looking up."

He hunched his shoulders higher, thrust his hands deep into his overcoat pockets, and leaned further into the wind.